MY FIGHT

MEN OF NEW YORK BOOK THREE

SAMANTHA SKYE

ISBN 978-0-6452730-4-5 (ebook)
ISBN 978-0-6452730-6-9 (paperback)

Cover Design: Angela Haddon
www.angelahaddon.com

Editor: Nice Girl Naughty Edits
www.nicegirlnaughtyedits.com

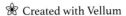 Created with Vellum

CONTENT DISCOVERY

If you are not familiar with my writing I am going to be honest and let you know a few things.

In this book there is spice, lots of spice. There is also violence, the kind that is descriptive in nature and most certainly on the page. There is also descriptions of family violence and partner violence throughout.

1

CARTER GRANGE

If only Benji would shut the hell up so the pain in my head can subside, that would be a fucking godsend. He is acting like my personal bodyguard, currently shouting at everyone who comes near me as we make our way into the emergency department.

Clearly, he is worried about me, but he doesn't need to be. Even though my heart is racing, and my chest feels tight, my anxiety at an all-time high. Though he doesn't know that bit; just that I'm injured.

This hospital is not my usual medical clinic, but it's closer to the warehouse where my fight was. So, Benji, in his world of panic, sped his way here through the dark streets of Philly, and now the bright lights beaming off the stark white walls is enough to blind me.

The one time my boys aren't with me and the whole night goes to shit.

"Benji, slow down. I'm fine," I grit through my teeth, as he powers through the mass of people here on this manic Saturday night.

"Nico tasked me with taking care of you. So, I am doing what he asked, and he said to bring you here," Benji spits out, his eyes laser focused on our surroundings.

Although it is rare that I need a hospital visit after a fight, it does happen on occasion. Usually, ice and pain medication see me through a few days of aches and pains before I start recovery sessions and training for the next fight.

Tonight is no different except for this power trip that Benji is on, only to ensure I am not more injured than usual. I'm not, but no amount of telling him that will get him to let up on the situation, so I've let him take the lead. If for no other reason but to focus on breathing through the pain and trying to quiet the thumping in my head.

Pushing through the double glass doors, we make our way inside the busy hospital, where a trauma nurse greets us immediately. Benji called Nico on the way here, and apparently there is a doctor who Dante recommends that can help us. He relayed that the doctor will be discreet, and that they're on top of their game. They'll be able to fix me up, no questions asked, and send me on my way. The sooner they can do that, the better, because I already feel my pulse thumping harder and faster after taking two steps inside the door.

The problem with underground fighting is that it's all on the downlow—underground—or if you want to get technical... illegal. That combined with the fact I work with the head mob family in New York, it means that anything I do can be a point of interest for some people.

Those that have a morbid interest in the inner workings of our family. The men who want to be part of something, the women who want to be wrapped around one of us, neither of whom will ever get a glimpse of what or who we truly are. Although many of them prefer to run away instead.

I walk like a fucking invalid next to Benji as sweat beads form on my forehead simply from being in this place. All the while, he continues to bark orders at everyone in sight. I hope Nico and Dante are right about this doctor, because the smell of disinfectant is piercing my nostrils and the need to get the hell out of here crawls up my spine, making me shiver. My throat tightens as the memories of my past escape my subconscious, infiltrating my mind. I've got no time to reminisce, though, and have no desire to take a trip down memory lane. Especially not tonight.

How Nico and Dante know a doctor here in Philly, I have no idea. They only ever come down here to watch me fight and ensure that I win, preferring to be in New York with the rest of the team. I used to always be right alongside them, but as of recently, I am spending more and more time down here, building up my gym business with Benji and making new acquaintances for the mob. It works in everyone's favor.

As we walk farther down the hall, my grip around my torso tightens. Each inhale I take, brings a renewed twinge of pain, and I wonder if coming to this hospital was actually a good idea for once. Even though my hands feel clammy, and I now feel slightly nauseous.

"We need Dr. Wakeford," Benji barks at a young

nurse. She looks totally intimidated by his erratic manner, and rightfully so.

"I'm... I'm not sure..." she stammers before Benji interrupts her.

"We want to see Dr. Wakeford!" he shouts at her, and she jumps, startled by his tone, rushing away to the nurses' station.

"Benji, fucking calm down," I barely manage to say, while holding back a groan. My arm remains wrapped around my torso, and I hiss as the pain shoots across my rib cage.

It was a tough fight tonight, that much is sinking in now. My face feels swollen, my ribs hurt, my hands are bruised and covered in blood. Hopefully nothing's broken because that will put me out for a while. The thing is, though, it's not much worse than how I find myself after most fights. If anything, my nerves are what's really causing me the most aggravation. And Benji's crazy ass isn't helping either.

I look up in time to see a male nurse walking up to us.

"I'm Ian. I can assess you today," he says calmly, taking in the sight of me.

Before I can respond, Benji pipes up again. "No one is touching him except for Doctor Wakeford." His finger points in my direction, and my eyes roll.

"I can appreciate that, but I am the Nursing Manager for Doctor Wakeford's office, so I can do an initial assessment before I call the doctor." He's not taking any crap from Benji, and I need to smother my smile. As I look at Benji, I can tell he's about to explode, yet he's holding it in and going bright red in the face in the process.

"Relax, Benji. Let him do the paperwork." I'm too tired and sore to argue, and really just want to leave this place as soon as possible.

We follow Nurse Ian into an examination room, and I sit on the edge of the hospital bed. He passes me an ice pack, and I nod in appreciation as I press it onto my face to try to contain the swelling before it gets out of hand.

"Would you like to tell me what happened?" Ian asks as he grabs my wrist and feels for my pulse.

"Just a fight, nothing major," I reply steadily. I can tell by his expression he doesn't believe me, but continues with his initial assessment by noting a few details on his paperwork.

"When will the doctor be here?" Benji asks with a huff. His two minutes of silence must've given him a second wind, his demanding attitude back in full force. He paces the small room, not yet settled. Maybe the pressure of being held accountable by the mob if, God forbid, I croak under his watch, is getting the better of him.

"I'm afraid that Doctor Wakeford is—" Ian starts to say before he's cut off, much more confidently than the previous young nurse.

"Tell her that Dante Luciano from New York has sent us," Benji tells him slowly, almost calculating, and I narrow my eyes as I look at him. *What pull does Dante have in this hospital?*

Ian sighs. "Fine, give me a few minutes. I will page Doctor Wakeford for you," He concedes, before grabbing his clipboard and walking out the door, leaving us in silence.

Taking a strangled breath, I glance around the room,

trying to distract myself. Only, there's not much to see. Everything is stark and bland, white and clean, and I squint under the bright lights, the pounding in my head increasing. It's a small room, made even smaller by Benji and me in it, the two of us both tall and broad. Our daily sessions at the gym give us the bulk many men envy and women cower from. The bed linen is scratchy, and while it is quiet in the room, I can hear the running around on the other side of our door, machines beeping, people talking, many of them frantic, probably not unusual for a Saturday night. I hear the security team struggling nearby with what I can assume is some drunk idiot, and I fleetingly think that could have been me had it not been for Sebastian and Dante picking me up off the streets all those years ago.

"How does Dante know a doctor down here?" I give in to my curiosity, turning to face his direction.

Tonight, shit was going down in New York, and the boys couldn't make it to my fight. Hell, I nearly didn't make it either, because family comes first, and I should be with them. But Sebastian is aware I am trying to build my life down here and told me they had it under control.

"Nico said the doctor that fixed up Annie after the shooting now works here. That's why I brought you here instead of that other shithole you usually go to get checked." He finally sits down in the white plastic chair that looks about as comfortable as a pile of rocks. Rubbing his head, he's visibly exhausted, his adrenalin wearing off.

It's a good thing. I think this power trip of being my manager while the boys are away is chipping at his sanity.

I would yell at him if my fucking head didn't hurt so much. Instead, I close my eyes, attempting to calm my breathing once again.

I fucking hate hospitals.

This doctor better hurry up before I lose my mind.

2

DR. CATHERINE WAKEFORD

Pushing my chair out, I stand up from my desk and roll my shoulders, trying to relieve my constantly tight, sore muscles from my stressful daily grind. It has been a long night already. Saturday night at the hospital is always crazy, though. Usually that means the late shift goes fast, which I am grateful for.

Since performing surgery for a man injured in a car accident, I have been back here in my office, combatting the mountain of paperwork requiring my attention. The most important being the plans and project outlines for the new Emergency Department that the hospital is in the midst of building. While our current facilities are good, they will soon be one of the most technologically advanced in the country. I am super proud that I get to lead it.

When I made my rounds on the floor earlier, I could see all the usual suspects had come in. Saturday afternoons we were full of kids and families, since the sporting days ensure we are busy with broken bones, sprained limbs, and deep cuts. But Saturday nights are my least favorite, because that is when we get the drunks, fighters, and other questionable characters who have indulged in drugs and other such activities. All of which warrants the high number of security guards we now have down on the floor.

It is unbelievable that we need security to protect the people who help and heal.

Walking over to my door, I grab my white coat from my coat rack and put it on, ready to check on what craziness is currently happening outside my door. Something I try to do on the hour, every hour.

I shouldn't complain, it is my only form of exercise, and the thousands of steps I do per shift far outweigh any I could accomplish in a run around the park.

When I accepted this job nine months ago, I negotiated that I only work one Saturday night per month. I love medicine; it has been in my blood for generations, but there is an eight-year-old I love more. Although she enjoys spending the night at her aunt's house, I miss her when I am away.

Already I can't wait to see her for breakfast, before I delve into my Sunday soccer mom duties, and then attempt to fix the leaky tap that appeared in my kitchen this morning. Sighing, I grab the photo of Ivy from my desk, willing it to give me the energy I need. As much as I cherish every moment spent with my daughter, the single mom life can be tiring at times.

I'm lost in thought when my desk phone rings, and immediately my adrenaline kicks in. Being a doctor means hard work and long hours, especially in the ED, where you need to prepare yourself for anything.

"Doctor Wakeford," I say as I answer the call.

"Catherine, we have a few guys down here that are requesting you," Ian, my head nurse and closest friend, tells me.

"Requesting me?" I ask in surprise. I can't say that anyone has ever requested me personally like this before. That piques my interest.

"Yes. White male, late twenties, presented himself with what looks like injuries to his face, abdomen, and hands."

"A fight?" My brow furrows, wanting Ian to get more specific.

"Yes. A pretty brutal one, if you ask me. But they won't let me assess. His friend is highly agitated and said that a Mr. Dante Luciano sent them to see you."

I still for a moment, memories flooding my mind.

"Fine, Ian. Tell them I will be down in five minutes," I reply, before hanging up the phone.

Dante Luciano. Second in command of the New York Mob. He brought his girlfriend to the emergency room with a gunshot wound back when I worked in New York over a year ago. Something I should have reported to the police, but instead, I kept it quiet because he offered cash to do so. While it wasn't my finest hour, I needed the money to get Ivy and I to safety.

I hope karma doesn't come back to bite me.

Accepting money from the mob was also not the smartest thing to do; I recognize that now. As a woman who worked her ass off at med school and received top honors, becoming the youngest woman to lead an Emergency Department in the country at the age of thirty-five, I am held in high regard. I followed in my dad's footsteps, and if he, or anyone else, ever found out about my small indiscretion, then I would lose the career and reputation I have worked so hard to build.

But, if I had to do it all over again, I would still take the money. For Ivy. While I love being a doctor, I love her more. She will come first every single time, and getting out of New York was something I had to do. Even though my father is still seething about the move and constantly trying to make me move back.

I fix my white coat and brush down my navy dress underneath. Quickly, I check my cell phone to make sure my sister hasn't called with any issues with Ivy, and with a sigh of relief, I get into business mode.

The mixture of noises hits me first as I step out of my soundproofed office. Rushed voices of panicked patients, and firm assurance from our nurses and doctors. Rattling wheels of gurneys and beeps of medical equipment. Calls over the speaker, and the distant whir of a siren. This is chaos to anyone else, but to me, the sounds belonging to a hospital immediately get my head in the game. Striding down the corridor, I duck and weave past a few staff and patients and make my way to the nurses' station to see Ian.

Ian is one of the best nurses I have had the pleasure of working with, and is not only professional, but also a lot of fun.

"Okay, what should I know?" I ask as I sidle up to him behind the counter.

"As I mentioned, white male, abdominal bruising, cut above his eye, swollen cheeks, bruised and swollen hands…" He passes me a clipboard, and I quickly look over his vitals, but find the paperwork mostly blank.

"Ian, there is nothing on here? Just his pulse?" I usually get a full write-up of a patient's condition before I see them.

"They only wanted you, so I was lucky to get that. His friend wouldn't let me touch him. They scared poor Kate out of her skin when they arrived," he says, shooting his gaze to Kate, who's smiling shyly and biting her lip with obvious nerves. She is a sweet, friendly new nurse, with a great bedside manner, but I am not sure the ED is the right place for her.

"Anything else?" I press.

"Well, the friend is an asshole, but the patient is mighty fine," he whispers before wiggling his eyebrows at me.

"Ian!" I admonish with a laugh, whacking him in the shoulder with the clipboard. "All right, lead the way." Might as well get this over with.

3

CARTER

"Benji!" I yell this time. I am sick of him creating a scene here with every goddamn nurse and doctor that walks past. "Shut the fuck up, man. Just let the nurses treat me."

I still haven't been seen since the male nurse left. My anxiety is rising, and I want to climb the walls at this point. I'm tired, hungry, hurting, and all I want is to fucking go home.

"No, the boys left me in charge. I'm doing what they asked of me and waiting for Doctor Wakeford."

I roll my eyes and drop my gaze back to the floor, willing the pain to subside. I have been sitting here on the edge of the bed, legs hanging off, my head down, waiting for this magical fucking doctor to appear. They're apparently the only one who can fix me, when all I need is fucking ice and my bed. Fucking Benji. This is ridiculous.

I love him, I do. We have been best friends since we were eight, so he's basically a brother. We met at the local police station because the cops had picked us up for shoplifting. Me at the supermarket, stealing food, because my mom was too busy with her new boyfriend, and we didn't have anything in the trailer for days. And Benji for stealing a packet of smokes from the local gas station.

We formed a bond that day as we both waited at the police station for our respective parents to pick us up and have been friends ever since. Always by each other's side. While his current power trip is pissing me off, he is doing a good job of looking after me. Benji has been chomping at the bit to manage me, and despite the fact he has no formal qualifications, he is pretty good at it, often helping me mend after each fight.

I am about to say something else to him, because I can see his impatience growing by the second, when the door opens. All I can do is keep my head down. I don't want to look at another nurse while Benji yells at them.

"We want the fucking head of ER now!" he roars, and without looking, I know that his face is red and the thick vein in his throat is probably throbbing. I wait to hear if the nurse scurries off like the rest of them have. But whoever is in the room doesn't run off and whimper like the last few.

My eyes lift from the tiled floor to see the sexiest fucking black stilettos, then higher to her smooth, long legs and pristine navy dress. A crisp white coat covers what I'd like to see more of, but then my gaze settles on the shiniest brown hair and most perfect skin that I have ever seen in real life. As I take in her captivating features, I find that it's impossible to look away.

"I am Doctor Wakeford, Head of the ER, and if you raise your voice to me or my staff like that again, you will be escorted out of this hospital and will need to drive another hour to Mass General to be assisted. Do I make myself clear?" Sounds like she means business.

I sit in shock for a moment because I was expecting the Head of the ER to be a man. A middle-aged, play golf on the weekends, white hair and pretentious polos, type of douche, but Doctor Wakeford none of those things.

I rub my temples because my head is pounding, but I can hear Benji breathing heavily and starting to calm down. Ordinarily, he doesn't like to be challenged, but I have a feeling he will let this slide.

"Good, you're here. You need to look at Carter," he mumbles, like the chastised man he is, raising his arm in my direction. Then she's turning on her heel and moving toward me.

My head is still down, because it is throbbing like a motherfucker, but I watch her shoes come into view with every step she takes in my direction, not stopping until she is right in front of me, my knees nearly touching her body. I take a deep breath to get some air, which seems to have all but left me the moment she arrived, and I get a lungful of her instead. She smells like fucking springtime, flowers and freshness and sunshine, and I close my eyes and fist my hands in the scratchy white sheets underneath me. From the pain in my torso, or her scent, which one I am not sure.

"Mr. Grange," she says quietly, as she places the clipboard down on the bed next to me. "What happened?" Her hand grabs one of mine, her fingers curling around my wrist as she checks my pulse, and it's like I have been slammed in the chest. Her hands feel so fucking soft, so small in comparison to mine. My heart is racing, and I thank God I am not hooked up to a machine for her to hear it because it would be beeping off the charts.

I don't say anything, leaving it to Benji to do the talking.

"He had a fight. We just need you to check him over. He got a few punches to the head and a few to the ribs. Nothing crazy, but I want him checked before we go home," Benji states, now acting like the perfect kid in Sunday school.

She doesn't respond, or react, as she looks at her watch, timing my pulse. While Benji continues talking, she turns my hand over and looks at my knuckles, assessing the damage with her delicate hands.

"I need you to lie down, Mr. Grange, so I can check your ribs and face, please," she instructs delicately. The contrast between her gentle tone and Benji's fucking insane yelling is significant. I don't think I know anyone who speaks so firmly, yet so softly.

Delicate is not a word I would use to describe anything in my life. Violent, criminal, dark and hardened are more my history.

"Mr. Grange?" she says again, prompting me. *Shit, how long have I ignored her for, because I was lost in my own thoughts?* I start to move gingerly because my ribs are on fire and my head feels like a bowling ball. Closing my eyes, I lower my body onto the bed and swing my legs up so I am lying on my back, my eyes squinting shut due to the lights.

"Ian, turn the lights a little lower, please." I internally thank her for that as she stands at my bedside, still holding my hand. Why is it so fucking comforting? And that's just another word that doesn't usually describe me or my life.

She lets go of my hand, and for a moment, I feel cold, colder than I did before her touch. But then they're on my body, as she slowly runs her hands up my bare torso, checking each rib, gently pushing and prodding, searching for pain points and possible fractures.

Suddenly, she hits a sore spot, and I nearly jump off the bed. "Fuck!" I spit out, and my eyes fling open and lock right onto her beautiful brown ones. We stare at each other for a few beats, her glossy, plump lips parting slightly as I gawk at her. Benji clears his throat, and it is enough to startle both of us back to reality.

"I apologize, Mr. Grange, I will try to be more gentle," she says, a blush pinkening her cheeks. Continuing to explore my body for wounds, she checks each rib delicately before moving back to the original sore spot and prodding some more.

"Call me Carter, none of this Mr. Grange shit," I say to her, and it comes out rougher than I wanted, but she nods as she presses her lips together, her eyes staying focused on my body.

Now I have seen her, I can't stop fucking looking at her. Chestnut hair, shiny and long, half up so I can see her face set in concentration, but it flows down her back, itching for me to grab onto it. Her eyes are like coffee, her skin is cream, and her lips are shining like fucking cherries. This is a visual that I know won't leave my mind for days.

She is fucking stunning.

While she is writing things down on the clipboard, I continue to let my gaze wander over her. She is polished. Her fingernails are painted soft pink, flawlessly, with no chips, and she is wearing a small amount of jewelery that looks to be of the highest quality. While I'm at it, I notice no ring on her finger, bringing a smile to my lips that I immediately straighten. The dress she's wearing under her doctor's coat is pressed to perfection, refined and unrevealing. It's the kind of dress you long to unzip with the thoughts of what delectable curves she's hiding from the world underneath.

She is not over the top, but classic. She is what you would call *way* out of my league. I bet this princess has never had to go without.

I fucking hate princesses, yet I can't say I mind her hands on my body right now.

Fuck my life.

"No broken ribs, but they are certainly bruised, and I am a little concerned about internal bleeding too," she says, and my eyes flick back to hers.

"Doc, just some pain medication, some ice, and I will be on my way." I start to sit up, willing the thumping in my head to stop as I do.

"Oh no, no, no." Her hands land on my shoulders, and she pushes me back down. "*You* are not going anywhere."

Out of the corner of my eye, I see Benji stand, and I feel her stiffen slightly.

"I am going to organize a scan for you." I remain still,

but give her a small nod at the same time Benji marches over to the bed beside me.

"A scan? What for?" Benji barks at her.

"Benji, enough," I say sternly. I can tell she is a little frightened of him, and I don't blame her because he is back to being an ass. "Let's do the tests and get home. I'm tired."

"Ian, please arrange for Carter to get an CT scan, specifically for the upper body please. I want to check for internal bleeding," she says to her nurse, who nods while taking notes, and I begin to feel like a fucking invalid.

"Further, we need to assess for concussion and.." She stops as she looks back at me. Her hand comes up to my face, where she cups my cheek and turns my head slightly. "We will need a few stitches in his left eyebrow, please."

"Carter," she says softly. "Ian will look after you, and I will return with your results as soon as they come through. In the meantime, we will also get you settled in a private room at the end of the hall for your comfort, and I'll get you some medication for the pain and some more ice for the swelling. However... we will need to admit you here overnight." One of her hands swoops under her coat and lands on her hip, like she is daring me to argue with her. I like her sass, and I don't miss her bust and the curve of her ass with the movement either. Both of which I would like to explore. But there is no way I am staying here overnight.

"No. I'll stay for the scan. But as I said, just some pain meds and ice, and I will be fine." I'm trying to sound like I am not in pain, but I don't think she's buying it.

"I wasn't asking. If Dante sent you, then you need to do as I say," she insists, with no room for argument, and I tilt my head and look at her. Let's see how far she will go with this.

"I don't particularly like people telling me what to do, Doc..."

"Well, get used to it, because you are here for the night, and I expect you to do everything I say," she replies, with one eyebrow lifted in a challenge, and as I remain silent, she grabs the clipboard from Ian, who is observing our conversation wide-eyed, and walks out the door. As soon as she leaves, my annoyance skyrockets.

Ian rushes out after her and Benji stalks over to the bed, a stupid smirk on his face.

"Fuck, she told you!" he says as he starts to laugh. Like she didn't just pull the same shit with him.

"Shut the fuck up," I grit out as I lie back down, easing my head on the pillow.

I hate hospitals, I hate doctors, and I fucking hate perfect princesses who probably survive on daddy's money and live their perfect fucking lives in perfect mansions, with perfect gardens, all behind a perfect fucking white picket fence.

I bet she has a boyfriend named Chad. I silently fume to myself, while Benji gets busy calling Nico to fill him in on the latest.

Closing my eyes, I just want this night to be over with.

4

CATHERINE

I pace back to the nurses' station, my heart thumping out of my chest. Usually, when the hectic atmosphere of the hospital envelopes me, it's like a warm hug, making me feel secure. But right now, my happy place is doing nothing to calm me down. I suck in deep breaths as I sign off on the forms to get Carter into a scan and then admitted. As the staff move in an organized chaos around me, I am thankful they pay little attention to me and what my body is doing.

Carter Grange is something.

The minute I walked into that examination room, I felt an energy unlike anything else. I can't explain it, but whatever it was, it was rolling off Carter in tsunami-like waves as he sat on the edge of the bed, head down, in nothing but a pair of shorts, which hid nothing. His body is truly spectacular; he has muscles in places I've only ever seen in my medical academia books. Every inch of him is carved to perfection and covered in ink. I like tattoos, although I don't have any myself. To be honest, I haven't really seen that many, only a few on some patients over the years.

From his shoulders down his torso, his body is a masterpiece, and all I wanted to do was keep exploring. That's when I pulled my hands back from him like they touched fire. I don't know if it's the lack of sleep or if I need another coffee, but touching a patient's body even a moment more than necessary is so unbelievably unprofessional. I am the Head of ER. There are protocols, rules, regulations. *What is wrong with me!* I have never had a reaction like that before.

It was not my finest hour, that is for sure.

Maybe it is the fact that the only place I see men is here at the hospital. Maybe I need to get out more?

My ex, Daniel, was my last and only intimate partner and he is the typical prep school prototype. Not a hair out of place, not a feather ruffled, and certainly no tattoos. But seeing them on Carter tonight... I needed to escape that room before I melted into a puddle right in front of him.

And his hungry, unwavering eyes on me didn't help matters either.

Ian steps up beside me. "Do you need a cool drink of water to quench that thirst?" he asks with a bit of sass. I raise my eyebrow at him, trying to remain stoic.

"Oh, c'mon," he whispers. "The two of you were eye-fucking each other so hard I got pregnant." I hit him in the arm with the stack of papers I'm holding while looking around to see who heard him. Thank God everyone is too busy.

"*Seriously*, he is a patient. You know I can't go there." Keeping my head down, I finalize the paperwork.

"The pink blush of your cheeks tells me otherwise..." he murmurs, and I roll my eyes. "I'm not sure how you can be so professional around an Adonis like him without losing your mind. Give me those forms so I can wheel him down to the scan team. I am happy to take him off your hands," he adds playfully, his eyes searching me, obviously trying to assess what my true feelings are. Which is completely understandable after just witnessing his boss being thrown a little off kilter by a patient. He's aware that's very unlike me.

I stack the small pile of papers on the desk to get them in order and hand them over to Ian with a smirk.

"It is easy to be professional because I am a professional, Ian." I swivel around to face him, trying my best to erase the vision of a half-naked Carter Grange from my mind. My stern face is in place, to remind me that he is just another patient and I am his doctor.

"Who is this Dante person you all keep talking about anyway?" Ian asks as he looks through the paperwork, and I stiffen.

"A mutual friend. Someone from New York." I wave my hand a little, trying to remain impassive, while also taking another look around to ensure no one is in earshot of our conversation.

He glances up at me and his eyes widen slightly. "Don't say some more bad history? Anything to do with your ex?" he asks, and I shake my head. Ian knows all about Daniel. He knows everything that happened and why I am in Philly.

"How long has it been since you've heard from him?" All playfulness is gone from his expression, replaced by concern, his eyes boring into mine for full honesty.

"Too long," I answer. "Lately, I feel uneasy about it. I know he is going to come and find me soon, and I am not looking forward to that." Ian is the only one who knows about my history at work, and I plan to keep it that way. I don't need to be the hot news and I certainly don't need anyone's pity.

"Well, you do have a restraining order against him so that might keep him away?" Ian offers, and while my lips turn upward at him, it is not a true smile.

"Nothing will keep him away. He is a rich, pompous jerk who has always gotten whatever he wants." Taking a breath, I shake my head from that spiral. "Anyway... do you want security to escort you down to the scan room? His friend seemed a little agitated."

Luckily, Ian lets me get away with the subject change.

"Agitated or asshole?" He looks at me incredulously, and I let a small chuckle escape. "No, I can handle him." And I know he can.

"Fine, let me know how it goes. Once you have him settled, I can come down and do the stitches and deliver the results."

"Oh, so you want to personally stitch his eye, then?" Ian teases, a smirk on his face.

"Well, we can't have you slipping on your own drool and falling into his lap now, can we?" I taunt him right back.

"I don't think he swings my way, *Doc*, but I bet he sure

swings yours." I don't miss that he called me the same nickname Carter did just now.

"The last thing I need in my life is another man to tell me what to do and how things are going to be done." Huffing, I dig my hands in my white coat, checking that I have all my things, while trying to keep busy as the nerves *still* thrum through my body. I feel only pens and gum since my stethoscope is hanging around my neck. An accessory I always forget is even there.

"Speaking of all the things you get done, how is my darling Princess Ivy? I meant to ask you earlier."

"Great!" I smile as I look at my watch, seeing that it is now after 1am. "In fact, I have soccer mom duties with her in approximately seven hours." Ian winces.

"I have no idea how you do it. I am dead on my feet by the time I get home after this shift."

"Well, she really wanted to play soccer this year, and it is a great way to get to know more people here, so I encouraged her. I will take a nap later in the day and drink copious amounts of coffee when I get home." I smile at him and watch as he takes a few steps over to the wall of wheelchairs. I can't help but laugh.

"What?" he asks, stopping mid-stride, looking between me and the chair.

"Good luck with that." I point to the wheelchair and before he can reply, I grab my paperwork and leave him to look after Carter Grange and his obnoxious friend.

I have coffee to drink.

5

CARTER

"Fuck, she is a hot piece of ass," Benji says the minute he gets off the phone to Nico, and I glare at him.

"What! She is," he whines, taking a seat back in the white plastic chair at the edge of the room. "Don't tell me you didn't enjoy that little examination just now." Wiggling his eyebrows, his stupid grin taunts me.

For once tonight, I actually agree with him. She had a presence from the moment she walked into the room. I didn't want to come here, I hate being here, but she made me forget it all. The feel of her soft hands on my body still lingers on my skin.

My mother was always in and out of the hospital when I was younger. After whatever asshole boyfriend she had at the time used her as a punching bag. I spent many nights between the ages of five and ten asleep on the hard plastic chairs in the waiting room as doctors worked on her and nurses continually doted on me, bringing me soft drinks and chocolate from the vending machine. I even got to first name basis with some of the nurses, which isn't something to be proud of.

Then, one day when I was fifteen, after a particularly bad beating, she left me at home instead. I waited in our trailer for days, pacing non-stop, telling myself she'd be okay. Only, she never came home. And when I found out why, I became desperate.

That night, I hit the streets and tried to pickpocket Sebastian. I needed money for food, and having not eaten a thing for two days straight, I was out of options. He offered me a job, and I haven't looked back since.

"What is taking them so long!" Benji grumbles, frustrated once again. We are both tired and just want to go home. Since that doesn't look like it is happening tonight, the need to get settled into a quiet room is strong.

"What did Nico say?" I ask, trying to distract myself. I also want to gleam some information from him on what is going on in New York. I'm keen to know what the boys are doing, wishing I was with them. Wishing I was anywhere else but here.

"They're busy. He couldn't really talk, but he wanted to know how you were. I think they need you back in New York soon." I nod, though I already knew that. Benji wasn't so lucky in life to find someone like Sebastian, so when I was whisked up by the mob and moved to New York as a teenager, he stayed here in Philly. He continued his rough life, until I found him years later and put my money into the gym. A gym that he now manages for me and does a pretty good job of it too.

I wince again as I try to take another big breath, and the smell of disinfectant brings back a host of memories that I would rather forget. I clench my hands, feeling overheated again, my chest tightening, and I wonder if I should just up and leave. I take another slower breath to inflate my sore lungs and catch a hint of Doctor Wakeford. It instantly calms me, so much so, my hands relax, and my mind wanders back to everything *her*. Cherry lips, long dark hair, sexy body.

Benji is right, she is a hot piece of ass, with a sassy mouth to match. I find myself shaking my head in frustration. What am I doing daydreaming about a hot doctor? I've already established she is not someone for me. And I am certainly not the man for someone like her. Buttoned-up and straitlaced is not my life.

I can't be thinking about her. I need to keep my mind on my next fight, and getting my body right with training. It is twelve weeks away, so I have enough time to mend.

Tonight was a hard fought win. I knew it would be. I am now in my late twenties, and my fighting years are nearly behind me. There are some strong young kids coming through the ranks, many of them like me with a big fucking chip on their shoulder and a history not worth repeating. That's what gives us all enough anger to explode in the cage like we need to. But the fights are getting tougher as the years go on, and I am thinking my next one may well be my last.

"Any news on Reggie?" I ask, not because I care. When I am in the cage, the last thing I think about is the wellbeing of my opponent. But I sure as fuck hope he is doing worse than me, since these pains are a bitch.

"Apparently, he is in ER too, needing stitches, and I

think his ribs are broken from what I hear," Benji relays with a sly smile, one that is contagious.

It took me six rounds to knock Reggie out; everyone else usually only takes two. My stamina was tested, my fitness was pushed, and because I was in the ring longer than normal, it meant more hits to my body. Which is the sole reason why I'm here.

My next opponent I'm facing will be Big Dom and, like me, he hasn't lost a fight yet. He has been around the cage for a few years, and we have never come against each other, the two of us both undefeated. The organizers of our MMA have been trying to get our fight together for years, but timing and injuries have prevented it up until now.

Promotion will start soon, but we already know that it is going to be deadly. We are well matched in weight and height, with him slightly younger, but I have more experience. This fight will be a guaranteed sell out, held in one of the biggest warehouses in Philly. Big Dom won't give me even an inch of reprieve, so that's just another reason to focus on recovery.

"Big Dom will be harder," Benji states, reading my mind, and I glare at him.

"As if I don't already fucking know," I snarl. Big Dom is an asshole too. One who is extremely unpredictable and one hundred percent conniving.

"We need to get you recovered and onto training as soon as possible. Where is the fucking nurse?" Benji starts up, pulling at his chair.

I continue to lie on the bed, uncomfortable but too

sore to complain. A moment later, the door swings open, with Ian walking back in, pushing a wheelchair.

"No fucking way," I say as soon as I see it. "There is no way I am sitting in that fucking thing and getting wheeled around this fucking hospital."

"You have had some hits to the head tonight and most likely have a concussion. You can't walk to the scan room," Ian tells me simply, his hands coming to his hips, and it appears that he is feeling sassy tonight as well.

"No. Fucking. Way," I grit out to ensure he knows I mean business. I would rather fall to the floor than sit my ass in that.

Sighing, he pushes the chair back out the room, before holding the door open for Benji and I. "This way, gentlemen. We need to head down the hall and to the right." I gingerly rise from the bed and follow Benji out the door, shuffling my way down the godawful corridor in this godawful place.

6

CATHERINE

The lights are dimmed as I step into the room, closing the door on the small amount of noise outside. I see Carter lying still as the dead on the bed, eyes shut, hands clasped over his bare chest. It is now very early morning, and so I take a few quiet steps in his direction. I look over and see his friend Benji snoring, drool on his chin as he sleeps over in the armchair. Not leaving his side for a moment. It is nice that he has such a good friend, even if he's been a jerk to the medical staff here.

I set my equipment tray on the table and wheel it closer to Carter. His breathing is steady, but his face looks tense. Hopefully he is in no pain. Grabbing the clipboard from the side of his bed, I look over the stats Ian has recorded over the past few hours to ensure he is still doing okay.

"Am I going to live?" he asks me, his lips twitching into a small smirk. His deep voice feels like velvet across my skin, and I struggle to not let it show as a shiver moves down my spine. He wasn't asleep as I had thought. I look at him, but his eyes remain closed, his hands still locked together across his broad chest.

"Yes, you'll live to see another day. There is no internal bleeding, and you should be recovered in no time. But you have a slightly elevated blood pressure rate, so I'm just going to check your pulse." I put the clipboard down and move to grab his hand, and as my eyes flick to his neck, I can see his pulse thumping.

"Are you feeling all right?" I ask him as my fingers grip around his wrist. I internally count the beats, not missing his sweaty palms, and I am wondering what is going on. What he might not be sharing that's ailing him.

"Fine," he says much too quickly, and I narrow my eyes at him just slightly.

"Are you sure? Your pulse is moving pretty fast for someone who's lying down?" I offer him an opportunity, and with him not looking at me, I don't think he'll bite. But then I hear him take a breath.

"I just hate hospitals," he admits. I continue to count the beats, seeing if I can slow it down by keeping him talking. Rule out any other cause and take his word for it. It's not an uncommon fear, that's for sure.

"Any reason? Or you just don't like us prodding doctors?" I tease to try to lighten the mood.

He huffs out a laugh. "Pretty ones, you mean." My eyes flick to him again, as his words don't quite register.

"You think I'm pretty?" I ask in jest, still counting, and I feel his hand relax in mine.

"Beautiful," he says seriously, and even though his pulse has now slowed, mine starts to race. My stomach flutters, so I have no choice but to bring the conversation back to where we started. That's my only option.

"Have you spent a lot of time in hospitals in the past?" I ask him, needing this to remain strictly professional.

"Too much. I was always in here as a kid." I can hear the unease in his voice. Just as I am about to let go of his hand, I feel his muscle tense again.

"Really? Did you have lots of falls or injuries?" Grabbing the clipboard, I note his pulse.

"My mom. I was in and out of hospitals with her, until she passed." I pause my movements, bringing my gaze back to him. The room is quiet for a beat, his expression unreadable. But I've seen enough pain to know what it looks like.

"I'm sorry you lost your mom, Carter. It is hard to lose a parent so young," I say, swallowing roughly as I place the clipboard down and lean against the bed.

"Yeah, well, she had a big heart. Fell in love with the wrong men. She gave herself to them, and they treated her like shit. Love killed her in the end."

I look at him with understanding. "I lost my mom too when I was a teenager. The pain never really goes away, does it?"

"What happened?" he asks, and while I normally don't share personal details with my patients, he has just opened up to me, so I try.

"Car accident. She never drank, she always stuck to the limit, yet this one night, both apparently were a factor. It is still hard to believe," I say with a sigh. I miss her every day.

"Sorry you had to lose her like that." Such a simple

statement, but the look in his eyes is filled with such deep understanding. It makes me want to hug him. I feel entirely too comfortable around this man, and that's a problem.

Clearing my throat, I smile softly. "So, have you been able to get some rest? Your friend seems pretty cozy? His snoring is loud enough to cause an earthquake." Pushing the trolley closer to him, I prepare everything to stitch the cut above his eye.

"If you have a bandage, I can wrap around Benji's nose to shut him up. That would be great." I can't help but huff out a laugh as I smile and shake my head.

"No, sorry. You need to find another friend who isn't so loud, I am afraid." I give him a shrug, and he smiles at my banter.

"Nah. I have had him around for years; I don't think I will get rid of him yet," Carter replies, giving me a small glimpse into their relationship.

"What time is it?" he asks me, and I meet his deep blue eyes that are staring straight at me. They are vibrant, almost sparkling, as they go from my head down my body and back again. It feels like he is undressing me with his eyes and my blood heats.

I internally scold myself while hearing my father's voice on repeat in my mind, "*You are nothing. An unwed single mother, no one wants you.*" Which causes me to shake my head to dislodge the thoughts. I need to pull myself together. I have been in the medical field for years, treating all manner of people, yet this is the first time I have had such an instant reaction to a patient. This is ridiculous and so unprofessional.

"Just after 3am. I'm going to quickly do your stitches and then you can rest some more. I'm sure you're exhausted," I say gently, aware that he has had little to no sleep tonight, and also wanting to remove his eyes from me before I lose focus entirely.

"I'll be fine. What about you?" he asks, and I pause, the question catching me off guard.

"Oh. Tired, actually. It's been a long week." I try to busy my hands with prepping the medical tray as I stifle a yawn. Talking about being tired makes me more tired.

"What time do you finish?" That question has me looking at him, wondering why he wants to know. His eyes pierce mine, appearing open, wanting to have a genuine conversation, and I will admit, it is nice. Not many patients ask me how I am or what my hours are like. Actually, not many people outside of work do either.

"A few more hours yet." I lean over to look at his cut, and I am suddenly aware of how close our bodies are. My waist nearly comes into contact with his, and I tilt my head so I am looking him in the eyes. The air around us crackles, his nostrils flare, and I feel the electricity of this moment as it zaps me to my core.

And I ignore it, ignore it, ignore it.

"Can you move your head this way a little?" I say in my most formal doctor voice I can muster, trying to get my betraying body to fall back into line. As my hand touches his jaw, I pull his face toward me, feeling the scratchy stubble on his cheek.

"I can see the cut better in the light," I tell him. In the ER room earlier, I could see the lights were harsh, and now as he is resting, I didn't want to make them too bright again.

His eyes continue to drill into mine, and I blush under his gaze. It is incredibly intense, and I am not yet sure if that is a good thing or not. Who am I kidding? It can't be a good thing. And that's confirmed when my stomach flips into itself, and I suddenly have the urge to squirm my legs together. Yet I refrain.

"So you're the doctor that fixed up Annie, then?" he asks, as I run the numbing cream around his cut, not missing the way he is white knuckled, locking his hands together. I'm not sure if the cream is causing him pain, or if he is feeling things he shouldn't as well.

The mention of Annie brings me back to reality, since he must know her from Dante. Which means... he must be close to the mob. *How close* is the question, because, like me, he could merely be an acquaintance. The fact that I know Dante is enough to get me in trouble with work, not to mention I have a small daughter to worry about. Getting closer to anyone even associated with them and their lifestyle is not something that I should be doing.

"Yes. She is a lovely girl. I am so glad things worked out for her. I spoke with her only a month or so ago, actually, and she sounded happy," I say with a smile on my face as I think of the beautiful young woman who was shot back in New York. I still have regular check-ups with her. How someone like her became involved with the mob is a whole other story.

"She is," he replies simply, watching me pretend to tidy up my tray of supplies as I wait for the numbing cream to take effect. My mind is swirling with questions that I shouldn't even want to ask, but I don't have to wait long until he gives me more clarity. Completely unprompted, like he could see my thoughts all over my face.

"Dante never leaves her side now," he says with a huff and a small smile, and with that, it's clear he knows them both well. It's slightly unnerving. Everyone knows the New York mob, and most people stay right out of their way. Except me, it seems. *They just walk straight into my life, apparently,* I think to myself with a dose of sarcasm. And for some reason, I'm feeling content in his presence. Enough so that I can't help but keep talking.

"Hmmm, well, it is good that she has someone to look after her," I murmur. And as I say the words it sinks in that that luxury isn't one afforded to a woman like me. Exhaustion nips at my heels again, knowing that there is no rest for me, no one to help with Ivy or to lift any of the heavy load I carry.

Taking a breath, I grab the tools I need from the tray and lean toward him again, trying to concentrate on the task at hand and not his muscled chest.

"So you moved here from New York?" he asks as I put the first stitch in, not even flinching as I pierce his skin. I concentrate on the work before me as I think about how to reply. I want to be honest, because in the quiet of the night, it feels like just the two of us. It is almost intimate as we talk in hushed tones. His deep voice surrounds me like a protective shield, one that makes me want curl up in his lap and stay there forever. Who he is outside of these walls, I am not sure, but I feel strangely safe around him. Something that is new for me, given that I feel the exact opposite with the existing men in my life.

"Yep. About nine months ago," I say as I continue stitching, ensuring that I make them nice and neat to prevent scarring.

"New York not your scene?" he asks, peering up at me.

"Hmmm..." is all I get out, my eyes like a hawk on his cut. My need for precision when doing stitches is almost comical. I wonder what he is trying to establish, but I leave it open for him to continue.

"I can't imagine Philly being a place someone like you would prefer?" he remarks, and I finally stop what I am doing and look at him.

"Someone like me?"

"You know. Rich, pretty, daddy's little girl and all that shit." I squint my eyes in question. Did he really just say that? My hand hovers above his face mid-stich, and I think about pricking him deliberately, but that would really take my unprofessionalism to new heights. I take a calming breath instead.

"Is that what you think of me?" Is he truly a nice guy, or just a chauvinistic pig? With an observation like that, I'm leaning toward the latter. I can feel my mask slide back into place as I wait for his response.

"You look too polished to be anything other than a New York girl. Manhattan, no doubt," he says with confidence, and my eyes flick to his. *Polished?* Clearly, if he saw me drag myself out of here at 5am to parent Ivy, then he would understand that polished is not necessarily how I would describe myself. I try to look my best, sure. I am a leader at this hospital, and I need to be a good example for my daughter, so I try to at least *look* like I have my shit together, even if the reality is somewhat different. As I stare at him, I wonder if he is serious or just trying to get under my skin. Unsure of which one it is, and not really caring either way, I lean over toward him again and begin the next stitch. He can think what he wants about me. What does it matter?

"It appears you know everything about me, Carter," I say, not hiding my annoyance as well as I should. Although I can't blame him for coming to the conclusion he did... I was that person up until a few years ago, I suppose.

"How is your head? Are these stitches going okay for you?" I ask when I notice he's looking uncomfortable.

"Fine, Doc. I've had much worse." I bet he has. Even though he is covered in tattoos, I can still see scars covering his body, and he has a lot of them. If I had to guess, I would say knife wounds mainly, but there are one or two that could be from bullets. Thinking about this, I decide to ask him a few questions. He's already made his assumptions about me, so it's time I find out if mine are correct.

"So, how do you know Dante?"

"Dante and Sebastian Romano are my brothers." Although my hands remain steady, and I continue with the stitching, my heart beats erratically. Everyone knows who Sebastian Romano is. It is suddenly apparent to me that this man underneath my hands is not just a friend of the mob, but a part of the mob.

"Hmmm, sounds like you're more New York than me, then," I say with more sass than intended, as I try to calm my insides and snip the last thread. Putting down the scissors, I place my hands on either side of his head and look closer to see if he needs another stitch. As my hands cup his face, I feel his eyes on me. The way he's making me feel, just from his gaze, there is no denying some chemistry between us. But I have to.

Out of the corner of my eye, I see his mouth turn up into a smirk, obviously amused by my retort, and I melt a little inside. My eyes meet his, and I offer a small smile in return.

"I think this will do. I have put them in as close to the hairline as possible and I don't think it will leave a scar, although you may have a thin red line for a little while," I tell him as I lean back and pull off my gloves.

"I'm not too worried about scarring, Doc. It comes with the territory." He rests back down in the same position he was in when I entered the room. The comment has my eyes back on his bare torso, again looking at the black ink, but also lingering on the scars this time. Being in my profession, I don't like seeing people in pain. My natural instinct is to stop it, heal them, fix them where I can. With the number of scars on his body, I only hope he's had caring doctors when he's needed them.

"Ian will check on you later. Is there anything you need before I go?" I ask, feeling the push to get out of this room. I need to get away from this man. My emotions are all over the place and the last thing I need is to be on friendly terms with another member of the mob. First, his eyes peer into my soul, then he insults me by calling me a rich daddy's girl before giving me that sly sexy smirk. I want to care for him, slap him, and kiss him all at once.

Carter stares at me for a beat. "How about your number?" he asks, his deep blues set on me, and I just about choke on a swallow. I still for a beat. It has been a long time since anyone asked me for my number. Again, my father's voice repeats in my mind. "*No one wants you, Catherine. You are washed up.*" And even if those insecurities weren't running rampant... this is dangerous territory for me to ever entertain. I need to do everything in my power to keep my daughter safe, and that means keeping a healthy distance from anything mob related.

"I don't think so, Carter. Why don't you rest up, and you can go home in the morning once your stats are taken after breakfast." I pat his hand, a habit I have with all of my patients. But when I go to move, he grabs onto it, stopping me in place.

"Being a polished girl from Manhattan is a nice thing... just so you know," he says as his thumb sweeps across my hand. It sounds like an apology of sorts, like he knows what he said earlier hit a sore spot within me. I stand there, looking at him for a beat, shocked that he bothered to acknowledge it.

I'm not sure I can form words. His hand gripping mine is steady, not threatening or harmful, but strong and reassuring. Like he knows I need it. But I can't let myself think like that. I need to be strong on my own; I know there is no one coming to save me.

"Good to know," I manage to whisper, before he lets go of my hand, and I grab onto my tray, gripping it like it is my lifeline.

"Goodbye, Carter."

I have never had a reaction like I have with Carter tonight. I don't know why, but I would be lying to myself if I said I didn't want more of it. Good thing I'll probably never see him again.

"Bye, Doc," he says, and it's like he knows it too.

7

CARTER

After lying in this fucking uncomfortable bed all night, I wake from the few hours of sleep I managed to get, and all I can smell is her. My nose so attuned to her scent now that I think I would be able to follow it and find her. But I don't. I lean forward and grab the clipboard from its holder on the side of my bed and flick through the pages. I am no doctor, but I've been around enough hospitals and have had enough injuries myself to be able to read most of the jargon on these pages.

Small concussion – not surprising.

No broken ribs – that is good, but that *is* surprising, because my body hurts like a motherfucker.

No internal bleeding, which I already knew, since Doc told me last night. But my ribs still hurt, and I feel like my organs are jumbled. Reggie got me good. I remember the punch too; a quick hard jab at the same time I twisted my body, and when the two of us collided, I felt the pain deep within.

My eyes scan farther, and then I catch her name. Doctor Catherine Wakeford. Fuck, even her name is beautiful, delicate, fucking feminine as shit. Most of the women I know are Rhonda, Tobi, or even Megan, which are all nice names, don't get me wrong. But Catherine Wakeford is refined. Elegant, even. *She is not for me*, I have to chant in my mind, over and over again, because even her name causes me to want her more.

But we are opposites. Like night and day. We move in totally different circles. She works in a hospital, helping, caring. I punch the shit out of people. I even kill a few of them too, if need be. She is too good for me. A man like me can't give her the kind of life she is accustomed to, so I need to stop fucking thinking about her.

I groan at the image I have of her in my mind as I cup my dick, which is already standing to attention. I can't say I minded having her body so close to mine last night. I had to keep my hands gripped together to refrain from latching onto her. If it were up to me, I'd be trading places with her, exploring her body instead. I've already dreamed up the countless ways I'd love to hear her scream my name.

She was open with me too, her answers were genuine. I could also tell when I stepped over the line. I didn't miss her body as it stilled when I called her a "daddy's girl," so I know I hit a nerve. Perhaps because I am right, and she just doesn't like to admit it. Although I think there is more to it than that.

I never ask a woman for her number either. But as soon as I opened my mouth, that request came out, the thought of her leaving and not seeing her again making me speak without thought. It shocked both of us, I think. I hated the rejection, but I saw her contemplating it for just a moment. That intrigued me, even if I had to man up and get over her knock back.

Then, I couldn't just let her leave when I had ruffled her feathers. So, like an idiot, I grabbed her hand. I couldn't even stop myself from caressing her skin, and I didn't even realize I was doing it at first. What is wrong with me? Now I'm daydreaming about holding her hand? My mind is out of control because of this woman. Hell, even now, with her not even in the room, I am still thinking of her. I am putting it down to the drugs and lack of sleep as I rub my eyes.

I look over at Benji, who is still asleep, snoring in the armchair in the corner of the room, his head at an odd angle and drool dripping on his chin. He can sleep through a hurricane and is clearly just as tired as I am, even though his sleep count doubled mine last night. I touch my head, the small stitches reminding me that I must have fallen asleep as soon as Doc left due to the pain meds. The hospital is quiet now, and I see the sun breaking through the cracks in the curtain.

Whilst I am still in pain, the throbbing in my head has subsided and the swelling has reduced and moved south to my crotch. I want to go home. If my relentless dick is any indication, then I *need* to go home. I need a cold fucking shower and to get my head on right.

I put the clipboard back and press the call button to wait impatiently for a nurse.

Ian comes in too fucking bright and cheery. "Good

morning! Everything all right, Carter?" he asks as he checks the fluid bag connected to my arm.

"I want to be discharged." I leave no room for argument with my demand. I am cranky, I am horny, and I want my own fucking bed, preferably with my doctor in it, naked, bouncing up and down on my cock. But, I'll have to do without, I suppose.

He looks at me with wide eyes at my grumpiness, but it isn't his fault his boss is the hottest fucking woman to ever appear in my life.

"Oh, well, I will need to get the doctor for you. They will check you over again and give you an update on your condition before the release papers can be signed." He places the clipboard back into the holder.

I nod like a damn pushover, because even though I want to leave, I want to see her one more time even more. And it will be the last time; our paths will never cross again. I am a masochist, and if one last look is all I can get, then I'll take it.

Ian walks out to make the calls, and I bark at Benji to wake up.

"Wake up, motherfucker." I throw my pillow at his face, and he jumps up with a start.

"What the fuck, man? I was having the best fucking dream," he whines, dragging a hand down his face.

"We're leaving."

"Fuck, okay. How you feeling?" he asks through a yawn, sitting up and stretching his arms above his head.

"Sore, but fine. They fixed me up. I need to rest, and I want to do that in my own fucking bed," I grumble. I am an asshole in the mornings. Actually, most of the time, but particularly in the mornings.

"Do you think that sexy doctor does house calls, because I have a swelling down below that I think she can alleviate," Benji says with an eyebrow wiggle I'd like to smack off, cupping his junk as he stands.

"You say one word about her again, and I will knock you out," I grit out. Benji stops suddenly, eyes wide with surprise.

"Fuck, you like her?" he whispers, gaping at me in shock.

"Fuck off, Benji. Let's get our shit together. The doctor will be here any minute, and I want to go home as soon as she's done."

Benji grins. He knows me too well. *Do I like her?* She is fucking beautiful, I can't lie. But I don't date. I fuck. Often. That is how my life is and, unfortunately, as much as I would like a taste of the pretty doctor, I don't think she is the *fuck and run* type.

As Benji hands me some clothes, Ian walks back in with an older man following him.

"Who the fuck is this?" Benji asks, and I am glad he did because I was wondering the same thing.

"Good morning, Mr. Grange. I am Doctor Gregory. I believe you would like to be released?" he says as he looks over my chart.

"Yes, I do, but where is Doctor Wakeford? She is my doctor." I look between him and Ian.

"Ahh, Dr. Wakeford finished a few hours ago. She came to see you before she left, but you were sleeping, and she didn't want to wake you. Dr. Gregory here will need to check you quickly and then you can be on your way," Ian answers me.

Fuck, I missed her. I rub my hand over my face and wince, forgetting about my bruises. This is probably a good thing. I made enough of an asshole of myself in the early hours while she stitched me up. I'm sure she is happy to see the back of me.

The doctor does his duty of checking my vitals and telling me I need to come back in a few days for the stitches to be removed before he signs my papers.

"You're free to go," Ian says with a grin as he looks between Benji and I. I nod to him in thanks as he retreats, before I slide off the bed and change.

"I think I prefer Doctor Wakeford too," Benji says, eyeing the door where the two men just left.

I look at him as I change quickly, then I grab the rest of my things before the two of us walk out the door. Because as much as I have enjoyed Doc these past few hours, I want to get the hell out of here.

8

CATHERINE

I rush to my sister's place, where she has breakfast waiting for me. God, I love her. Eighteen months younger than I, Maggie has it all together. A husband who is a professional accountant—one of which she works for as a well-paid accountant herself—a gorgeous child, and the pristine white picket fence. Yes, my father is extremely pleased with Maggie.

Me? I am a mess in comparison. Yes, I have an amazing job that pays well, but it leaves me too tired for anything else apart from Ivy. I always have a to-do list a mile long and suffer from rushing woman's syndrome, where I am always running from one thing to another. This morning a stark reminder of that.

Slumping at Maggie's kitchen table, I rest my head in my hands. I am exhausted. I always am after a night shift, but with managing Carter all night, I had less rest time than usual, and I feel like I could sleep for days.

"Rough night?" Maggie asks me as she slides a fresh

cup of coffee across to me, and I sit up and feel my body relax as I smell the comforting aroma.

"Yeah. Saturday nights always are," I reply, my voice devoid of all energy. How am I going to survive this day?

"You don't have to come to soccer, you know? I can take Ivy with us," she says, pursing her lips. She really is the best sister.

"I know. But it is her first game, and I really want to be there." I sip my coffee, willing the caffeine to work a miracle as it flows through my body.

"Here." She slides over a plate with a freshly made omelette, the kind with lots of cheese and bacon, greasy and buttery deliciousness. My mouth immediately waters.

"I love your omelettes," I moan as I take my first bite. Maggie is not only my sister, but my best friend. I love her to eternity and back, and I knew leaving New York and moving here to be closer to her would help heal my wounds.

She takes a seat next to me, watching me with concerned eyes.

"I'm fine, really. Just a busy night with a demanding patient," I say, answering her look.

Her eyebrows rise at that. "Patient? Were you working on the floor last night?" she asks in surprise. While Maggie isn't a doctor, we grew up with a surgeon for a father, so she knows the lingo and how odd it is for an ED Department Head to be still working directly with patients. It is a rare occurrence, although I do tend to make a habit of it. I like to keep up my skills but also show the other staff that I am still willing to roll my sleeves up.

"Yeah. They requested me." She looks at me, puzzled. I wait for the penny to drop, and it does.

"Something to do with Dante?" she whispers as she leans in, even though it is 7am and no one else is awake. Her eyes flit around the room, and I need to stifle my laugh because she is acting like the FBI is listening and about to pounce on us at any moment. I tell my sister everything, so stitching up the girlfriend of a mob boss and supplying him with the bullet for hundreds of thousands of dollars was not something I could keep to myself. It would have eaten me alive.

I nod silently. "His name is Carter. Needed a few stitches and tests after a fight, nothing too dramatic. He was... nice." My mind wanders back to the man I spent time with last night and how his body is now firmly etched into my memory.

"Only nice?" she presses, taking a sip of her coffee, her eyes glued to me over the rim of her cup. I raise my eyebrow to her in question.

"The blush on your cheeks right now as you remember him makes me think he was a little more than nice, dear sister?" she mocks me with widening eyes.

"Yeah, well, he is brothers with Dante, soooo..." I can visibly see the air whipped from her lungs.

"Shit."

I hum in agreeance as I take another bite of her amazing omelette, letting the activities of the past twelve hours come back to me. I'm not able to reconcile any of it yet, but knowing that Carter is now long gone and I will never see him again. I'm not sure why, but that thought disappointments me. Although we clearly had a connection, I thought it would have deteriorated the minute I left the hospital parking lot this morning. But it still lingers, following me even now, hours later.

As I take the last bite of breakfast, my face splits wide into a grin as I see Ivy running toward me from the hallway, and she tackles me in my chair. Oh, my little girl. Eight years old and full of attitude, outspoken and kind and smart. I love her so much. She's the best thing to ever happen to me.

She loves staying with Auntie Maggie and playing with my niece, Abby. The two of them are around the same age, go to the same school, and play soccer together. It's nice to see them get along so well; it reminds me of my sister and I.

"Hey, sweetheart, how was your sleepover?" I ask her, squeezing her tight. It was only a twelve- hour shift, but any time away from her leaves me feeling empty.

"Mom, did you know that in the olden days, they used beetles to make red lipstick?" she asks me, and I feel that it is too early for her fact sharing, but I nod and smile at my wondrous child before my eyes flick to Maggie in question. She shrugs. I have no idea how Ivy remembers all these animal facts, but she blurts them out all day, any chance she gets. She enjoys learning new things; reading every night, watching a lot of animal documentaries on TV, talking to anyone and everyone. One day, I even saw her flicking through the newspaper, looking like her late grandmother.

"Sounds... interesting?" I say with a smile, before

watching her run back down the hallway to get ready for her soccer match.

I sigh as I watch her, taking another sip of coffee. My precious girl, who I would do anything for, including keeping her away from the man who should love her the most. The pressure I feel to keep everything together mounts at the thought. I take a deep breath, willing the tears to remain hidden, and that quickly turns into a yawn.

"You work too hard. I'm worried about you," Maggie says to me quietly as she steps up behind me, rubbing a soothing hand over my shoulder.

"This crazy life I have is normal to me, so I just get on with it. What choice do I have?" There's no use in getting caught up with *what ifs*. This is my reality.

"You moved here so that you and Ivy could be safe, but that hasn't stopped Daniel," Maggie states, concern etched in her brow.

"Ivy is safe. He won't touch her."

"I know. He doesn't care about her; he doesn't want her. But what about you? He wants you. His verbal attacks have escalated, and I am not going to lie; it is frightening me," Maggie presses, and she is right. It is frightening, but I can just take each day as it comes right now.

"I'm fine. Having Ivy safe is my main priority, so please don't worry about me." I wave her off, really not wanting her to be concerned for me. She has enough going on, she doesn't need my stress added to it.

"But I do, and I know it has been a few months, so Daniel is most likely going to show up soon. I want you to be protected... so I got you this." She reaches for an envelope I didn't notice and hands it to me.

I open it up and look at the paper inside. It's a sign-up sheet for 10 self self-defense classes at a gym I haven't heard of on the edge of the city. I look up at her with questioning eyes.

"His behavior is escalating. When you were together, he trapped you financially, was verbally abusive to you, and I know even though you haven't told me, that he has been physically tough to you too. He is crazy, Cat, and he will keep going, keep pushing, until he wins. I am really scared of what will happen. I want you to be armed with everything you can be in case he ever tries to touch you again." Maggie has tears in her eyes, but she continues.

"You are my older sister. You carry everything. You have excelled at your career and have done such a great job with Ivy. Dad is too concerned with getting you and Daniel back together, to even contemplate what he does is wrong, so us girls need to stick together. I want us to be prepared."

"I don't know what to say," I murmur, lost for words. I am thankful that she looks after me, but I'm upset by the fact I have to learn to defend myself at all.

I lean across the table to hug her. "Thanks, Maggie."

"I am always here for you, always," she whispers.

9

CARTER

I t has been a few days now since I discharged myself from the hospital. The swelling in my face has completely gone, my bruises are lightening, and the pain in my ribs has decreased. I wish I could say the same thing for my cock, which has been permanently hard since I met Doc on Saturday night. My new habit of daydreaming has continued, despite the lack of medication in my system. Cold showers are now a daily occurrence, anything to get the vision of her face out of my head or the way I want her pretty, pouty mouth wrapped around my cock.

I have been doing light training, nothing too strenuous, but I need to start prepping for the next fight, regardless of how I'm feeling, both mentally and physically.

Leaning back into my office chair, Nico sits opposite me after arriving in Philly this morning.

"Tomorrow you should start reviewing footage of his previous five fights, so we can look for his tells and his most repeated actions. Learn where to hit hard and when," Nico states, as the faint pounding of fists connecting with punching bags in my gym below sneaks through my office walls.

Benji is on duty in the gym tonight, because it is self-defense night. He stations himself at the reception desk and signs in every female that walks in, knowing that some of them are too scared to even step through the doors in the first place. Whilst he is big and burly and somewhat intimidating, he knows how important these classes are for the women in our community, so he puts on a smile and ensures every woman feels comfortable and confident once they sign up for some sessions.

"Big Dom is going to come at me with everything, but I got him, don't worry, Nico." Although the fight will be one of the tougher ones of my career, it will be nothing I can't handle.

I plan to get the jump on him early. I know how he fights; I have seen a few and heard a lot. He can only win if I drag the fight out, which is what I normally do for entertainment value—and because I am a sick bastard that likes to toy with my opponents. But Big Dom needs to go down hard and fast, so I won't be making this fight a spectacle. The promoters won't be getting their usual song and dance from me. It'll hopefully be a one-and-done kind of fight.

I also haven't voiced my thoughts on this potentially being my last fight, otherwise they'd be blowing this fight up even more than they already are. I'd rather not have the questions of why, or the pressures to continue. My body just isn't what it used to be, and it will be good to ease off a little, I think. Keep my mind more focused on the gym and what Sebastian needs from me in New York. Between the two, it keeps me busy, and although I love to fight, it's seeming like time to step aside.

"Shit is heating up in New York. Things are moving, business is going well, but we have some issues that are arising," Nico says with deep concern.

I am about to ask Nico to elaborate, when Benji bursts through the door, eyes wide and his mouth gaping like a fish.

"What?" I stand quickly, ready for what I'm sure is a problem. The shock on his face has me up in arms.

"She's here!" he shrieks.

"Who?" I bark in return, my heart racing. It'd be nice if he could get to the fucking point.

"The doctor!" he shrieks again, throwing his hands in the air, as if I'm the idiot here.

"What doctor?" He is not making any sense. I clench my fits, waiting to jump into action, still thinking I'll need to take somebody down.

"*YOUR* DOCTOR!" Benji yells, looking exasperated, and then it clicks.

My eyes widen as I stare at him, and I try and get my head around this information. My doctor. Catherine Wakeford. Is here? In my gym?

"She is *here*?" I ask tentatively. There is no way anyone as classy as Catherine Wakeford would be in my gym.

"Yes, she is here for the self-defense class," he breaths out, now finally able to chill out.

"Fuck." My heart is now pumping out of my chest as I walk to the window in my office that overlooks the entire gym. Sure enough, I spot her immediately. Looking so sexy, it is dangerous, in matching yoga pants and a crop top, her shiny, thick brown hair pulled back in a bouncy ponytail. She is chatting animatedly to a woman next to her who is dressed in a similar fashion.

They look like they belong in a fucking sports commercial. They are gorgeous. My gaze stays on Catherine, taking her in from top to toe. Her body is as tight and curvy as I have been dreaming about. I'm itching to grab that tiny waist, or that glorious, round and perky ass. Then I get to her smile, and I know I'm fucked. She is beautiful, too fucking beautiful for my gym, that is for sure.

Nico comes up next to me and peers out the window. "Your doctor, huh?" he asks, digging for information that he is not going to get. "I met her in New York a few times. Annie and Dante love her. I'm glad she could help you out the other night."

I grunt in reply as I watch her, and she must sense it because her eyes rise and catch mine. But I don't flinch, staring at her openly, drinking her in, tasting her with my eyes, really wishing I was fucking her with my tongue. She looks away when her friend pulls her arm to get ready for the class. Thank fuck I don't teach the self-defense classes because my dick is so hard right now, I don't think I could even manage a pose on my own, let alone run a full class.

The new classes are a real hit, and it makes me fucking sad that so many women need protection. But growing up with a mother who had the shit beaten out of her on more than one occasion, it was something I pushed Benji to offer once the gym opened.

Seeing Doc here has my mind racing. It is a popular class, sure, but our members are mostly from disadvantaged backgrounds, those who are in danger of violence at home and an abusive partner. They are not aimed at a sexy as fuck, rich, spoiled doctor, who has every resource at their fingertips and probably doesn't even need self-defense training because they live in a perfect bubble, surrounded by perfect things and a perfect family.

I stand unmoving at my office windows, my arms crossed across my chest. Nico continues to discuss our plans for the week, as Benji goes back downstairs to look after the gym. Whilst I am listening to Nico, my mind and eyes are on Catherine, and how good her ass looks in those tight fucking pants.

"Are you even fucking listening to me?" Nico barks, and I turn my head and look at him. He is my friend. One of my closest, but on the pecking order, he is much lower than me and he knows it. A fantastic soldier, Sebastian picked him up in Sicily a while ago, and he has settled in well in New York and loves to come and help me with my fights. But speaking to me like that, it's not how I operate. Sebastian and Dante are the only people on this earth who get away with that behavior, and as I look at Nico, flames coming from my eyes, I see the way his face changes as it dawns on him that he needs to rein in his commentary.

"It's the doctor, isn't it?" he prods, walking on very fucking thin ice. I squint my eyes at him, waiting for him to dig a whole big enough to not escape from.

"Fine," he sighs, putting his hands up in mock surrender. "I'm teasing you." He has the nerve to roll his eyes.

"But if you fuck her, you need to tell Dante, because she is still Annie's doctor and he will not compromise Annie's health for your sex life."

"I am not fucking her, and who I fuck is none of your or Dante's business," I grit out, furious that he is even talking about Catherine in this way. Why I am so protective of her, I have no fucking idea.

"Fine, but get your head in the game, then. We need you in New York, and you have your fight to concentrate on while you're down here. You can't go looking at pretty ladies, who are *waaaaay* out of your league, getting distracted. That's how you die."

10

CATHERINE

I feel so out of place.

Maggie booked us into this class tonight because I have a few days off, and her husband Brian was available to watch the kids. Walking in, I saw Benji at the front desk, and immediately, my stomach dropped. I just knew that meant Carter had to be close by. Benji didn't say anything to me as he checked us in. In fact, he looked like he had seen a ghost as I smiled and said hello. But soon after, I watched as he sprinted up some stairs into what looks like an office.

I don't have to think too hard about who might be up there.

My heart is racing, and my body is sweating, and I haven't even started the class yet.

"Maggie, I'm not sure..." I start to say to her as we walk farther into the gym.

"Stop. We have been through this. You need to know how to defend yourself and this gym is apparently the

best place to come for self-defense training," she whis-
per-yells.

"But I think this—" I try to say again, to tell her that I
think Carter is here, and maybe a gym owned by the mob
is not the best place for us to train. But she doesn't let me
finish.

"Cat." She stops and stands in front of me. "We are
doing this. We are doing this to protect you, to protect
Ivy," she says firmly, determination on her face, and it is
like she sucker punched me in the gut. She knows using
Ivy in her argument will get me every time.

Taking a few deep breaths, trying to calm my nerves. I
feel on edge, but I'm willing to make the most of this. As I
turn to set my drink bottle on a seat, my skin bristles...
it's him.

Glancing around, I look up to the room where Benji
ran to, and sure enough, there he is.

Carter is standing in the window that overlooks the
gym, staring right at me. His eyes are penetrating mine,
and I can't look away. I can't move. I can barely breathe.
I'm stuck in the gaze of the man who is so totally wrong
for me on every level, but it is the same man who I
haven't stopped thinking about since I treated him on
Saturday night.

The rush of memories floods back of his perfect body,
his firm grip of my hand, and the sound of his voice.
Clearly the fact that I haven't been with a man in years is
wreaking havoc on me, because one look from this man,
and I'm hot all over.

Maggie pulls me by the arm, grabbing my attention,
and leads me over to some soft mats, since the class is

about to start. We look like two barbie dolls in this gym full of muscle, tattoos, and women who look to be as strong as the men. We are sticking out, every pair of eyes looking us over. I squirm a little, not liking the attention.

The class starts, and our trainer Cliff is a young, good-looking guy. Like the rest of the men in here, he is huge and tattooed. It must be a prerequisite. There needs to be a sign on the front of the gym that reads '*WELCOME ALL LARGE, HANDSOME, TATTOOED MUSCLE MEN.*'

I look around at the women here for class. There's a mix of ages, all from different backgrounds. But I notice there is one similarity. It is fear mixed with resilience and a sprinkle of defiance, and I can see it in every single woman's eyes.

We are all different, yet we are all the same.

Cliff talks to us for a few minutes, explaining what the classes will consist of and how they will be conducted.

"Everyone has the right to feel safe. Unfortunately, we live in a society where it's become vital to be able to effectively protect ourselves and our loved ones." Cliffs voice hit me in the chest, and I feel my strength wavering for a moment. I am still dismayed that the people I need to be protecting myself and Ivy from are part of our own family.

"Here in this class, we will teach you the techniques, strategies, and mindset to effectively and efficiently take control of any dangerous situation quickly," Cliff says as we all hang on his every word. The guys around us are noisy, with some sparring in a boxing ring, and others punching bags. There are more over in the weights area too, along with music playing over the loud speaker, yet

Cliff and his instructions are clear. I am starting to feel empowered already, and I am thankful that Maggie did this for me.

"Now, ladies, I am going to start by showing you a few moves, none of which I expect you to get right tonight. But I did want to showcase what we will be going through over the next few weeks so you can get comfortable with the physical aspect of what we teach here. While I am here to teach you self-defense, I won't go easy on you. Because your attackers won't go easy on you, and I want you prepared for that." His eyes sweep across all of us, before they land on me. He gives me a brief smile. "Now I need a volunteer."

All the women are quiet, no one offering to be a helper until Maggie pushes me forward with enough force to have me nearly tripping over my own feet. I whip my head around and scowl at her.

"Great! Step up here and tell us your name." I want the earth to open up and swallow me whole.

"Sure," I say with a fake smile, one I have perfected, as I imagine how I am going to put food coloring in Maggie's shampoo as a payback. "I am Catherine, but my friends call me Cat." As I walk up to him, I ensure I look confident, even though I feel anything but.

"Welcome, Cat," he says with a smile I can tell is genuine. "Now stand up next to me, with your back against my chest. I am going to show everyone what to do if you are attacked from behind." I sidle up to him as he takes in my body.

I hate my sister right now.

He remains professional as he positions me right next

to him. My body is now in front of him, his chest to my back, as his hands firmly grab my arms from behind. I feel extremely out of my depth, and although his grip is not hard, it is firm. My heart races a little, because Daniel has held me in this position before, and its familiarity is near stifling. I am seriously not cut out for this, and I look at Maggie, begging her with my eyes to get me out of this situation. But she ignores me and continues to watch on attentively.

Red. That'll be the color I put into her shampoo.

Cliff is talking about what to do when a man approaches you from behind. His hands slowly lower and as he puts his hands on my hips. Gripping me firmly and pulling me to him. I'm growing even more nervous, as I'm not exactly sure what move he is going to do, or how I need to handle it, but before he does anything, I hear a smash.

We all turn around in time to see the office door from upstairs slam open and crash against the wall. Everyone's eyes snap to Carter as he runs purposefully down the stairs, his gaze not leaving Cliff's. He looks murderous, and I am slightly worried for our trainer.

"Cliff, a word," he grits out as he stalks past us to the corner of the gym.

"Excuse me, ladies," he says as he turns and follows Carter, and we all stand there, not sure what to do or where to look. I make my way back to Maggie and take a sip of water, and we watch Carter talking quietly to Cliff, his veins pumping in his neck and his fists clenching at his sides. I should be scared, but I am not. I see some of the women looking away, but my eyes are glued. Glued to the man who towers over everyone in this place, his air of authority palpable.

Cliff, in turn, looks like a scared little rabbit.

They finish their conversation and Carter walks away, but not before his eyes land on mine. All the noise and surrounding people become mere blurs as we look at each other.

"Carter?" I whisper in question before he takes a few steps closer to me.

"He is not putting his hands on you," he grits out to me quietly as his nostrils flare. I'm taken aback a little, but then a warm feeling washes over me. I don't even know this man, and he makes me feel safe.

I have no words, so I simply nod in return, before he strides back up the stairs to his office. As I watch him, I see another man at the top waiting at the door and it is one I recognize. It's Nico, another mob soldier, the one who stayed at the hospital with Annie in New York. I smile up at him, and he nods in acknowledgement, before Carter pushes past him, nudging him back into the room and slamming the door.

We finish our class as if nothing happened, only Cliff won't make eye contact with me again.

11

CARTER

I was going to kill him. I was literally going to kill Cliff. His blood was going to spatter all over the gym mats if he touched her for a minute longer. He is a known flirt, and he clearly took a liking to her, and although he is professional and would never cross the line of coach and client in my gym, he knew what he was doing, and he was nearly a dead man for it.

From my office upstairs, I stayed at the windows and watched every step she made since she walked into my gym. I saw her when she looked unsure about doing the class and didn't miss the way the other woman she was with grabbed her arm to lead her over. I also didn't miss when she bent down to place her water bottle on the floor, the amazing view I got of her peach ass now ingrained in my brain, never to be erased.

I was watching the whole fucking time as Cliff pulled her to his body, and when his hands rested on her hips, I couldn't take it a second longer. I was going to kill him. He had to die.

I can't explain it. I have no idea why I reacted that way, and I still don't even know why the perfect princess is in my fucking gym. But the sight of a man touching her was all it took for me to totally lose my shit.

It is out of character for me. I have never had a jealous moment in my life, and it has ruffled my feathers a bit as I try to piece together my actions.

Standing, heart pounding, watching them again from above in my office, I am glad to see he now has a different volunteer and has learned his lesson. *Don't touch the doctor.* I know every member of the club saw me as I stalked down the stairs and I didn't give a fuck. I will get plenty of ribbing for it later, but right now, I need this lesson finished and I need her out of my gym. She is driving me crazy.

"What the fuck was that about?" Nico says, and I would like to say it is none of his business, but he knows exactly who she is. He is like a little brother to me, not to mention my fight manager, so it is his business to ensure both my physical and mental health is on point. A slight hiccup could mean the difference between winning and dying, so he takes his job of keeping me in check very seriously.

"Nothing," I lie, trying to shrug it all off as it's no big deal, even though I am asking myself the same question in my mind.

"The fuck it wasn't." He's angry now. I get it, but he needs to back off. He's sensing how this could be a problem, one that he might struggle to fix for me.

"You don't need to be concerned with it. I'll handle it," I grit out.

"I can ask her to leave?" Nico offers.

"No!" I snap, a little too quickly, and a little too loudly.

He raises his eyebrows at me, concerned, sure, but also surprised. He has never known me to be like this with a woman. And that's because I never have. I never get close enough to them. I have loved only one woman in my life, and she died when I was a teenager. The pain of losing my mother still burns to this day. I never want to feel that loss again.

I should have come right back to my office after speaking with Cliff. But I couldn't. My gaze connected with hers all on its own. The sound of my whispered, breathy name on her lips was like a feather brushing against my tough exterior, testing my wavering restraint. The look in her eyes heated my blood, siphoning every ounce of strength within me to tell her what I did without throwing her over my shoulder.

I usually treat women like they are only good for one thing and, to be honest, most of the women I usually meet are. But this one. Fuck, this one, I don't know what is different about her, but something is and that makes it dangerous for me.

I realize Nico is observing me and my inner turmoil with a growing frown, and as he goes to speak, I shut him down for the last time.

"Just leave it alone," I say, articulating every word as I sit back at my desk and shuffle the paperwork in front of me. Not that I can concentrate on anything now.

Letting out a huge sigh, I lean back in my chair and rub my hand over my face. Nico walks over and sits down opposite me.

"So, like I mentioned, Sebastian wants you back in New York. I need to give you the details."

"What is happening?" I ask, narrowing my eyes. It's pretty bad that I already forgot this was exactly what we didn't get to finish discussing earlier.

Damn that sexy brunette downstairs.

"Senate elections. Senator Roy is up for re-election, as you know," Nico states with fire in his eyes. He loves this shit. Business, management, politics.

"And?" Our guy, Senator Roy Suitor, always wins because we make the outcome that way.

"Well, some rich men in New York are putting their dirty noses into the business, throwing another guy into the running. They haven't named him yet. Their plan is to not only shut down most of our existing business dealings with the city and police, but it also appears they are not as clean as everyone is thinking. If they're successful, it's going to be a huge problem for us. They have already-established supply chains and contacts, and wouldn't hesitate to make moves to take us down in order to grow their pockets." While I have no idea what is really going on, I know that things are about to get busy and stressful.

Having rich businessmen stepping over lines with us is nothing new. We are the mob, but we are fair, we negotiate and ensure deals are done for everyone involved. If this situation is escalating, then the other guys must be total assholes. We could kill them, but oftentimes our intimidation tactics work much better, and usually that involves me.

"Our drug supply chains are strong, the strongest they have been for years. Supplies are clean, everyone is paid well." Nico continues not yet telling me anything I don't already know. "But if a new senator wins the election, then it will all cease overnight and not only will we need to start from scratch, but we may also have some serious competition as well. Sebastian is *not* happy." Nico scratches his jaw, looking at me in contemplation.

"Fine, I'll be there later this week," I say as I stand. Nico nods, standing with me, and we walk to the door with a quick hug before he steps out and leaves.

Knowing I'll be traveling, I need to put my head down and try to make my way through the monthly profits of the gym, so I can leave it in Benji's hands while I am away.

I look down at my hands and think about the lives they have taken. I would do it all again for Sebastian. He lifted me up when there was no one else reaching out. But the older I get, the more I realize that Philly offers something soothing, a break from the hustle. Building the gym business, working with Benji, being in my old hood, it is all feeling good for me at this point in my life. It gives me something to do outside of New York, a city that takes so much from me at times. Flipping my hands over, the scars and damage that remains tell a story, the visual of dark memories that can't be erased. But I owe Sebastian and Dante with my life, and I will be with them until the end. They have made me the man I am today. Smart, savvy, wealthy beyond measure, and although it took a lot of blood on my hands to get here, I am forever indebted.

My leg muscles tense, as I grip onto my desk, willing my body not to move, but I can't stop it. I stand and walk back to the windows and watch her once more. Her face deep in concentration at what Cliff is saying, their lesson almost finished.

Nothing good can come of it. We're total opposites.

That thought lasts for all of one minute, until she's glancing up at me. Her brown eyes locking onto mine from the distance without any hesitation.

I'm fucked. Totally fucked.

Once their class has finished, despite my better judgement, I decide to walk down and ask how it went. *It is only right of me as the gym owner to make sure they had a good experience*, I bullshit to myself as I take the stairs at lightning speed.

I see her with her friend and head right over. She looks up at me as I approach her, and my heart starts thumping like a fucking fool.

"Hey," she says with a small smile, a little breathless. She pushes her hair back, some falling from her ponytail after the exercise. It's nice to see she got a good workout in. Not that she needs it. Her body is incredible.

"Hey, Catherine. How did you go?" I ask, feeling like a teenager with a crush as I get closer.

"Call me Cat, please. It was great. Carter, this is my sister, Maggie. Maggie, this is Carter Grange." As I look at Maggie, I can now see the family resemblance.

"Hey, Maggie, did you like the class too?"

"It was great. It was exactly what I was looking for when I got Cat the gift certificate for the ten sessions. The instructor was very thorough," Maggie says, looking at me with a look I can't quite decipher. Although I didn't introduce myself as a brother of the mob, she seems to know it. She looks a little nervous around me, jumpy even, and her words all stumble out together.

"Well, I own this place, and I was keen to bring in self-defense classes for the local women. It is important to know how to protect yourself." I look back to Cat when I see her twitch out of the corner of my eye. It makes me even more curious as to why she is here. Why her sister got her these classes as a gift in the first place.

"How are your ribs going?" Cat asks, and her concern for me smooths over me like warm honey.

"Fine, Doc. I've had worse. Although I think it helped that you were the one to fix me up," I say, my eyes now not leaving hers, and I see a soft pink appear on her cheeks. We stare at each other for a moment, and I can't wipe the smile coming to my lips. She is adorable when she blushes.

"Okaaayy..." Maggie cuts through the moment with a huffed laugh. "I'm going to go and wait in the car while you two chat. Great to meet you, Carter." Then she's grabbing her things and walking out of the gym like her ass is on fire.

We both watch her leave before I look back at Cat.

"I should be going too." She sighs, but makes no move to leave. So I take the opportunity to ask the question at the forefront of my mind.

"You in trouble?" I need to know if someone's hurt her.

"It's a bit complicated." We are standing close to each other, close enough for me to reach out and grab her hand, squeezing it in mine. She looks from me to our joined hands and back again, but doesn't let go. I know I shouldn't touch her. At the hospital, at least I could blame it on the drugs, but now there's nothing else to blame but my draw to her. Fuck, I just want to mark her mine. Facing her now, I can see the confident, elegant woman I met this weekend change a little. It is probably not noticeable to anyone else, but I can feel her hands shake in my soft grip, her facial features soften, and her chest rises and falls at a faster pace.

"You know I can help you with your complications, Cat," I say quietly, lowering my mouth to her ear so only she can hear. When I pull back, her eyes widen, and she swallows roughly, my own eyes tracking the movement. I know she understands exactly what I am telling her.

As she steadies herself, I watch the change in her again, her confident mask slipping into place as she pushes her shoulders back and smiles. "It's fine, Carter, you don't need to get involved. I can handle it." Anyone else might believe her reassurance, but I can tell that it isn't.

I nod to her, though, letting her off the hook for now, and already itching to hurt the asshole who is obviously making her so uncomfortable.

"So this is your gym, then?" she asks, looking around the expansive space. Her hand is still encased in mine, showing no interest to let me go either.

"Sure is. It is my space, my vision." Feeling so at ease carrying on a casual, honest conversation is unusual for me, but with her, I just want to keep it going. I also like that she's yet to bolt out of here, and instead of nerves, she's wearing a smile and twinkling eyes. Both of which are aimed at me.

"How long have you been open?" My chest puffs out, happy with her interest.

"It is something I have wanted to do for a long time. It was hard always being in New York to find the time I needed to designate getting it up and going. But Benji helped on the ground when I couldn't, and we finally opened a few months ago. We have multiple training programs and classes, something for everyone. Our youth programs got it started, and we went from there."

"Do you teach kids how to fight? I mean, you're a fighter, right? I assumed you were in a random bar brawl or something when you came in Saturday, but I guess that's not the case." She lets out the prettiest chuckle at herself, her eyes now firmly back on me. Exactly where I want them to be.

"No bar brawls for me. Not recently, at least," I say with a laugh, and her eyes widen again, just a fraction. "But yeah, I fight. I've trained in MMA for years, so this has always been a goal of mine. I only ever learned the hard way that I had to know how to defend myself, so I didn't want others to fall victim to that. The kids who come in are sometimes in a rough place. They need to know basic skills, give them a space to come to get off the streets, and help them channel their anger in positive ways." Her smile grows as I speak, and I fucking love that I put it there.

"That is amazing. And really admirable. It must take a lot of determination to get something like this up and running."

"About as much determination to ask for your number again..." My heart stops as the words leave my mouth. I'm not sure if my ego can handle another rejection.

She blushes a little, biting her plush lip. "You are my patient. I can't date a patient, Carter." Her tone isn't very convincing, and I smirk.

"*Was.*" I feel like I just got the checkmate, and I squeeze her hand in mine, noticing that she still hasn't pulled away from me.

"Was what?" she asks, eyebrows furrowing in the most adorable way.

"*Was* your patient. Now I am just a man asking for your number." I'm enjoying her flush way too much.

As my thumb brushes her hand, she changes the subject. "It looks like a popular place you've built here, Carter. You must be proud." I still for a moment, because I haven't really ever reflected on the success I have had.

"I am not proud of a lot of things I have done, but yeah, I guess this gym is the one thing I am proud of." The honesty this woman pulls from me leaves me a little unsettled. What is she doing to me?

"You're not a bad man, Carter," she says softly as she looks up to me, and I have never wanted to take a woman in my arms, kiss every part of her body, and fuck her, all in the same breath, as much as I do right now. She must feel it too, because her body is moving even closer to mine, and it will be a miracle if I ever walk away from her. I rub her hand with my thumb, caressing it in mine, keeping myself grounded. Not only is she fucking beautiful, but if she can see any good in a man like me, then she is even a better person than I thought possible.

"Believe me, when I leave this earth, the elevator is

taking me straight down," I say to her firmly, because it is a fact. There is no place in heaven for a man like me.

"Oh, I don't know about that. Seems to me"—she takes another look around my gym—"that maybe the stairway to heaven will welcome you with open arms."

I laugh then, before releasing her hand and moving my touch up her arm a little, itching to feel more of her bare skin, yet respecting her and still giving her some space. She has stars in her eyes if she thinks I am anyone else other than the angry, murderous mob soldier I am. I skim her skin with my fingertips, reveling in the goose-bumps that appear beneath them. We're toe to toe as we stand in the center of my gym, and with her body so close, the desire to strip her clothes off runs strong.

I want every fucker in this gym to know that she is mine, even though we are merely getting acquainted.

"Your life might be sunshine and rainbows, Cat," I say, and I don't miss the flinch of her eyes as I do, but I continue, "but I'm shrouded in darkness, and I have no idea how to live in the light." My hand wanders up her arm and to her shoulder, lifting to brush a loose hair off her face before I reach down and grab her hand again.

"Oh, that's easy…" She scoffs at me, and I squint at her in question.

"Oh, yeah?"

"Mmmhmm… you just take one step at a time," is all she says before she's stepping away from me, smiling as she grabs her things, walking out of my gym.

"Bye, Carter." She gives me a small wave, and I can't hold back the stupid grin that takes over my face as I nod to her, standing there like a fool as I watch her go.

Once she is out the door, I look around the gym. Yes, I am fucking proud. I poured so much of myself into this gym to get it exactly how I wanted it. So to have someone else acknowledge that effort makes it all the more special.

As I see boys and men working out their grief or anger or whatever emotion they need to unleash on the punching bags, I feel a renewed sense of accomplishment. I'm seeing the space through a new lens, and I am even more excited for what this place now offers, not only me but to the kids and women in the community.

And as I slowly walk to the stairs to make my way back to my office, I feel light on my feet. Benji comes up to me as I take the first step up, making me pause.

"They're over there," he says with a nod of his head toward the front door of the gym.

"What?" I ask, looking around, wondering what the fuck he is talking about this time.

"Your balls. Doc just walked out the door with them." He bursts out laughing, walking away before I can get a punch in.

12

CATHERINE

I t has been a few days since my self-defense class and my body is still sore. I can now understand how Carter is so immaculately carved, his body like something you see on the cover of fitness magazines.

I have to say, even though I only learned a move or two, I am feeling more confident. It was a great idea by Maggie to enroll us. After class, it was clear that this energy I have around Carter is not one-sided and I don't know what to make of it.

Maggie had twenty questions in the car on the way home. We have no secrets, my sister and I, and when I told her all about my conversation with Carter and the feelings that are starting to develop, she nearly drove off the road. At first, I thought it was because she felt unsettled that we are going to a gym owned by the mob, and thinking her sister is crazy for wanting to be close to a man who probably murders people before breakfast. But she smiled instead, happy with the fact that my interest has been sparked after not thinking about men or dating for a long time now. Not able to trust them enough to even considerate it.

I see a lot of good in Carter, despite what he may have done, or continues to do in New York. It's odd for me to be this sure, this secure in the type of person that he is. I just hope that I am right, since my history shows that my instincts with men are not always on point.

I keep thinking about Carter and his display at the gym with Cliff. Was it possessive? Yes. Is he a bit of an asshole? Also, yes. Is he hot as hell and does my body melt under his gaze? Does his voice give me a weird inner calm, soothing and soft, yet gruff and protective. Absolutely yes and yes.

I have never had this type of attraction to a man before. At school, I was a bit of a nerd, head of the chess club, always had my head buried in my textbooks. That's what I had to do in order to be a surgeon. It was my dad's dream for me to follow in his footsteps, and I worked my butt off in college to make sure that I did everything he wanted. So, there was no time for boys.

Then I was always with Daniel. Our fathers pushed us together the moment we both graduated from med school. While he seemed nice at first, there were definitely no butterflies for me, but back then, I would've done anything to have my father's approval and so I went on a few dates and we became a couple. Given we both worked in medicine, we had little time for each other due to our work, and I suppose that is why I stayed for so long. Too long. When Ivy was conceived, it became apparent that he wasn't the man I thought he was.

I shake my head of the thoughts as I stroll around the

grocery store with Ivy. We are grabbing a few things for the week before we go home and snuggle on the sofa together for a movie night with popcorn, ice-cream, and candy. It is my last day off with her before the onslaught of crazy hours start up again for the next week, so I like our nights together to be special.

We come to this store weekly, even though it is a little farther away from our house. It is a small, family-run store, and the owners always give Ivy a little treat. It is nice to visit and feel like part of the community. In between work and Ivy, I don't have a lot of time to make friends, so coming here is like my weekly ritual of socialisation.

I am looking over the labels on some new candy and Ivy is off chatting to Tony, the owner, about her soccer game she scored at this past weekend. Being an older man, he enjoys hearing about her antics, and she is a great storyteller.

As I try to decide between peanut butter cups and chocolate-covered marshmallows, my skin prickles with unease, and a shiver runs through my bones. I feel him before I see him, and as my heart rate increases, I try not to panic. It has been months, so I knew he would turn up soon. Even though I have a restraining order, he must have been following me, because this is not a chance encounter. There is no way he would be in the small grocery store in this neighborhood.

I have never hidden where I am; he always knows where to find me. There is no point in hiding, since being a doctor himself, he can make a few enquiries and get my location within an hour. But Philly isn't really his scene and he never got along with my sister, so I didn't think he would bother following me here.

But he did.

I slowly put the candy back on the shelf and look around for Ivy, but I can't see her, so she must still be with Tony. Turning around, as expected, Daniel's standing a few steps away, arms by his sides, looking straight at me. I can't move. I am like a deer caught in headlights. He always makes me feel like this. Like I am stuck. The air has left my lungs, and my hands begin to shake.

There is something different about him since I saw him last, though. His eyes look more vacant. He is angry. Angry at me for not giving him what he wants. *Me.* He doesn't care about Ivy, even though she is his blood. All he wants is me.

As he takes steps to move toward me, I automatically step back. My spine is straight, my limbs are tight. I don't want to be near him, don't even want to be in the same town as him. He takes another step forward, and I take another backwards, my daughter's voice cutting through my fear.

"Mommy!" she breathes out, frightened, as her little arms wrap around my legs, and she hides behind me. She knows that Daniel is her father, she knows that he is not a nice man, and she also knows that he wants to take me back to New York. She's never felt his love or compassion, because he has none to give. I still can't quite comprehend it all, actually. How could you not love your own child?

I fell pregnant when he forced himself on me one night and didn't stop to put a condom on. We always used condoms, because he never wanted children. He hates them, and made that clear only after he knew I was committed to our relationship. But that's all it took. One time. I didn't realize I was pregnant for months, with a busy work schedule and the stress of the job, I have never been regular, so I thought nothing of it when my period didn't come. By the time I found out I was carrying a child, I was 22 weeks, and I didn't even consider not having her, even though I didn't want to be tied to Daniel. Even back then, I knew he wasn't the man for me.

The minute he found out I was pregnant, he became filled with resentment and rage. When she was born, he never held her. Once I was out of hospital and home, he ignored her completely. Never changed her nappy, never put her to sleep, never fed her or played with her. Tried to take all my attention, excluding her at every opportunity, until one day I found the strength to mention something to him.

The way he acted that night... it cemented the fact that he was never going to be the man I needed him to be. There was no escaping him then, though. With a little child and no support, I was hostage to the situation. Maggie overseas at the time, and my father not at all helpful or sympathetic.

Ivy and I have both been through a lot of counseling together, and for such a little girl, she is handling the situation reasonably well. I shield her from a lot of it, but she knows the kind of man he is. She's frightened of her father, and I don't blame her, because I am too.

His eyes quickly flick down to Ivy, and his lips turn

into a snarl as he looks at her. It is because she has my heart, not him. He is jealous of his own daughter.

His fascination with me started years ago, and back then, I thought it was young love. I thought that was how it was meant to be. As the years passed, I began to feel restricted. He took ownership of our finances, my salary going into a joint bank account, one that he seemed to continually change, and I lost track of it. Instead, I lived off an allowance he gave me, trusting that he was investing the rest.

Looking back to me, he takes another step toward us, and I step back again, not wanting the space between us to get any smaller. Ivy shuffles back with me, my hands now guiding her behind me, her grip tight on my legs. He takes another step, now smirking. It is like a game of cat and mouse and whilst the grocery store is usually quiet, today it seems totally empty. Where are people when you want them?

Then, he's right in front of me. Tall, domineering, and dressed impeccably in slacks and a pressed shirt, looking like he is about to play a round of golf, not abuse his ex-girlfriend. He is leaning down, looking me in the eyes, trying to intimidate me. Our eyes are locked, and I feel sick, but I can't back down. I can't show him weakness.

"Well, nice to see you, my dear," he sneers, and I don't know what it is, but he seems even more unhinged.

"What do you want, Daniel? You are not meant to be near me. The restraining order is in place. You need to stay at least 200 yards away from us," I say to him, all the while trying to remain confident and unaffected by his standover tactics. My heart thumps in my chest as my eyes flick around the store to see if I can find a way out for us. I subtly rub my sweaty palms against my legs.

"I came to pick you up and bring you back to New York, Catherine." He smiles then, his facial features relaxing, before Ivy's movements grab his attention, and he is back to being angry again.

"We have discussed this, Daniel. We broke up, we are not together. I am not your girlfriend." I can hear the quiver in my voice. I need to get us out of here, but I still can't move. I swallow, my dry throat nearly making me choke.

"We are not fucking over until I say we are over, so you need to stop playing these fucking games," he spits out, loud enough for only me to hear. Dread washes over me.

"Daniel..." I try to gather my strength, but I am slowly losing out over my fear of him, and I begin to tremble. I know he'll notice.

"Please, Daniel, just go," I plead to him as he takes one small step forward, ready to unleash his venom, but before he says anything further, my body is pushed away from him by the back of a man, startling me until I breathe in. I know his scent. I have been dreaming of it for days.

Standing in front of me, like he is my protector, is Carter Grange.

13

CARTER

I pull up to the rundown house on the outskirts of town, wondering what I am about to get myself into. Checking the photo and the address in the text Sebastian sent me this morning, it matches, so I know I am in the right place.

I look around the street. It is quiet, uncomfortably so. After shoving my gun into the back of my belt, I ensure I have my knife strapped to my calf as well. I don't often do visits on my own. We usually work in teams of two, or small groups, but Sebastian said I could handle this solo without issue.

Stepping out of the car, I hear a dog bark in the distance and notice a few cars parked farther up, but aside from my feet crunching on the gravel, there is nothing else of interest.

I am here to send a message. Sebastian had a tip-off that one of the men who knows the inner workings for the new drug syndicate we have running on the east side has come down here to a safe house. He is hiding from us because he attempted to take money that wasn't his to take. As I step up to the front door, I huff out and shake my head, because this house is the most ridiculous safe house I have ever seen. Even the front window is wide open to catch the breeze.

I try the door handle, and it opens straight away. It could be good luck or it could be a trap, so I keep my eyes trained on everything as I quietly push open the door and step through. I should have brought Benji with me. At the very least, he could have stayed in the car for a quick getaway. Although I know he would never stay in the car. Benji would be next to me the entire time. Which is exactly why I didn't bring him.

Noise from the TV blares at me from the back of the house, and I walk slowly down the hall, peering into each room as I go. I am about to keep going, when a man comes at me from the side.

"Arrggh!" he yells, his hands up, no gun or knife in sight, which gives me quick relief, before the air is pushed out of my lungs as he throws me against the wall.

"Fuck," I grit. Being caught by surprise isn't a good start, but as he pulls back to take a swing, I realize he really is no match.

Ducking his punch, his hand hits straight through the drywall, and I jump up beside him, punching him in the side, cracking a rib on contact.

"What the fuck!" As he grabs his side, I send an uppercut into his jaw, smashing his teeth together so hard I feel the vibration through my wrist.

"That is for sticking your nose in our business," I say as I step back, and then kick his legs out from under him.

I grab his by the collar and lift him straight up, before my fist connects with his cheekbone. "That is for thinking you could take our money."

I hit him again, connecting with his nose, the crunch of bones a familiar noise to me, as his face collapses into itself, and his eyes roll into the back of his head. Letting go of his shirt, his body falls back to the floor with a hard thump.

"And that is for trying to fuck with the mob." I wipe the sweat from my brow, huffing out a breath. Taking a quick look around the house, I see no one else, so I step over his body and walk out, leaving the front door wide open.

Sebastian said to leave a message and this one says, "Don't fuck with the Men of New York."

*****

I clench my hands together, my knuckles aching and in dire need of some ice. I cleaned myself up as best I could in the car, but detoured to the grocery store, which is closer than home, in need of an ice pack and pain relief. Seeing the store owner, Big Tony, talking to a little girl, I decide to walk over to say hello.

"Hey, Carter," Tony says as we shake hands. We have known each other for years. Tony is one of the few people who knew me as a delinquent teenager, and many times in my younger years, he offered me food or a roof when I needed it. I was too young to appreciate it back then; I was just a kid with a giant chip on my shoulder, but I made it right once I grew into a man. I helped him financially and offered any other support he needed and still do.

"Hey, Tony." He sends me a knowing look, as I cringe a little in his hard grip, but before I can say anything, we are interrupted by the little girl.

"Hi! My name is Ivy. What's your name?" a little voice squeaks out. I look down at two pigtails, big brown eyes, and a cute purple dress.

"Hello, my name is Carter. Pleased to meet you, Ivy." I put out my hand to shake hers, which she accepts and shakes with confidence. *Who is this kid?*

"Did you know that the oldest turtle in the world is 190 years old?" she asks me, and I raise my eyebrows.

"No, I didn't know that," I grumble back. I look at Tony, and he is smiling, so I have a feeling he knows her well.

"Did you know that a giraffe's tongue is over 45cm long?" Ivy asks again, and Tony laughs.

"You sure know a lot about animals," I say to her, scratching my chin. I'm not usually one for kids, and try to stay right away from them beyond any training at the gym, but she has got spunk and is clearly a smart one. The kind of kid that parents would be lucky to have.

"I want to be a zoologist one day. My mommy said I can be anything I want to be, and I want to be that."

Tony stiffens a little beside me, and I snap my gaze to him.

"Who's that man with your mommy, Ivy?" he asks, and she turns to look.

"Mommy!" I hear her gasp before she runs to the woman, whose back is to us. Ivy slams into her mom's legs, hiding behind her, and her mom's hands come around to secure Ivy to her body. But her eyes don't leave the man approaching her like she is a bird about to fly away. He doesn't seem to have good intentions. Not from the way mom and daughter are behaving either.

"What's that about?" I ask Tony quickly, not taking my eyes off Ivy and her mother.

The man steps closer to them, and her mom steps back, and it's confirmed that the man is a danger. It is then that I get a glimpse of her face, and my body stills. It's Cat.

My anger rises, and as he gets right in her face, I am on him before I even realize my feet have moved.

I push my way between them, Cat at my back, and I hear her gasp in surprise. But I see red at the moment. I am staring at him, my face a mere inch from his.

"You like to come into the grocery store and intimidate women?" I growl as my face contorts in rage, my eyes piercing his. I could never protect my mom, but I sure as hell will protect Cat. I notice his nostrils flare, and his eyes flick between me and her.

"Do we have a problem here, or are you going to turn around and walk out and not come back again?" I bite out when he doesn't respond, wanting nothing more than to punch him out.

He is eyeing me, trying to figure out how much of a threat I am. We are similar in height, but I know that under his khakis and shirt, his body is soft and fatty; he is more of a casual golfer type than a fighter. He gives me a smirk, which has me clenching my hands at my sides. But then I feel her hand, gently placed on my back, and I calm slightly, knowing that she is all right, scared but all right, safely tucked behind me.

The shirt-wearing dickhead takes a step back and smiles, a wide, psychotic smile. "I will see you soon, Catherine. I miss you," he sing-songs before he walks out of the store. I notice Tony follows him, watching him to ensure he leaves the parking lot.

I turn around, and for the first time, I look at the beautiful woman who is standing behind me. She has her hair tied back in a loose ponytail, some of her hair having fallen around her face, and I can't help it, my hand comes up and I brush it away.

"You okay?" I ask quietly as my fingers touch her cheek. It is the softest I have ever touched another person. The stark contrast of my punches from this morning to the gentle touches this afternoon is rewiring my brain. I am not sure what I am doing, but I can't stop it. I am touching her like she is a precious jewel. A rare diamond. And she is.

She is looking at me, her head tilted upward slightly, relief overtaking her face. My thumb caresses her cheek again, looking out of place given the fresh bruising, yet I am itching to cup her face and kiss her. She looks so beautiful in this moment.

"Mommy..." Ivy whispers from behind her, and our eye contact is broken. Cat squats down and hugs Ivy, smoothing her hair as she comforts her.

"It's okay, honey. He is gone."

"But he will come back... he always comes back," she says in a small, shaky voice. Poor Ivy is now a scared little girl, not the same one I met only moments ago. Her comment doesn't sit well with me. This man, whoever he is, is obviously a problem.

"C'mon, Ivy. I have some new ice cream at the back of the store. I need you to try it and tell me what you think before I stock it," Tony says, as he walks back to us, reaching out his hand. Cat nods to her.

"It's okay. I'll be there in a minute to join you," she says, and Ivy takes Tony's hand as Cat and I watch them walk down the grocery aisle.

I stand looking at her until she meets my eyes again.

"Just, don't say anything," she whispers, looking embarrassed, and I now understand why she is at my gym getting self-defense classes.

"Okay. Do you need—" I begin to say, but she cuts me off.

"Thank you, but I'm fine. It wasn't the first time he's come near me, and it won't be the last. It's fine." She tries to brush it off with a small, firm smile. One that doesn't reach her eyes. One that I have seen before. Her mask slowly slips back into place. This is the second time I have seen her hide her vulnerability, and my protective instincts are kicking in each and every time.

"What's his name?" I ask her, because I will fucking make sure it is the last time he comes near her.

"Carter..." she warns as she starts to turn back around, trying to put distance between us. I don't let her. I grab her around the waist and pull her back to me. My breath catches as I wait to see her response. I need to stop touching her. I am no good for her. But every time I see her, my body betrays my mind as I want to get closer.

"I will make sure he doesn't come near you again," I

promise, and I know she understands what I am saying. She looks up at me, her eyes glassy, and my heart thumps wildly in my chest. I can tell she is trying to be strong. She is still shaking a little, so I squeeze her around the waist and run my thumb across her body. I hear her let go of her breath and her body falls into me. I want to give her the strength she needs, even if just for a moment.

"It's fine, really. You don't need to get involved." Her mouth is saying one thing, but as her hand rests on my chest and grips onto my top, her body is telling me another. Her leaning into me feels like the most natural feeling ever, and I don't want to move. So, I decide to push my luck.

"Give me your phone." It's not a question this time, and she tilts her head inquisitively.

"You're very demanding today," she mumbles, and I like to hear her attitude coming back.

"Just gimme your phone," I say again, softer this time, and she reaches into her handbag and pulls out her cell.

"Unlock it," I say to her, which enlists another scowl, and I grin as I watch her put in her code, then hand it to me.

"Why, what are you doing?" she asks as she watches me with interest.

"You won't give me your number, so I am giving you mine," I grunt out, and I watch her mouth curve into a small smile.

I put in my cell number. A number I have never given out to anyone before.

"Carter, what happened to your hands?" she asks with

surprise as I type in my digits, unfortunately noticing the outcome of this morning's visit.

"Nothing. Just work," I mumble, keeping my eyes schooled on her phone.

"Oh my God, let me get some frozen peas." She takes a few steps to the freezers and grabs a large pack before coming back and taking her phone from my hands and shoving the peas there instead.

"You call me the minute you see him," I say to her, leaving no room for discussion. "I don't want him touching you. I don't want him anywhere near you or your daughter."

She nods, and I notice her eyes fill with tears, but she is trying to remain composed as she takes a deep breath and exhales slowly.

"Fuck." My one good hand wraps around her waist, and I pull her to me, her head reaching my chest, where she settles against my pounding heart. Her hands wrap around my torso, and I toss the peas onto the floor as my other hand grabs the back of her head. Holding her close to me, I bury my nose into her hair, something I have wanted to do since I first met her in the ER. It is so soft and smells too good to be in my damaged hands, yet I don't move them, preferring to have the silkiness in my grip.

She is fucking small in my arms, and I have the strong desire to pick her up and take her home with me. Usually, I would, but this is different. *She* is different.

"Mom?" Ivy's voice is quiet, and Cat and I pull away from each other like we are on fire.

"Hey, Ivy," I say as I squat down to Ivy's height.

"I'm friends with your mom, and I just gave her my cell number. I want you to call me any time you need to, okay? No matter what the time, or what is happening, you just give me a call." As a kid, I wish that I had an adult who offered an out, someone who I could pass on my worries to.

"Okay," she says quietly, her eyes skirting from me to her mom and back again. I see Cat nod to her out the corner of my eye, and then Ivy smiles to us both as I stand back up.

"Carter, did you know that there are over one thousand different ice cream flavors in the world?" And now she's back to her bubbly self, licking a chocolate ice cream, with Tony nowhere in sight.

"I don't eat ice cream," I mumble, though it looks fucking delicious.

"What?" Both Cat and Ivy baulk, looking at me like I have grown two heads.

"I'm a fighter. I need a clean diet." I shrug, but that explanation isn't enough for them.

"Is he serious?" little Ivy whispers to her mom, even though I can hear every word, and I need to hide my grin.

"Afraid so, honey," she says in a disappointed tone.

"So I guess he can't come to our movie nights, then?" she asks, looking up at Cat.

"I'm not sure we can trust a man who doesn't eat ice cream, Ivy," Cat says back, the two of them whispering about me like I am not even here. Although Cat gives me a cheeky wink, making my heart thump, the feeling then traveling directly south. Her face has now relaxed a little more, her eyes twinkling as she chats with her daughter.

She looks good with a smile. And I bet she would look even better in my bed.

"What about candy? Do you eat candy?" Ivy asks as she looks at me with a penetrating gaze like I am a suspect in a trial, and I am glad she is back to her original self.

"Nope. No candy," I say, shaking my head, and both their eyes grow wider than they did about the ice cream.

"No candy?!" Ivy whisper-shouts to Cat again, and even she needs to stifle her grin.

"What do you think? Do you think he can be friends with us if he doesn't eat candy?" she asks Ivy.

"Hmm... maybe..." Ivy thinks it over as she continues to lick her ice cream, assessing me.

Cat looks at me and smiles again, which I find myself returning. I'm fucking mush in front of this woman. I need to get a grip.

"Thanks, Carter. For helping earlier. I appreciate it." The way she says it, it's like I have given her the world. Who he is to her, I still don't know.

"I will see you at the self-defense class next week, right?" I want her to have every tool in her arsenal in case that dickhead ever comes back and I am not around. I also want to see her again. Badly.

She sighs and raises her eyebrows. "Yep, I will be there." There's exhaustion in her expression, and it's then I find myself in awe. How does she do it? A doctor, at the top of her game, with a daughter full of energy and sass, having to deal with a man who seems intent on hurting her, and then moving to a new city only a few months ago.

The urge to protect her runs through my body. And now, to know she also has a little girl to protect as well, it has me thinking about when I was a kid. I know how that shit affects a person, and that sweet girl doesn't need that in her life. All I want to do is wrap them both in my arms and take them to my place, where I know they'll be safe and cared for.

Cat is too good for me, I know this. My job is dangerous, I fight, I hate almost everyone and everything... but none of that has helped to push her from my mind.

Maybe I just need to get her out of my system? Maybe we just need something from each other, and one time would be enough.

Only, I know even as I think it, that could never be true. That would never be enough.

14

CATHERINE

Sitting in my office, shuffling paperwork, my mind drifts to how much better I'm feeling since taking that class with Maggie. It is astounding what can happen when you step out of your comfort zone, and being amongst other women experiencing a similar issue has opened my eyes.

"What are you thinking about?" Ian asks as he strolls into my office. The afternoon is a little quieter for us, so we are taking the time to talk through rosters for the next fortnight and catch up on work admin.

"What are you talking about?" I shuffle in my desk chair, grabbing some more files from my drawer.

"You just have this faraway look in your eye, one I haven't seen before."

"I went to a self-defense class the other night with Maggie." Might as well tell him all about it.

"Amazing, good for you! How was it?" He sits down, pushing his paperwork to the side as he gets comfortable with his coffee in hand.

"It was fine. Really good, actually. After one class, I already feel more empowered."

"That's great, but what aren't you telling me?" Ian prods, and I sigh. He knows me too well.

"The gym we went to... Maggie booked it... I had no idea.." I start blabbering on, stumbling over my words.

"No idea about what?" Ian asks.

"Carter Grange owns the gym." I say, looking him dead in the eye as I wait for his reaction.

It takes a minute for him to remember, but I can tell the moment he does because Ian's eyes go wide and his jaw drops.

"Stop it!" His grin now a mile wide.

"Totally serious, he was, um, how should I put it, very attentive," I say, and I feel my cheeks heat.

"OMG. As I live and breathe!" Ian flaps his hand near his cheek to mimic cooling himself down. So dramatic. "Doctor Wakeford has a crush!" he exclaims, and I choke on my coffee.

"Stop it, I do not." I know I am not winning this argument. Why do I bother?

"Your red cheeks tell me otherwise, Cat. Now, when are you going to jump into bed with this Adonis?" Ian asks with a little shoulder dance, and I roll my eyes.

"Stop it. I went to gym class, we talked afterwards, there was nothing to it," I say simply, and he eyes me with suspicion.

"Again, what else aren't you telling me?"

I heave a sigh. "Daniel came up to me at the grocery store yesterday."

"WHAT? He isn't supposed to be anywhere near you!" Ian practically shouts.

"I know, I know, but a piece of paper is not going to stop him. Anyway, he got all up in my face and started threatening me, and then... Carter stepped in—"

"Carter?! The same Carter?! What?" Ian cuts me off, looking totally bamboozled.

"Yes, Carter was at the store when Daniel approached me, and he stepped in and got rid of him for me."

"Oh my God. Carter saved you?" Ian asks, totally astonished, just like I was when it happened.

"Yes, I mean, I guess. He was just in the right place at the right time," I mutter, with a shrug of my shoulders, trying to remain casual, but my insides turn with a mix of feelings I'd rather not address about my situation.

"So Carter Grange is kinda, like, your hero now, then?" Ian says teasingly.

"Oh, it's nothing. He would have done the same thing for any other woman, I am sure." I scoff at him.

"Oh, let's be honest, Carter Grange is not nothing. He is EVERYTHING!" Ian exclaims, and we both burst out laughing at the silliness of it all.

"Seriously, though, even though I will admit there is a strong chemistry there when we are together, and I can't stop thinking about him, I just don't think it would ever work." I chew my lip, having let the cat out of the bag. Now that Ian knows I'm interested, he won't be letting it go any time soon.

"Cat, we are talking about having sex, not getting into a lifelong commitment with the guy. Just have some fun, live a little. You deserve it," Ian says softly, and I give him a weak smile.

"Maybe..." But one-time things are not really my style. In fact, I don't know what my style is because I haven't been with anyone aside from Daniel.

"Definitely, Cat, because I have a feeling that Carter Grange could make you feel otherworldly, if you know what I mean." He winks, not once, but twice, and I roll my eyes at him, shaking my head.

"Let's get these done, shall we." I pull the stack of papers front and center, signifying the end of our chit-chat. I don't have the strength to tell Ian that I don't know. I don't know what it is like to feel *otherworldly*, as Ian puts it. Daniel never made me feel anything but less than. My father continues to tell me I am worthless. I have never had a man in my life that treats me like I am his everything, and so I have no idea what Carter Grange is capable of. But a part of me really wants to find out.

An hour later, our paperwork is done, rosters are confirmed, and I have approved a few more deliverables on the new building. I feel accomplished as Ian and I both stand to leave. He has another hour on his shift, but I am on my way home for the day.

As I step over to grab my coat, my office phone rings, and Ian leans over the desk to answer it.

"Doctor Wakeford's office, this is Ian," he chirps in his professional phone manner. I smile to myself at having such great employees, before my smile fades as Ian looks at me in shock.

"Certainly, I will let her know." Ian's eyes don't leave mine, and I get an uneasy feeling in my stomach. He hangs up without saying goodbye, and I take a few steps over to him.

"What is it?" I ask him as he puts the phone back down.

"That was a man called Benji," Ian says, and I don't need to think too hard, because I only know one Benji.

"And?" I say, confused about what is going on. Why the hell would Benji be calling my office.

"And he is requesting your services at the gym. Carter needs his stitches checked after taking a few punches to the head in training today." His shocked face slowly morphs into a wide shit-eating grin.

"What?" My brows crease together, as I try to piece together what the hell is going on.

"Well, it appears that Carter Grange requires your services and has called to see if you will make a house call to him at his gym," Ian states again as he moves past me to grab my coat from the hook on the back of my door. "So, now that your shift is over, best you grab your medical kit and drive on over to the gym. See if you can't help the man."

"Oh my God, are you serious? I haven't done house calls in years!" I absentmindedly put on my jacket, regardless.

"Honey, when a man like Carter Grange calls, you don't question it. You run." Ian hands me my bag, basically pushing me out the door.

"Ian—"

"Look, Cat, I would LOVE it if I had a cute little nurse's uniform to give you, but I don't. So put on your big girl panties and go and show that guy what you've got because he is asking for you, and you my dear are a catch," Ian says, his tone the perfect mix of playful and business, as we step out into the hall.

"But I..." I stammer, still bewildered and not at all ready for what could possibly happen.

"But nothing, Cat. Remember, you don't have to marry the man, just get to know him, have a little fun. You deserve it." He keeps talking as he walks me straight to the staff exit, then opens the door for me, sending me off.

I turn around to say something else, but Ian only lifts an eyebrow at me.

"Go!" he says forcefully, a small grin on his face.

"Fine! I'm going!" I say, before turning and walking down the hall to my car, trying to work out if I have got what it takes to seduce a man like Carter Grange, yet letting my body lead the way anyway.

15

CARTER

I am hot and sweaty, but my training session today is on point. Benji has been barking orders to everyone, but now I am in the ring, thrashing it out with my sparring partner to ensure my fitness levels don't drop.

I spend hours a day on fitness, working on agility, flexibility, weights, and boxing. My diet is clean, my mindset is strong, and I am in the zone.

"C'mon, Carter, you've got more than that!" Jamie, my partner, yells at me, egging me on, and I pay him well to do so. There are not many men who would willingly step into the ring with me. I tried Benji once, and that was a disaster. One that left him with a broken nose because he didn't duck and weave like he was supposed to. Now he sticks to watching from the sidelines.

I keep my eyes on Jamie, my punches coming out strong, my breathing consistent as I twist and turn, alternating between jabs and uppercuts, then bringing in a knee strike to surprise him.

The door of the gym opens and out the corner of my eye, I see Benji approaching with someone behind him. Which is unusual, since we are currently closed. I continue to dance around the ring, throwing punches and taking some too, and in between it all, I quickly look over and see her. I'm shocked for a moment, not sure why she is here. But from my second's-long glances while dodging Jamie's punches, I somehow relax.

I like that she is in my space again.

Every time I see her, she looks beautiful and today is no exception. A black pencil skirt and white shirt flattering her every curve, and those sexy as fuck black high heels elongating her already long legs. I may be in the ring, dancing around my opponent, but my eyes are firmly on her.

I look up and down her body, before I settle on her face. Her eyes pierce mine, and I give her a wink before I go back and focus on Jamie, now with renewed enthusiasm.

I can spot her flinching each time I take a hit. I don't even feel them, though. I am used to the bashing my body takes.

"Time!" Benji yells, and Jaime and I stop, hitting gloves. I don't hesitate to jump through the ropes and stride over to where Benji and Cat are standing.

"I called Doc to come and take out your stitches and look at your ribs," Benji says as my eyes remain on her, and I try to catch my breath. My eyebrows shoot up. I had no idea he called her, but looking at her now, I am sure glad he did.

"I'm fine." I sigh, waving him off, and he leaves us to return to the front desk.

"I'm here now, so I might as well take a look, make sure your heart is still beating." I smile at her sassy tone.

"Oh, my heart is beating, all right." I hide my smirk as I see her eyebrows shoot up at how direct I am. Grabbing her hand, I pull her along with me, the need to touch her thrumming through my body once again. How can any man be near a woman like this and not want to touch her? "Let's go to the clinic, though. That'll be a better place for you to work."

One of the things I made sure to build when constructing this gym is a medic center. Something small but professional where I can get cleaned, iced, and taped up during training, but more so somewhere that the kids can come and be looked after with any of their medical needs. Many don't have healthcare, many don't even have a doctor, so kids turn up all the time needing help with one thing or another. The problem is finding medical staff. Working here at the gym, helping kids with small ailments, is not really what a medical professional wants to do, so I have a great new clinic, but no doctor. Something I am trying to rectify.

"This is amazing," Cat says as I pull her through the door, closing it behind us. She stands still at the entrance and looks around at everything like she is in a museum.

"I built it for the kids, so they have somewhere to go for medical assistance," I say as I watch her. "We need a doctor, if you know of anyone?" I can't help but tease a little. "Unless you want the job?" There is no way in hell someone of her calibre would work here, but I am interested to hear what she says.

She walks around the space, taking in all the equipment and products. Hopefully impressed, since everything in here is of the highest quality. When she stops and looks at me over her shoulder, my eyes are already on her. And from her sharp intake of breath, I think she notices. "I think it would be great, but I heard the boss is too tough," she replies with one eyebrow raised and a dazzling smile.

"I think he turns to mush when he sees you," I mumble out, not sure if she heard me or not.

"You need to be careful, Carter. You tell me that you are a dangerous man, but with all these good deeds you do, people will start to think you are a nice guy."

The room feels smaller with the two of us in it, and the electricity we have is amplified. I know that I won't be able to hold myself back from her for much longer.

She places her medical bag on the table, realizing she isn't going to need much from it, and turns to me.

I laugh. "No chance of that happening," I respond as she walks over to me. Every step she takes, every click of her heels, making my heartbeat pick up pace.

"Hmmm, I'm not convinced." She tuts, standing before me. Looking up at me, her eyes are bright, and her smile is breathtaking. My gaze falters when hers does, roaming down my chest, and mine does the same. I get an impressive view right down the front of her shirt, and I want to rip it off her. Instead, I opt for gripping her waist, something that I find myself wanting to do each time I am near her. The need to have her close to me is near stifling.

"So where should we start..." she asks softly, probably thinking about her reason for being here, but that is the last thing on my mind. Her voice skirts up my skin, following her hands as they run up my naked chest. I'm sweaty from my session, but she doesn't seem to care and neither do I. I want to take her touching me like this as a signal that we're on the same page. The feel of her soft hands on me is everything. I growl low and deep, but she doesn't react, her touch remaining gentle as her perfume fills my senses.

Her hands continue traveling up to my neck, her eyes following the path up my body and resting on my face. She has too many clothes on, and I need her in my bed. With how close we are, there's no way she can't feel how hard I am for her. In my gym shorts, there's no hiding it either.

"How about here?" I say to her, one hand remaining on her lower back, keeping her close to me, as I bring my other hand up her body. My palm molds to her, feeling the curves of her hips, then the dip of her waist, before I move up her chest, softly skimming the outside of her breast. Her lips part as she takes a breath, and I watch for any sign she isn't into this, but I don't get one. And so, I'm done waiting.

Cupping her jaw with my hand, my fingers grip into the back of her neck and pull her face forward, bringing her lips to meet mine. She lets out a small moan, one that I know I will remember for a long fucking time.

She is timid, so I go slow, my lips meeting hers in

smooth caresses before I slip my tongue across her bottom lip. She tastes like cherries, exactly like I had imagined.

"Carter," she breathes out against my lips, and my other hand comes up, gripping her other cheek. I keep her face with mine, not wanting to let her go.

I plant my lips on hers again, this time harder, so she knows exactly what I want, and she opens for me on another moan. As I hold her body flush with mine, her hands reach up and grab onto my shoulders, pulling me closer, wanting more. My tongue swirls with hers, our lips moving in tandem, and I don't miss the feeling of her fingers as they thread into my hair at the nape of my neck. The slight pull showing me she wants me just as much as I want her.

I move away slightly because I need air. This woman is intoxicating, and I can't get enough. Pushing my forehead to hers, I see the rise and fall of her chest, she too caught a little off guard with our desire for each other. We look at each other for a beat, both of us panting, but neither of us pulling away.

"You taste so damn good, Cat," I grit out, running my tongue over my lips, licking her cherry gloss off them and wanting to eat her whole.

She hums, the sound vibrating across my mouth.

"Too fucking good for me, that is for sure," I growl, my nose trailing down her cheek, inhaling all of her. She lets another moan escape when I reach her neck, leaving light, teasing kisses down to her collarbone. Every press of my mouth elicits a pretty sound from her lips or rewarding shiver and tightening grip from her body.

"Taste me again. I think you might be my favorite flavor too," she says breathily, and I groan louder as my lips find hers again, before moving down her jaw, to the most sensitive spot of her neck. Kissing with more force, I trail my tongue to her earlobe and nibble, before moving lower. Her hands run through my hair, her fingers massaging my head, and this spot right here, tucked into her neck, with her hold keeping me in place for her pleasure, is magic.

Her body arches into mine, as I lean against the medical bed. My hands find her ribs as I follow the line of her bra, and she jumps a little at the contact, so I pull back to look at her. Maybe I've pushed too far.

"Sorry... ticklish." She giggles as she leans back from me, secure in my grip, and I smile cheekily.

"You're ticklish, huh?"

"Sorry, yes, extremely," she says with a blush and a smile, and I take full advantage of it.

"Where? Here?" I ask as my hands and fingers start tickling her around the waist.

"Arghhh! Yes!" she screams in delight, her laughter bouncing around the room. It is a sound that has never been inside these walls, but fuck, I really want it to be.

"Carter, stop! Carter!" she screams at me, as she flops around in my arms, like a jumping bunny. I'm laughing as I pick her up and place her on the medical bed, standing in front of her so she can't move.

"Good to know you have a weakness," I say to her, grinning, pleased with myself that not only am I getting to know her better, but I just had my hands all over her.

"Tell me, are you ticklish here?" I ask her, before my

lips find the crook of her neck again, and I feel her relax instantly as I taste her skin.

"No..." she says in a whisper as her hands run up my arms, her fingernails lightly scratching my skin.

"What about here?" I ask her, my lips going lower, trailing down the neckline of her top, and she leans back, her hands gripping my neck, keeping me with her.

"No..." she almost moans, and my hands wrap around her middle as my lips start to go even lower, my tongue licking the skin at the top of her bra.

"Carter," she moans my name then, and I lift my head to look at her.

She stares up at me, and I kiss her again, before her hands cup my face and she pulls back slightly.

"You have gloss on your face," she whispers, taking her thumb and wiping my lips.

"You have my sweat all over you," I say in response, because girls hate that shit.

"I don't mind." I growl at the hungry look on her face, as my forehead bumps hers gently. I probably look like I want to devour her whole. And I do.

I see her swallow and take a small breath. "C'mon, let me fix you up." Even though I know she is right, and we should stop before we take it too far, I groan loudly as I remove myself from her. She giggles at my grumble, and I grip her waist again, pulling her with me. I try to be a gentleman as I lift her off the bed and place her back onto her feet.

"Fine, no more tasting for now," I murmur, and she smiles.

"For now," she confirms as she straightens her clothes and fixes her hair. The two of us a little disheveled.

I swap places with her as I take a seat on the medic bed, letting her get to work.

"So Benji called you?" I ask as she gets a few things from her bag.

"Yeah, he called the office. Said you need your stitches checked and that you had a few hits to your head," she says, looking at me with a quirked brow.

"I'm a fighter, Cat. I always get hits to the head. Not that I mind you looking me over."

She smiles, almost shyly, and my lips curve in response.

"So what's Benji's deal anyway?" she asks, stepping toward me with scissors.

"He is my best friend. I have known him since we were teenagers. He is a good guy, just got mixed up with a bad crowd when he was younger. All good now, though."

"I assumed he must be a close friend. He was very protective of you." She's being too nice.

"He was an ass that night, Doc. You can say it." I tilt my head, giving her an expectant look, and she laughs.

"Well, he doesn't seem to be like that any other time I see him. You must've had him stressed out." She shrugs, smirking.

"No, he's just dramatic."

Huffing a small laugh, she shakes her head.

"Okay, look down a little so I can see the stitches." As she stands before me, my hands immediately go to her waist. I pull her closer, so she is firmly standing in between my legs as I caress her sides.

"Go for it," I say, tilting my head down, again getting a great view of her fucking amazing tits under her shirt. They are in what looks like a black lace bra and my fingers twitch at wanting to unwrap her. It would be like the Christmas I never had.

"How often do you train like that? In the ring?" she asks as she gets busy with removing my stitches.

"Most days. It keeps me agile, light on my feet, and gives me great spatial awareness." As I look at her, I get the feeling she isn't comfortable with my answer. It's too soon to think I can read her like I book, but I know I'm right before I even ask.

"What are you thinking?"

"I am a doctor, and I know it is a sport, boxing, wrestling, fighting, but I help, not harm... so seeing it in the flesh just now, and seeing people wanting to hurt you is not my idea of a good time." I smile at the thought that she cares. That is something that has never happened with anyone before.

"What are you smiling at?" she asks warily.

"You worried about me, Cat?" I ask her teasingly as I lean in again, quickly tasting her lips once more.

"Maybe." I like that she is coy, bashful even. She shows so much strength, yet lets her vulnerabilities shine for me on occasion. She is totally different from any woman I have ever been with.

"You don't need to worry about me. I can handle it. Is there anything else that worries you about me?" She knows I work with the mob, so that has to be playing on her mind, and I've been curious to know how she feels about it. She remains quiet as she bites the inside of her cheek, her eyes flicking to mine briefly before she looks back at my wound.

"Because I kind of like having my hands on your body and seeing you on the regular, so might as well get everything out on the table now," I state, watching her for her reaction.

Her eyebrows rise, a little shocked that I am so forward, and I am too. But I don't think I can let her go now. A taste wasn't enough to satiate my craving for her, my desire to be around her. The feeling of her under my hands is incomparable.

She finishes off removing the stitches and steps away from me slightly, but my grip on her remains. Her body language is not as sure as it was, and I see her take a breath before looking at me.

"We are total opposites, Carter. Besides, my life is a mess. I can't offer you anything. Why would a man like you even think about someone like me?" My head rears back as I take in her words.

"Someone like you? What does that mean?" There was an underlying insecurity in her statement that's completely throwing me off.

She steps back to me, bringing a wipe to my forehead, cleaning my wound with an ever-gentle touch.

"It doesn't matter. Forget I said anything."

"Oh no, you are not getting out of it that easy. Tell me. Tell me who you think you are?" I ask her again. I'm not willing to let her leave here without knowing what she's talking about. How could she ever think she's the reason we can't be together? *I'm* the problem here.

"You know, a tired single mom, with a crazy ex-boyfriend. I have a father who lost any sense of morality when my mom died and is the devil incarnate. Not to mention, I work too hard, I am the worst soccer mom ever, and the tap in my kitchen has been leaking for weeks because I have no idea how to fix it. Why the hell would anyone want to be with me? I am a mess. I am too old for you, Carter. You deserve someone young, vibrant, and beautiful. Not someone like me." The words rush out of her so quickly it is hard to grasp them, hard to interject and argue her points. She's talking down about herself with nonsense, as if they are facts. I'm so taken aback; it takes me a moment to digest it all.

She looks back at me with her eyebrows high like she is saying *I told you so.*

"Nope. You got that all wrong," I say, my tone serious. My hands still on her body pull her closer to me, until she's flush with my chest.

"That's not what I see." I grill her with my eyes, my stare keeping her quiet.

"I see a strong woman, a tiger mom who would do anything for her cub." When I see her about to scoff, I continue.

"I see a hard-working doctor who has worked for years to be taken seriously and climb the medical ladder." Bringing my hand to cup her face, her eyes don't leave mine.

"I see a woman, who despite it all, continues to show up for everyone around her. I also see a sexy woman, one who hasn't had the right man in her life to show her exactly how she's supposed to be treated."

"Hmmm... maybe you do have a concussion," she

murmurs, trying to use humor to get out of this. But I shake my head.

"No. I'm serious, Cat. Don't brush me off. I am this close to ripping these fucking clothes off you and showing you exactly what I mean," I growl out.

I hear her gasp. "Carter—" she starts, looking at me wide-eyed, but I cut her off.

"I'm dead serious. No one is to talk to you like that, not even yourself. You are strong and beautiful and kind and fucking classy as shit. I have no idea how this"—I point between her and me—"is ever going to work, but the need to be around you, it's all I can think about. To have you screaming my name over and over again... it's fucking leaving me harder than I have ever been." I grit out every word, and I'm made aware all over again just how fucked I am.

She is standing still, her eyes remaining wide with surprise. Just as she's about to say something, Benji barges in.

"Carter, we've got a problem with the—" Benji says, looking at some paperwork and not at us so he has no fucking idea that he is interrupting.

"Benji!" I bark at him, and I don't miss Cat jumping at my tone. I internally cringe. Benji stops mid-stride and looks between her and I.

"Shit, sorry," he mutters before turning around and walking back out the door.

Cat takes that moment to stride away from me and back to the table holding her medical kit, and starts packing up. Creating distance between us that I just don't like.

I slip off the bed and walk to her.

"Carter, I need to go. I have to pick Ivy up from school." Her eyes won't meet mine.

"Hey…" I grab her hands from the bag, turning her to look at me. "Don't be scared of me. I will never hurt you."

"I'm not scared of you, Carter," she whispers as she pulls her hands away and zips up her bag. "I'm scared of what I feel when I am with you." Then she's turning on her heel and walking out the door.

A grin comes to my face as I watch her leave.

I'm not the only one who feels this connection.

16

CATHERINE

As Maggie and I walk into the gym for our second class, I see Benji at the front desk again. However, instead of running away to his buddy this time, he actually greets us with a smile.

"Ladies, welcome back!" he says, his voice full of energy. He really is like a totally different person than the one I met weeks ago. It almost feels like we're friends now.

"Thanks, Benji. This is my sister, Maggie," I say, formally introducing them, and he nods to her with a smile.

"And this is Ivy!" I state with pride, gripping my daughter's hand tight in mine. She wanted to hang with us tonight, and I know she would find this class interesting. It's a good opportunity for her to see women being strong and independent.

"Great to meet you both." His smile is extra wide for my daughter, which I appreciate.

"You need to follow me," he says, and Maggie and I

look at each other, confused. It took me all afternoon to get my nerves in check. After the last encounter with Carter, I am not sure what will happen tonight if I see him. But I really want to. The feeling of his hands on my body has been in my dreams for days.

"What for? Are we meant to be in a different class?" Maggie asks as we all start following Benji toward the back of the gym.

"Yeah, well, kind of. A special class is a better way of explaining it." He leads us to the back of the massive gym to a door I haven't seen yet. When he opens it, we all walk in, and my eyes widen in surprise.

It is another space, completely empty of people, but full of state-of-the-art equipment. It has a large boxing ring in the middle of the room, mats over on one side, a weight room, mirrors, punching bags, everything that is in the front room, although this space looks a little newer, fresher and more professional. Maggie and I look around in awe, having never seen anything like this before.

"This is Carter's private area. You will both be taking self-defense with him tonight," Benji says, as my head snaps back to him.

"What?" My jaw would fall off my face if I didn't have to keep it together in front of my daughter.

I practically bolted from him a few days ago, and I still haven't been able to reconcile the feelings he brought out in me. And now, he'll be the one I'm face to face with, in close contact with...

"He will be here in a minute. He is finishing a call with New York," Benji says, looking at me knowingly, then glancing at Ivy and back to me. I need to take a breath to steady my nerves. *The mob. He is part of the mob.* I need to remind myself of that fact because it keeps slipping from my mind. Of course, he would be talking to them, of course I am now involved on a personal level with one of the head mobsters of New York. It can all only happen to me. *What the hell am I doing?*

Maggie looks at me wide-eyed, no doubt wondering what the hell I got us into, and I squeeze Ivy's hand even tighter.

"Thank you, Benji, but we are okay with the other group. We don't want to bother Carter," I say with a smile, albeit a shaky one.

"Too bad." *His* voice grumbles at me from behind, and I turn quickly, startled. "You need to be able to protect yourself for whenever he comes back, because according to your little cub," he says, stopping near Ivy and rubbing her head in greeting, "he always comes back."

I watch Ivy's smile beam when she sees him, and Carter puts out his fist for her to bump, which she does with glee.

"Hey, Ivy. Glad you can join us today." I'm in a state of shock, unmoving, as I was their interaction with interest.

"Can you teach me to fight, Carter? I want to learn all the moves!" she asks, throwing a mock punch that whooshes through the air. And this big, tattooed monster of a man laughs. He's laughing with my daughter, like nothing sounds more fun than that. He is probably the last man she needs to know, yet it warms my heart like I never knew it could.

"Sure thing, Little Cub." Ivy jumps with excitement, basically catching air, and his smile grows even wider.

Carter comes to stand next to Maggie and me, looking like a delicious contradiction. The most intimidating bouncer at a nightclub, his arms crossing his chest, challenging me to argue, yet there's a softness in his eyes that has my stomach fluttering.

"Cub?" Maggie asks with curiosity.

"Ivy," both Carter and I reply to her at the same time, and her eyebrows raise as she eyes us both suspiciously. No doubt she will fire a million questions at me later, because I haven't had time to fill her in on the latest.

I look back to Carter, whose gaze takes me in.

"What do you think, Ivy?" He turns to her, trying to get her on his side. He clearly hasn't forgotten what I was saying as he walked in.

"I want to learn, Carter! Teach me everything!" she says, her face lighting up in anticipation.

"Sure, I have a few ways you can get strong, just like your mom." His eyes flick back to me, but it's not teasing anymore. It's... reverent. It's a look I've never seen aimed at me before.

"Let me teach you how to protect yourself, Cat." His hand reaches out and connects with my hip, and he squeezes my waist. He gives me a sly grin, which I can't help but return, and I nod at him, knowing that in this moment, I would do anything he says. So, I nod my agreeance.

Maggie clears her throat, snapping the two of us back into reality, and Carter claps his hands. "Let's go, ladies," he says, spinning on his heel, and we follow him over to the mats for our session, but not before Maggie gives me a wink that makes me smile.

Ivy takes a seat to the side to watch, while Carter explains a few moves to us. Then Maggie and I each take a turn in trying to escape from his different holds. He and Maggie strike up a great rapport and when it is my turn, I don't miss the way he grabs my waist, runs his hands up and down my back, caressing my skin. With his hands on my body so much, it is hard to concentrate. I am so turned on by him, his strength, the way he teaches us the different moves with the utmost patience, his caring nature, his intelligence. There is a lot to like about this man and my fondness for him is growing by the minute.

"Go, Mom!" Ivy yells from the sidelines, and I hear Carter chuckle.

"She's a great kid, Cat." I smile, about to respond, but he grabs me and flips me over, showing me exactly why I need to keep my guard up.

After a rigorous session, Maggie and I lie on the mats, staring at the ceiling, both of us coated in a sheen of sweat as we try to catch our breath. Carter worked us hard, throwing each of us around, showing us techniques, getting our fitness up so we can harm and run. It is similar to what we were learning in the other class, but a little more advanced.

I watch Ivy with Carter, as he picks her up and throws her around like she weighs nothing. All I can hear is her elated giggles and a tear runs down my cheek, mixing with my sweat. I never thought I would see Ivy interact with a man like she is with Carter right now. Normally, she's hesitant with any male that comes near her, but it seems Carter not only has a special effect on me, but my daughter as well.

"Well," Maggie says as she sits up. "I'm done. Thanks, Carter!" she yells across the room, to where he is grabbing his water bottle.

"Good job, Maggie. See you next time," he says before taking a few gulps of his water, wiping the sweat off his brow. Clearly, he got a good workout in too.

She stands and looks at me, a knowing look on her face. "I will see you later, and I want all the details." It takes me a moment to catch up, but then she's answering my unspoken question.

"Ivy, let's go, your mom can meet us at my place. I need an ice cream stat." Ivy promptly gets up, running to her jacket with a squeal. And now I know what my sister's up to.

"Bye, Carter!" Ivy calls out to him, out of breath as she sprints across the room to meet Maggie. He smiles, giving her a wave, and I watch them both leave without another look back. Maggie's wobbling slightly, her legs feeling like Jell-O, no doubt, because mine sure are. I want to thank Carter for taking time out of his busy day for us, so I am slower to stand.

I peel myself off the soft mats of the gym floor and look at Carter who is walking back to me, his shirt is now gone. My eyes drop to his body, and I can say with certainty it's a sight I could never tire of.

"You're going to burn a hole through me, looking at me like that," Carter teases, and I blush at being caught gawking. I rub my face with my hands, laughing lightly, so out of practice with dealing with men.

"Come here," he says gruffly, lifting his arm out to me for me to take his hand. I don't hesitate to do just that, and as I do, he pulls me closer. My eyes automatically go to his hard chest again, landing on a woman's name he has tattooed. I have seen it before, but I haven't asked about it.

"What are you looking at now?" he asks before his gaze lowers to meet mine, and I lose my breath for a moment in his crystal-clear blue eyes.

I am so turned on right now, standing close to him, I can't think straight. His hands find my waist again, where his fingers run up and down my bare skin, making it prickle with heat. The way we act around each other is like infatuated teenagers.

How can I be so comfortable in his presence, when I know I should be anything but?

"I'm just looking at your tattoos," I answer, my hands skimming over his bare torso. The electricity between the two of us right now is off the charts. I swear I can feel it sparking with each touch we exchange.

"Hmmm, which one caught your eye?" There are many, so I could easily fib, but I want to be honest with him.

"This one." I trace the letters that are painted across his chest.

"Mmmm, I like your hands on my body way too much, Cat," he says, his tone filled with gravel, and as our eyes meet again, I feel myself burning up under his gaze.

"Who's Clara?" I ask nervously, as my eyes moving from the tattoo to his eyes to gauge his reaction.

"It was my mother's name," he answers honestly, and my heart breaks for the young boy Carter was.

"It's a beautiful name," I say in a whisper as I look back at the tattoo. He keeps his features schooled, but I can see a twitch in his jaw.

"So you ran away from me pretty fast the other day. Why is that?" Each caress of his hands against my bare waist has me melting into him.

"I didn't run..." I lie, building the courage to give him the truth.

"Are you scared of me?" he asks, his eyes now inquisitive, his hands remaining steady.

"No. Not at all," I rush to assure him, still trying to find the right words. His brows furrow in question, and I reach up and smooth the line between them, my fingers trailing down his cheek. That action is all it takes to confirm how soft he really is, under all this muscle. Maybe just for me, but he is. I feel him relax as he holds me, his gaze searching but patient.

He doesn't move, doesn't push for my answer... and that's what has my words flowing.

"I probably should be," I say, pausing to look into his eyes not straying from mine. He is steady, solid, simply waiting for me to say what I need to say.

"I shouldn't even be thinking about you. But I do," I whisper my admission, and I feel his hands caressing my skin once more.

"God, Carter... you are all I have been thinking about." He swallows roughly at my admission, his hands gripping me tight.

"You work with the god damn mob. I am a single

mother... I have a daughter to worry about. My career is taking off... being involved with a man like you..." I pause for a moment as I stare into his eyes, and he still waits, hearing me out without interruption.

"It is a risk..." His jaw clenches slightly, and my fingers automatically find his hair and massage his scalp.

"...but I know you would never hurt me, Carter..." I whisper, looking at his lips. God, I really wanting them on mine.

I should stay away, but I can't. I feel like I am totally sucked into his orbit and want nothing more than him. Right here, right now.

"I'm not scared of you, Carter. Not even a little." His stare has me breathless, and before I can even think of pressing my lips to his, he lifts me up and slams me onto the mat. A move he trained us on tonight, and catching me totally unawares.

I let out a squeal before he chuckles, looking down at me, his eyes searing into my skin. One of his hands holds his weight above me, the other one meeting my bare skin on my stomach, where his fingers trail up and down my side. The way he touches me, looks at me, it's like he wants to discover all of me, bit by bit. Internally, I beg him to.

"I'm not a good man, Cat," he repeats what he's already told me. As his face grows more serious, I feel the tension leave his body, so I strike.

"Yaaaaaa!" I yell as I move swiftly into position and maneuver us so that I am now on top of him. I am sure he could have stopped me, but he didn't. Now I sit straddling him, my hands resting on his bare chest, and his firmly wrapped around my waist.

"You're playing with fire, Cat," he says in a low growl, warning me again, but I don't heed his words.

"So what are you going to do about it, then?" I sass, flicking my eyes to his lips and back to his eyes in time to see the hunger in them.

"This." He grabs me around the neck and pulls me to him, sitting up and meeting me halfway, as he crashes his lips onto mine.

17

CARTER

She lands on top of me, a moan leaving her lips that I savor. Our bodies stick together, her breasts push hard against my bare chest, my hands sliding down to grab onto her hips as her lips move effortlessly with mine.

I hear her draw breath, and my eyes flick to hers. And all I see in those pretty browns is desire. Everything I'm feeling reflected back at me through her gaze.

I want her more than I have ever wanted another human being in my entire life.

She lowers her head, and our lips meet again in a hungry tangle.

I don't hesitate when I am fighting; if you hesitate, you lose, and I don't want to lose her. So, briefly, before I lose all self-control, I roll us over so she is on her back, lying underneath me again.

Our tongues clash as I settle on top of her, the feeling eliciting a groan to vibrate up my chest. I move my hand to grip her neck, pulling her closer, wanting to devour her completely.

I know I shouldn't. I know I shouldn't even be fucking touching her, but I've daydreamed of this moment, and I can't convince myself to be the bigger man and stop.

Her hands run up my body, feeling my tensing muscles, and I could fucking die happy right now. My gym shorts are now the only piece of clothing I have on, and they are no longer hiding my hard cock as it pulsates between us, begging to be released.

"Cat, tell me to stop. Tell me to fucking stop," I mumble against her lips in between our kisses.

I have to fucking stop.

She deserves better. Better than me and better than a quick, dirty fuck.

I'm no good for her. I need to get off her. I need to leave her alone.

But I can't.

"Oh, Carter, don't you dare stop. I need you, want you so bad…" she moans into my mouth, and hearing that plea from her lips has me feeling feral. Grinding my dick harder into her, I feel the heat radiating off her body, evident of her arousal.

Fuck, it's going to happen. This is going to fucking happen. If she's giving herself to me, then I'm taking her. No questions asked.

Her floral scent overpowers me, and I pepper kisses along her shoulder, her head falling back, my hands itching to grab her hair. I am such a greedy asshole; I need more of her right this fucking second. I sit up onto my knees abruptly and yank her pants and panties down over her hips in one go. She helps me shimmy them off as I pull my cock out, stroking from root to tip to give myself a reprieve before I explode too soon.

Her matching desperation is evident when she's up on her knees, half naked, in the next second, kissing me again. When her tongue caresses my lower lip, I groan, and she fucking smiles up at me. There's no more waiting when I see that. Not even another second.

I grab her around the waist, lifting her off the mats, setting her on my lap. Her wetness glides over my dick as her legs wrap around my hips, and I thrust inside of her, hard, fast, and fucking needier than I've ever been.

I hiss out at the contact, her warmth surrounding me making my eyes roll back. She moans in reply as I settle myself deep inside of her, and begin to move. Her arms circle my neck, nails digging into my shoulders, as she holds on for dear life through my powerful thrusts. Not able to stop, not able to slow.

"Fuck, Cat. Fuck," I growl as I nip at her neck and shoulders. Seeing her delicate, beautiful body wrapped around my roughened, tattooed one is doing things to my head. I'm not going to last.

"Mmmm... do that again," she moans, as my teeth bite into her skin, sucking on it like I need it to survive. "Yessss, Carter. More."

"I want you too damn much. *Fuck*," I grit out. My hands, my mouth, my cock, I want to be all over her in every way possible, and I can't get enough. I bite her neck again, and she arches her back on a moan, as her hand cups the back of my head, pulling me closer so I know that she likes it.

I leave little marks, before finding her now swollen lips again, and continue my assault, tasting her like she's my last meal. I am an animal for her, my desire unrivalled.

"Oh my God. Carter. Carter..." She pants and moans my name like a prayer as her hips move in rhythm with mine. It's like we were fucking made for each other. I grab her ass hard, which drives another breathy moan from her chest. And when I slap her plump cheek on impulse, she rewards me with another call of my name, her hands gripping into my shoulders and thighs tightening around me. I grab her ass in my palms to control her movements, pushing her and pulling her on and off my cock, making sure to grind her clit against me with each pass. Every clench of her pussy has me raging inside her.

"Don't stop. That feels so good," she pants out, pulling my lips to hers in a kiss that has me almost coming.

This is the fucking hottest sex I have ever had.

"You are so fucking hot. So fucking beautiful," I grit out, every second inside her becoming a test of my will. With one hand, I tug down her bra and free her breasts, needing to feel them, to see them in all their glory as her body bounces on top of me. And fuck, they are perfect. *She* is fucking perfection, and I am going to ruin her.

Or, she's going to ruin me.

I feel her convulsing around me, her body shaking in my arms, getting closer to her release. So I double down on my efforts, pulling her to me, harder and faster.

"That's it, Cat, give yourself to me. Come for me," I say just as she screams my name, continuing to move herself against me to draw out her pleasure.

My muscles tense as I watch her in rapture. She's the sweetest fucking thing I have ever seen. But I don't stop. I can't. I ravish her, gripping her ass in my hands strongly enough to leave marks, and thrusting up into her until I explode with a roar. My head falls forward, resting against hers, as we both catch our breath and come down from the high.

I squeeze my eyes shut as sudden paranoia settles over me, feeling her against me like this, being so in tune with her. What the fuck have I done? The most incredible woman I have ever met, and I go and fuck her on the gym mats? She is right. She has a successful career, an amazing daughter, a life she's proud of, and I fuck her on the floor.

I'm a fucking disgrace. I need to get far away from her. Far, far away. She deserves better.

This is how it is. I fuck and I leave. No expectation and nobody gets hurt.

Before I even pull out of her, I already know that this can't be whatever we were thinking it could be. It just can't. We are too different. I kill people for a fucking living, for Christ's sake.

I gently lift her off and stand up, giving me space to put myself back together and pull my shorts back up. I rub my hands over my face, and as she rises, she begins to talk.

"Carter, I—" But I don't let her finish.

"Bathrooms are over there," I say with a nod to my left, feeling sick that I didn't even use a fucking condom. I always wrap myself up, never go without it. I turn around, shaking my head at my stupidity, and grab my water bottle. I am so fucking dizzy, I think I will faint if I don't hydrate.

I hear her quietly gathering her things, and then she walks away, pushing into the bathrooms before I lower my head in shame.

I grab my top from the floor where I dropped it earlier and put it on, glimpsing her coming out of the bathroom, heading straight toward me.

"Carter, that was—" Again, I don't let her finish. I don't want her to say anything that could change my mind.

"A mistake," I state firmly, not looking at her. I know I will see hurt in her eyes, and that will fucking kill me. I should have stopped it all before it started.

"I don't deserve someone like you, Cat. I can't be with you. You deserve better than me... we can't be together."

"I'm sorry," I say, but it's barely out of my mouth before I'm walking away from her, not once looking at her face, and not giving her a chance to reply.

18

CATHERINE

I stand still, in shock. Is he really just going to walk away from me?

"Where the hell are you going?" I yell at him, and he pauses mid-stride. My chest heaves like I have just had another lesson.

He pauses in place, but doesn't turn to look at me, still facing the door like he is ready to run.

"What? You can't even look at me now?" He doesn't move his body, showing almost no reaction, but his hands clench at his sides.

"So, I'm okay to fuck, but I don't deserve the respect of a conversation afterward?" I spit at him.

"You were right!" he yells at me, finally turning to look at me with heat in his glare.

"I am no good for you. I am in the fucking mob. You have a daughter to protect, you have your career to manage. You can't even be seen with a man like me!" He throws my own words back at me.

I watch him for beat as realization dawns on me. *Was

I that bad? My father says that no one will ever want to be with me, so as I stand here on the gym mats, I can hear his voice in my head.

"You're no good, Catherine. No one will ever want you. Daniel is the only man for you. You are an old, single mother... who would ever want you?"

My words get stuck in my throat, unable to speak as he turns away from me and high-tails it out of the gym.

It has been years since I have been with a man, and despite my reservations, I wanted Carter more than anything tonight. What we just did was the hottest, most intense sexual experience I have ever had in my entire life, and I loved every minute of it. That is, until he walked away from me. I could feel him trying to remove himself from the situation, but no one can fake what we just did. Sure, it was lust, carnal need, but I felt that there was an undercurrent of so much more.

We have been dancing around each other for weeks and tonight we combusted. I thought it was amazing.

But to him, it was a "mistake."

My heart beats out of my chest, and I try to control my breathing.

He doesn't deserve someone like me? His words loop around in my mind as I try to get myself together, my legs still feeling shaky from both the workout tonight and the amazing sex.

Was sex all he was after? Did he use me, and I fell like prey into his hands?

I am so stupid. Such a naïve fool to think that a man like Carter would want anything other than that. I should have known better. The first man to pay me any real attention and I go and throw myself at him like a needy schoolgirl.

He is right. On paper, we don't fit. But when we're together, there is a real connection, and after what we just did, I know he feels it too. He has to...

But his rejection stings.

Swallowing down the tears that threaten to fill my eyes, I feel worthless and totally pathetic. We didn't even use protection, and I thank God that I am on the pill, because it only took one time with Ivy. What was I thinking?

I wasn't, that's the problem.

Looking around the empty gym I try to get myself together. Bending down, I swipe my drink bottle and grab my keys before rushing out the door. When I hit the main gym area, I don't stop. I have tunnel vision as I head for the door, my arms hugging my chest, thankful the music is loud to drown out my thoughts.

Benji is sitting at the front desk, and I make the mistake of meeting his eyes as I walk past. I try to stand tall, even though my dignity is slipping from my fingers at a fast pace.

"He didn't mean it, whatever he said or did. He's scared," he says softly, looking as glum as I feel. I don't say anything as I stop and stare at him. "You are both from two different worlds, and he likes you. Shit, does he like you. He feels like he isn't good enough for you. That's what it comes down to." The pain in my stomach tightens. I swallow, again trying to keep the tears at bay. "But he really likes you, Cat."

"I don't think so, Benji. If he liked me, he wouldn't

have treated me like he just did." I will myself not to cry. Not here. Not in his space. I don't want him to see me shed a tear for him.

"I need to go," I say to him before I put my head down again and walk out the door.

"See you next week!" Benji hollers to me, and I turn and look at him abruptly.

"For your class, he won't be here. He will be in New York, so you should still come," Benji says, like he is extending an olive branch. I simply nod quickly and keep walking. The last place I ever want to be is back in this gym.

Out in the fresh air, I take a deep breath and get into my car, locking the door behind me. Now in the dark of the night, in the quiet of my own space, a lone tear falls down my cheek. But I don't want to cry here, so I throw my things onto the passenger seat and turn on the ignition.

As I flick on my lights and drive away, I leave a piece of me behind.

19

CARTER

Seething as I sit in my office, I rub an ache in my chest. I watched her as she walked from the back room and through the gym, not looking at anyone, her beautiful head down, her posture broken, knowing that I did that to her.

It fucking kills me.

I have had sex with women, then carelessly left immediately after, plenty of times before. But this was different, much different. Because I didn't want to. I wanted to scoop her up and take her home.

Only I can't do that. I can't have her caught up in my life. It isn't fair.

So, I took my taste. Like a damn beast. I couldn't control myself, and I took from her what I have desired ever since the moment I met her, thinking maybe it would be enough. To quench the thirst I have for her. But it wasn't. And deep down, I knew that's exactly how it would be.

I am a fucking grade-A asshole.

Jumping up from my chair, I throw open my door and take the stairs down two at a time before walking back to the scene of the crime. Slamming my personal gym door shut, I head straight over to the punching bag and start hitting it.

I don't even bother with gloves or tape. As the anger in my body mounts, I throw my fists at the vinyl bag one after the other, over and over, each one more vicious than the last. Sweat pours down my face, my t-shirt now soaked again, as I continue my assault.

"You're going to wreck that bag," Benji says from behind me. He is a stealth motherfucker because I didn't even hear him come in.

"Fuck off, Benji," I grit out in between punches, not looking at him.

"She's gone, you know."

"I know."

"For what it is worth, I think you made the wrong decision tonight, Carter." Benji doesn't let up, and I stop punching to glare at him. My chest heaves rapidly as I try to catch my breath.

"I made the only decision there was to make."

"I've seen you two together. I know you like her. It's just, you think you don't deserve her. I get it. The life we had growing up, the life you have now, none of it is something that she could ever imagine. But she doesn't care about that, Carter. She likes you, regardless. That much is obvious to anyone."

"Goddamnit. Fuck. Off." I don't need to feel remorse. I don't want to feel the pain. I need to fight, punch, throttle this bag until my body is so weary, I can easily fall asleep tonight. If not, then Cat is going to be running through my mind until the sun comes up. I have known her for only a few weeks, and she has already taken over every spare thought.

She makes me crazy. She makes me weak. And I cannot be weak.

"You think you don't deserve a good woman. You think you can't get close to anyone because of what happened to your mom. But Doc is keen for you, man. I can see it!" His voice raises, trying to get through to me, and that's just pissing me off even more.

"What can I give her?!" I roar my feelings out to the empty room, thankful the music is blaring next door so the other patrons are oblivious. "What the fuck can I offer her, Benji?" I run my hands down my face in exasperation, noticing my bloody knuckles.

"I fucked her. I fucked her on the fucking floor. I am an animal! I fucking took what I wanted, and then ran away from her like a fucking pussy." I start to pace, my hands running through my hair and tugging at the roots. I'm completely losing my shit, not able to rein it in even if I tried. Benji just stands there, staring, knowing it's best if he keeps his distance.

"I am in the fucking mafia... I kill people for a fucking living, and she saves people. She has a daughter, Benji, a little girl! I know the dangers of being with a man like me. She doesn't deserve that." I'm screaming at this point, my chest heaving.

"She is fucking the most beautiful woman I have ever met, and I just treated her like she was disposable. I fucking hate myself for it."

All the fight has all but left me, and when I look up at my friend again, I see such a pitiful expression on his face for me that I groan.

Slumping on the floor, I hang my head in shame, feeling like the piece of shit I am.

"Have you told her what you do? Sure, she knows a little about what goes on, no doubt, and she was still here with you, spending time with you. Sounds like you need to tell her. Talk to her. Let her make the decision, and stop trying to make it for her," Benji states, before turning and walking out the door, closing it behind him. I sigh out my frustration.

I feel my cell vibrate and pull it from my pocket and see Sebastian's name on the screen.

"Yeah." My greeting is lackluster, at best.

"What's up your ass?" Sebastian asks with a bite.

"Nothing. What's happening?" I adjust my tone, needing to get my head back into the game.

"I need you back here earlier tomorrow. We have a meeting at 10am. We have some heavy shit to get through, so be prepared." I rub my eyes at the thought, already tired.

"No problem. I will be there."

"Good. Preferably in a better mood too." Sebastian says before he ends the call, and I throw my cell across the mats.

Thank God I am going back to New York tomorrow.

I can forget about all of this and move the fuck on.

All I need is some work to distract me, the kind that'll get my hands dirty and reaffirm that I did the right thing tonight. As much as it fucking guts me.

20

CATHERINE

Tears pour down my face as I sit with Maggie in her living room. We put the girls to bed half an hour ago, and Maggie firmly requested I spend the night, clearly seeing that I was upset.

I told her everything. I told her about Daniel's visit and Carter standing up to him. I told her about the moment Carter and I had in his medical room days ago, and then I told her about tonight. About what we did. About what he did.

My heart hurts, and I am exhausted. I stepped into his advances and got trodden on and thrown to the curb. The fact that he couldn't even look me in the eye is what's making me feel sick. My confidence has already been beaten down over the years, and now it's at an all-time low. Meeting someone like him, who I thought was different, who I was open to giving a chance to, and this is how I'm left feeling...

I want to dig a hole and hide away from him, from the world.

"You know, it is all probably for the best. There is no doubt you guys had sparks... any fool could see that. But he is right, Cat, you are both worlds apart, living two totally different lives. Maybe you need to sort out yours before you get involved with anyone else—even if it was the best sex you have ever had in your entire life," Maggie says, a small grin growing on her face, and I roll my eyes.

"I know you feel like shit now, but seriously, he would have put Daniel to shame. I know it." She isn't wrong. Daniel couldn't even make me orgasm.

"You're right," I say to her on a sigh, and she looks at me wide-eyed, her expression one of shock. She looks even more ridiculous with her hair now a soft red color from the food dye I put in her shampoo earlier today.

"Not about the sex. I mean, yes, you're right about that. But what I mean is, I need to take charge of my life. I need to get it sorted." As my tears dry, I feel a small amount of courage building inside me.

"I need to clean up my mess of a life before I can fully be open to anything or anyone else. Whether it is Carter, or someone else—if that is what I want in life—then I need to tackle my problems before I can drag anyone else into it," I say with more strength than I feel, my mind now racing a million miles an hour.

"What are you getting at?" Maggie eyes me suspiciously.

"For years, I let Dad and Daniel tell me I wasn't good enough. Whether it was with work, or as a mother, or even just as a woman. Maybe subconsciously I started to believe them. Or... honestly, I did believe them. When Carter first showed interest in me, I thought there was no way he could be. Then, when I pushed those thoughts aside, I realized being with Carter made me feel wanted again. Like someone could find me attractive and beautiful, but more than that... it felt like I mattered to someone. And that was nice. Until it wasn't, obviously." I swallow hard, pushing out a breath.

"Cat, you know that anything they say is wrong. Of course, you are beautiful, caring, smart, an excellent mother, and so many other wonderful things. Too many for me to list, that's for damn sure," Maggie says, her eyes welling with tears, and I squeeze her hand in mine.

"I feel that now." Even after everything that happened tonight, Carter still made me feel things I never thought I could. I'll always remember that.

"I have a battle to fight, Maggie. It's time to get more serious. I need a lawyer. I need to remove any permanent attachments to Daniel, sever all ties completely, including terminating any parental rights he has to Ivy. I haven't pushed it before now because I was too scared. But I can't keep living like this. Living every single day in fear, always on edge. It needs to stop. Now." She nods in agreement, probably having been onboard with my plan before I even laid it out. She's wanted me to do this for a while.

"What should we do about Dad?" Maggie asks, and that is the other dark cloud that continually circles me. I haven't heard from him in weeks. The last time was when he yelled down the phone at me, demanding I go back to Daniel. I have no idea why he still wants us together. I have told him about the abuse, about his horrible ways with Ivy, but if I'm honest with myself, the two of them are a lot alike.

Dad wasn't always controlling and cold, but when Mom died years ago, he changed. He started working longer hours, and that led to him getting caught up with new friends, New York businessmen who didn't have time for their wives or families. Maggie and I saw Dad less and less over the years until I left Daniel, then he swiftly got back in touch and told me exactly what I needed to do.

"His expectation of me is to be playing happy families with Daniel in New York, whether it is safe for me or not. He expects me to get my old job back, have a nanny look after Ivy, and to get into line, regardless of my own safety and happiness. I deserve better, Maggie. If I want a chance at life again, at love again, then I need to get rid of the baggage that is continually bringing me down. That includes Dad too." I feel lighter for verbalizing my thoughts, some that I didn't even know I had until right in this very moment.

"Let's start tonight," Maggie suggests, and I look at her in question. She jumps up and grabs her laptop from the kitchen bench, then sits next to me on the sofa.

"Let's find you the best family lawyer in the country and start building your new life." Her fingers are tapping on her keyboard before I even respond.

"I love you, Maggie." I have never been more grateful to have her in my life.

Looking up from the screen, she reaches over and squeezes my hand. "And I love you, Cat."

"Nice hair, by the way," I say to her with a smile, not able to hold it in any longer.

"Be afraid dear sister, be very afraid..." She shakes her head, laughing, and I already know she has put itching powder in her spare bed for me. It looks like I will be sleeping on the sofa tonight.

Maggie and I search for the best family lawyer our money can find. While I took no money when I left Daniel, him having looked after all of our combined assets, I know that on my current salary, along with a loan from Maggie, I can afford a lawyer who will at least give it all a red-hot go.

No one is coming to save me.

This is a fight that I have to win on my own.

21

CARTER

After arriving back at the compound and spending a few days with the boys, Dante and I are now sitting in the car outside a seedy bar on the edge of town. Running on intel, our team gleamed from a few people in the know, we are looking for a man called Henderson. Cliff Henderson. An associate close to the businessmen who we think are planning to upend Senator Roy's current term. We are here to find him and get information, hoping that it leads us to find the main culprits.

We take a look at the place from the outside. We've never been here, but it has an air of familiarity to it. Rundown and in desperate need of repair, the overweight bouncers at the door barely move as we step inside. The obnoxiously loud music insults my ears, and I see a few scantily clad women roaming around. They are the topless wait staff, but I can see them trying to make tips from other activities as I watch one of women grab the hand of an older guy, leading him out the back.

"Fuck, this place is a shithole," I murmur to Dante, who nods in agreement.

"There he is," Dante says, and I follow his line of sight, spotting the grey-haired man currently flirting with a woman who looks half his age.

"Fucking dirty prick."

We move in his direction, and as we get closer, two younger men stand, clearly his bodyguards, and I wonder why he needs them if his business dealings are supposedly so clean.

"Who the fuck are you?" the old guy spits out, and my jaw clenches. I am itching to get my anger and frustrations out, and this man will do just fine. I've been functioning on autopilot, drowning myself in work and training, not wanting to think about her.

But she's still there, ever present. I hear her laughter in my dreams, see her face in my mind daily, and even though New York is busy, there is always room in my head for her.

It's done nothing to lessen my self-loathing.

"Your worst fucking nightmare." I step closer, ready to rumble.

One of the younger guys steps forward, and I don't hesitate as I rear my arm back and hit him square across the jaw before he even has time to get his footing. He jerks back, his body hitting the table with a jostle, just as the other one steps toward me.

I look at Dante for a second and see him standing back, arms crossed, letting me have all the fun, which I don't mind at all.

"I think you need to step back, brother," the guys

warns me as he takes another tentative step in my direction.

"I'm not your brother," I spit back as my hand flies out and I connect with his nose. Blood spurts from the impact, but I don't stop as he lunges for me again.

He gets a hit into my ribs, and I yank his head back and head-but him in the face, further damaging his already broken nose.

"Fuck!" he groans, but doesn't pull away, his resilience admirable.

When he lunges for me again, I swivel, kicking him in the torso, before I step toward him and follow it up with another hard punch to the ribs, hearing two of them break. He staggers back, but still doesn't lay down. Unlike the other guy, who still hasn't risen from the floor.

"Not so fast," I hear Dante's voice rumble, as he grabs Henderson by the sleeve, just as he was trying to escape.

"Carter, stop playing, we've got what we came for," Dante says, pulling Henderson along, taking him out to the car.

I look back at the two men, both bloody and broken.

Throwing another punch, it lands right across his temple, sending his head whipping to the side. I see the lights in his eyes go out before his body even hits the floor.

"Goodnight, *brother*."

Straightening my shirt, I look around, all eyes in the place on me. So, I nod quickly, pacing out the door to meet Dante and Henderson.

Sebastian has some questions.

***

Turns out that Cliff Henderson was a dead end. After bringing him back to the compound and turning him black and blue, he didn't give us anything. Even though he was most definitely hiding something. Leaving us all frustrated, we kept him a few days before I stole his last breath. His soul joining all the others that I have taken in the depths of hell.

Dante and I have been out and about every few days, following the trails of businessmen, while Sebastian and Nico have been following the money, the paperwork.

Between the four of us, we know we are getting close, but as I look down at my knuckles, the bruises and cuts are not going away. Cementing to me that Cat and I just aren't meant to be.

Chalk and Cheese. Day and Night. Never meant to happen.

The small scar above my eyebrow has faded slowly, but the memory of the way her body felt under my touch, not so much.

Walking into our meeting room, I am the first one to arrive, and I slump in my chair as I pull my ringing cell phone from my pocket.

I see Benji's name on the screen, so I answer quickly.

"Hey, man," I say casually, when all I really want to do is ask if he has seen her, if she has been back at the gym this week. I don't need to know, of course. Because I already do. I like to taunt myself at night, watching the gym cameras, and I am glad she is still doing the classes.

That what I did hasn't deterred her from doing what she can to keep herself safe.

"Hey, I have news." I can hear him walking around, and I know he is at the gym, running up the stairs for privacy.

"What's going on?" I press, as I get myself settled, waiting for the boys and wanting him to get to the point. The gym has been going well, and all bills are paid. From what I can tell, there are no issues with the staff either, so I have no idea why he is calling.

"I saw Doc with another man this morning," he finally says, and I still. My heart pounds out of my chest, blood pumping through my body and heating me up in the worst way.

"And?" I grit out, as I crack my sore knuckles, hating the world right now.

"And I thought you might want to know. I saw them having coffee together and introduced myself. They looked pretty cozy." He continues, and with each word, my grip on my phone tightens. "He was sharp, full suit, fucking good looking guy, said his name was Donovan Wilson." Just as he tells me his name, the boys all walk into the room.

"I gotta go, Benji," I grit out and hang up, not wanting to hear anything more anyway. Donovan Wilson. I don't even know who he is, but I already want to stab him in the eyes for even looking at my woman.

I nod to the boys, and as they come in and take their seats, I slide over to the internet on my phone and type in his name. I scour the first few results before I find someone that might be who Benji is talking about. Clicking on the page, I see a smarmy guy by the name of Donovan Wilson. He's a family lawyer, probably better suited to Cat than I ever will be. Swiping out of the page with a huff, I drop my phone on the table, rubbing my hands through my hair.

It's probably better this way. She deserves someone on the right side of the law, someone that I will never be.

"What the fuck is up with you?" Sebastian barks as he looks at me from across the table, Dante likewise as he sits down next to him. Nico slumps into the seat next to me.

"Nothing," I reply quickly, not wanting to get into it.

"It's not nothing. You have been acting like a pain in the ass since you came back from Philly," Sebastian presses, making it clear I am not getting out of this one. His brows crease, waiting for my answer. I can't hide anything from him, never have and never will.

"Just the fights coming up. Training is busy, that's all," I tell him with a sigh, trying to look anywhere but at him.

"You want to try again, brother?" Dante interjects, and now both of them are staring at me from across the table.

"It's the doctor, isn't it?" Nico asks, and I have never wanted to punch the shit out of him more in my life. Snapping my head to him, I drill him with my eyes.

"What?" he says in mock surprise, even though he knows he just totally outed me.

"What doctor, Carter?" Sebastian presses, eyeing me up and down. "Are you okay? Something wrong with you?"

"I'm fine," I say with a short nod.

"Let me guess, you fucked her, then left? Isn't that

how it goes with you? It's your M.O. You don't get attached to women, ever," Nico adds, digging is grave with every damn word at this point. I clench and unclench my fists, because by the grin on his face, he knows exactly what he is doing.

"What doctor?" Dante is now narrowing his eyes at me, and I already know this meeting is going to shit.

Nico goes to speak again, and Sebastian gives him a look, which thankfully shuts him up real quick.

"Talk," Sebastian commands, leaving no room for any excuses.

"Doctor Catherine Wakeford..." I admit as my eyes flick to Dante in time to see his eyebrows raise.

"That's Annie's doctor," he says in confusion. "You fucked Annie's doctor?" All I can do is nod.

"If you have fucked anything up with her working with Annie, I swear to fucking God, Carter, I will—" I cut him off before he can get too angry. Nothing will ever tame him when it comes to Annie's health and wellbeing after everything they have been through. But I can sure try.

"No, Cat wouldn't do that, Dante. She wouldn't punish someone like that, all because of me."

"You fucked Doctor Wakeford?" Sebastian confirms as he leans back in his chair, and I nod again in reply. "So I take it she's the one, then?" My eyes snap to his, and I scowl.

"Well, as Nico said, you've fucked and ran from women most of your life, but you never have acted like this. So she has gotten under your skin?" he asks again, steepling his hands on the table as he waits for my response.

I take a big breath, feeling like my lungs are empty, before I talk.

"Maybe," I grit out.

But as much as I hate talking about this shit, I'm relieved for them to know. It is obviously affecting my work more than I thought.

I see Dante raise an eyebrow as he listens intently.

"Well, is she?" Sebastian presses, watching me.

"Is she what?" I try to dodge the questions, because there is no lying in our family. We speak the truth to each other 100% of the time.

"You know what I mean. Is she different, Carter?"

"Yes. Fucking yes! She is fucking different. She is ingrained into me now, and I can stop fucking thinking about her. But I did as you said, Nico. I fucked her and left, so it's over. It's done. I fucked it up before it even started." My voice gets louder with each statement, taxing frustration clawing at me every time I think about what I did.

Sebastian sits still and watches me as he waits for me to calm down.

"You are not your past, Carter. History doesn't define you. What you do in the present or future is fully in your control," he says simply, before leaning forward onto the table.

"You can be with someone like her if you want it. Look at Goldie. She is fucking way out of my league, yet she is here with me. You have a lot to give. Your family life hasn't taught you that, but don't miss out on what might be made for you, because I have never seen you act like a bear with a fucking sore head before these last few weeks. Do whatever it is you need to do to get yourself right." Sebastian nods at me, making sure I understand what he is saying. And I do.

I think about what Sebastian says for a beat. As much as I loved my mother, seeing her bounce from man to man only taught me to never rely on anyone for love. Not matter where my mother went or who she found, she never found what she yearned for, and I realize that I have been doing the same thing. I meet women, many of them, but I get into their bed and then leave, not interested, or too afraid of feeling more. Maybe it is time I stayed. Break the historic routine that has been so drilled into my brain.

Sebastian rubs his jaw and continues to watch me. "Sort it out. Now. You have a fight in a few weeks, and then we've got to figure out this fucking situation here in New York. They are going to announce who is running for senator soon, and I will need you here to help me fix that situation. If you make it work, then after things have settled again, you can go back to Philly and live happy fucking families."

Happy Families? That has never been a term ever associated with me, and after Benji's phone call earlier, it seems like Cat may have already moved on. I hope I am not too late.

"Her dad's an asshole," Dante says, and I nod. She has mentioned that to me before. I think she compared him to the devil... so that stood out.

"What do you know?" I ask, wanting the details.

"I looked into her after she treated Annie. Had to cover all bases." I nod, knowing that is what we do. Investigate people.

"He is retired now, but he was the county's leading heart surgeon. Fucking loaded and a scheming bastard."

I sigh and rub my face with my hands. She and I really did grow up in two totally different worlds.

"Enough about me. What's happening?" I need to get this back on track before I start spiraling again.

"Henderson gave us nothing, so now we are waiting to see who will be nominated for senator against Roy. We have a few people on the radar, but no firm nominees as of yet," Dante says, leaning back in his chair.

"So what? We just wait until something is announced?" I ask, looking at Sebastian.

"For the time being. We can't go messing up people who are not even in the job yet, although we did a good job of that with fucking Henderson. Besides, whoever they do nominate, we may be able to turn them into our way of thinking. So, it is a waiting game at the moment," Sebastian says as he grinds his teeth. He doesn't like to wait so I can tell this is killing him.

"We will do the investigating here. You go to Philly and see if you can make things right. I will call you when I need you." I look to Dante and Nico, who are both nodding in support.

I nod slowly in return, feeling overwhelmed and desperate to get back there as soon as possible. Sebastian's support means everything to me.

I have no idea if I can fix what I have broken, but for the first time in my life, I want to try.

22

CATHERINE

In the car, Ivy and I are singing at the top of our lungs as I try not to think about Carter. It has been weeks since our tryst in the gym and even though Maggie and I bit the bullet and continued with our self-defense classes, he hasn't been there, staying away in New York until the fight, as Benji tells me. Probably for the best, but I can't help feeling hurt that I meant nothing to him at all. Although I'm not sure what I would say or do if I saw him.

As we drive in the morning sunshine, I am becoming increasingly excited. Today is soccer day, and even though it has only been a few weeks, Ivy has picked it up well and is loving it. We are driving to Maggie's to pick her and Abby up for the game.

"Mom, I think the coach may put me into striker this morning," Ivy says enthusiastically, eager to score a goal today.

"Wherever he puts you, I know you will be great! That last game, you did such a great job!"

I'm about to tell her to enjoy the game, no matter where she's placed, but the words get stuck in my throat as I turn into Maggie's driveway to see my father's shiny black Bentley parked out front.

"What is Grandpa doing here?" Ivy whispers, knowing that visits from Grandpa normally come with commands, not cuddles.

"I don't know..." I say to her as I turn off the engine and try to drum up the courage I need to face my father.

"Mom, we can't be late for the game," Ivy whines from next to me, and I feel sad. Sad that her grandfather is here, who she never sees, and she is more excited for soccer than to see him.

"I know, honey. Let's just go inside and see what is happening, okay?" She nods through her visible unease, and I unclip my seatbelt with a deep breath. As we both get out of the car, she grabs my hand and we make our way inside.

As soon as I open the door, I can hear them. Maggie and my father have always clashed. While her life has gone exactly how he wanted, she still did it her way, and he doesn't like to be defied.

"Dad. She is happy, they are healthy. She is successful. Stop trying to put her into this perfect box where you think she belongs!" Clearly, they don't know we have arrived, because it is obvious that they are talking about me.

"She belongs in New York with Daniel!" he shouts, and Ivy stiffens beside me. She has seen both her grand-father and father be violent with words toward me, and even though she is my most fierce protector, it is still frightening.

"Daniel is an abusive asshole, Dad!" Maggie screams at him, and I stop. We have been telling Dad for years that Daniel is not the sweet, successful doctor everyone thinks he is, but no one, not even our own father, believes us.

"I don't care!" *He doesn't care?* He knows Daniel is abusive to his own daughter... and he doesn't care?

Ivy and I walk into the kitchen then, Maggie spotting us immediately. Looking into her eyes, she is ropeable, but I can also see her sadness.

"Ivy, go and find Abby in her room and get ready for soccer, okay?" I lean over to her and kiss her on the cheek, giving her my phone, like I always do. She doesn't go to her grandfather; she merely glances at him with fear, and then runs down the hall to Abby's room, where I'm sure she is hiding from her grandfather as well.

"Hi, Dad," I say cautiously, keeping my distance.

"You need to come back to New York and to Daniel," he states without greeting, me around like he's my boss and this is his meeting. There is no question, only demands, and my heart breaks all over again. No "*Hi, honey. How are you?* No "*Hi, how is my beautiful daughter and granddaughter this morning?* No, he hasn't spoken to us like any normal dad would in years.

"I left Daniel over nine months ago, and I have no plans on reuniting with him. He is verbally abusive, was starting to become physically abusive, and he doesn't accept Ivy," I say, but he cuts me off before I can continue.

"He will accept Ivy. He has no choice," Dad spits out, and I tilt my head.

"Why? Why, after all these years, would he accept Ivy? He never wanted kids. When I got pregnant, it was because he forced himself on me, Dad. He didn't use protection, then wanted me to get rid of the baby. He wants me, he doesn't want her, and he never has."

The worst part is, he already knows this. But every time I tell him, he either doesn't listen or doesn't want to believe it. And as his daughter, that hurts the most.

"Well, he has to fall into line now," Dad grits out, and I stare at him.

"What is going on, Dad?" Maggie asks, and like me, she looks at him in question.

"He is running for senator of New York. He needs to portray a perfect family, and that is what you are. So *you*"—he points his finger at me, taking a step toward me—"will get in line, do your fucking duty as the eldest of this family, and come back to New York and be his fucking wife."

While my father has always been a dominating asshole, he has never been this vicious. I find myself flinching from his aggressive tone and stance.

"No, Dad. I will not..." But the words get stuck on my lips as his hand flies through the air and straight across my cheek. I immediately fall into the armchair beside me, one hand bracing myself and keeping me upright, the other holding my cheek to stop the sting spreading across my skin.

Maggie and I gasp, a lump forms in my throat, and my eyes burn with tears. My own father hit me. The three of us stand in silence, all in shock, including my dad. The only sound I hear is my heart thumping, while my cheek throbs beneath my palm.

"Is this what we have come to? What would Mom think?" I whisper to him in disbelief, and he runs his hands through his hair. In frustration or panic or maybe both, I'm not sure, before he turns and walks out the door. Slamming it behind him. Not saying another word.

Maggie and I stand in the kitchen, lost for words, as we hear his car tear out of the driveway, and it isn't until he has left the property that we both take a breath.

"What the hell?" I breathe out, my eyes wide, my hands starting to shake and the tears now falling freely.

"I can't believe he did that..." Maggie shakes her head, completely at a loss, coming up to me. As her arms wrap around me, I fall into her embrace, the two of us crying.

"Why does he hate me so much?" My tone nearly begs her for the answer that neither of us knows as I pull back and we look at each other.

"Fuck them. You are not going. You cannot go back to New York or back to him," Maggie says with venom, now pissed as she releases me to throw the drink bottle and half-time oranges into a backpack on the kitchen bench. Then she's grabbing an ice pack and handing it to me.

I have no idea how to hide this from Ivy. I put the ice to my face and hiss at the contact.

"He was really angry this time..." I say, the words not forming in my mind right now. Daniel? Running for senator? This has to be my worst nightmare. If he is running for politics, then the stakes have now been lifted. He will have huge money behind him—from his own family who are one of the wealthiest in New York, but also from my father. Being one of the best doctors, he will also have the whole medical community backing him and his reputation. He will most likely look like the best man for the job. Young, energetic, intelligent, beautiful family, history of giving back through his career in medicine.

I need to sit down as my heart races. My breathing quickens, and I begin to feel slightly dizzy.

"Maggie?" My voice breaks as I'm starting to feel overwhelmed with what the future may hold. "Daniel's profile will be elevated, paparazzi, interviews... no matter if I go back to him or not, Ivy and I will be pulled into the circus. Journalists will follow us, asking questions I can't answer honestly. It will affect my work, Ivy's school. The safe, simple life I have created for us is about to implode... I have no idea what to do."

There is no way out for me.

23

CARTER

After our meeting, I walk down the hall to my apartment, an extra spring in my step that wasn't there before. Rounding the corner, I spot little Leo, Dante's son, coming in from the courtyard with his soccer ball.

"Hey, Leo!" I shout, and he turns around to face me, giving me a smile as he waits for me to catch up.

"Did you know the oldest turtle is 190 years old?" I ask, using one of Ivy's animal facts for him.

"Yeah, doesn't everyone?" he scoffs, rolling his eyes at me. He has turned into a smartass as he has gotten older, but I still love him just the same.

"Well, what other animal facts do you know?" I wonder if he can give me something good that I can take back to Ivy.

"A cockroach's brain is in its body..." he tells me as he spins his soccer ball in his hands.

"Really?" I ask, surprised. Cockroaches are not what I

was thinking of. I'm not sure my girls would like that particular fact. I was fishing for something... less creepy.

"Armadillos can catch leprosy..." he continues, and I sigh. Yep, I can't really use that one either. Although Cat might find that one interesting.

"Got anything a bit nicer for me?" I ask as we reach my apartment.

"Unicorns have glittery poo," he deadpans, and it is me that rolls my eyes as I scruff his hair and push him down the hall to his house. He has come out of his shell a lot these past few years, all thanks to Annie.

"Thanks, but no thanks!" I yell out to him as he kicks his ball to himself with a smirk on his face, his skills now extremely advanced, given all the practice he does.

"Hey, got a minute?" Dante says from behind me.

"Sure, come on in." I open the door to my apartment, and we walk inside to the kitchen.

"What's up?" I ask him, as I grab us some waters from the fridge.

"Doctor Wakeford."

"Go on." Stopping in front of him, I take a swig, wondering if he is going to ask me to stay away from her.

I want her. I want her more than anything.

"You know, finding Annie changed my life."

"I know. She's good for you. Good for Leo," I say, taking another swig as my anxiety starts to kick in a little.

"After the craziness I had with Angelina, I really didn't want to get involved with someone again. But Little Red, she flew into my life so unexpectedly, like someone pushed her right to me." My heart thumps the longer he takes to get to the point. If he asks me to stay away from Cat for the sake of keeping Annie's doctor for medical purposes only, then I need to do that. No question.

"Okay..."

"Fuck, this talking is bullshit," he mumbles as he rubs his head. "What I am trying to say, Carter, is that it is good having a woman by your side. What we do, the work we do, it isn't for everyone, and it is not something that everyone can understand either. But if you find a woman who knows what you do and can still see something good in you, then you need to hold on to her with both hands and not let her go."

A breath leaves me, feeling grateful for his support, but I'm immediately hit with the reality of what I've done all over again.

"Look, I don't even know if Cat is ever going to want to look in my direction again after what I did," I say, and it's the truth. She is probably hoping to see me injured in hospital again, just so she can prick me with that stitching needle deliberately. And I'd deserve so much worse than that.

"Maybe. But I'm here to tell you to try. Try really fucking hard. Because Annie is the best thing to ever happen to me, Carter, and you can have that too. I know you carry the memory of your mother, I know what we do is dangerous, but fuck, the grass is so green when you push through all that bullshit. So do whatever you need to do to make it right because you deserve all the good things too, Carter," Dante finishes with so much emotion, I am shocked. That was quite the speech, especially from him.

"Thanks," I mumble. "Do we, like, hug now or some shit?" I ask with a smirk.

"Fuck off," Dante says, pushing me in the shoulder. "We will call you when we need you back." He's already halfway out my front door, and I watch him step through and close it behind him.

In the silence of my apartment, I let his words sink in before I strut straight to my bedroom, pulling my bag out of the wardrobe to pack my things. Throwing some clothes in, I start thinking about my trip back to Philly.

Now that I have come to the realization that Cat and I could make a go of this, I want to get back there as soon as possible.

My cell rings, and I pick it up, and like I have conjured her, Cat's name flashes on the screen.

"Cat!" I say in a rush as I pick up the call, surprised but also elated that I'll get to hear her voice. It's been too long.

"Carter, did you know that dolphins sleep with one eye open?" Ivy voice greets me.

"No, Ivy, I didn't know that" I say to her with a laugh, as I continue to pack, slightly disappointed that it isn't Cat on the other end of the call, but still finding myself smiling from Ivy's never-ending facts. I pause for a minute, and then I decide to use what I've got.

"Ivy, did you know that a cockroach's brain is in their body?"

"Eww! That is gross, Carter. I hate cockroaches." She makes a fake gagging noise, acting exactly as I'd expected, like the little girl she is.

"Does your mom know that you are calling me?" I ask

her, becoming more curious as I don't hear Cat in the background. I would put money on the fact that she doesn't.

"No, Mom is in the kitchen..." Ivy replies, and I pause because her voice changes, like it did in the grocery store. Her vibrancy from when she first called has all disappeared.

"Ivy, are you okay?" I'm immediately ready for action as I await her answer, my packing forgotten.

"I'm hiding in the bedroom with Abby. We are okay..." she says, her voice small, scared even. And I don't like the pause she takes.

"Why are you hiding, Ivy?"

"He's yelling at her," she replies quietly.

"*Who* is yelling at her?" I press, my skin prickling.

"Grandpa." Her voice is now a mere whisper.

"Where are you?" My thoughts go right back to the earlier conversation with the boys about Cat's father being an asshole.

She doesn't respond, and my stomach drops.

"Ivy, is your mom there? Can you put her on the phone?" My heart is galloping at this point, desperate to hear her voice, wanting to make sure she is okay.

"No... Abby and I are hiding under her bed. We always hide when Grandpa comes. He isn't very nice. Just like my dad," Ivy says, and the air promptly leaves my lungs.

"What do you mean, just like your dad? Is anyone else with your mom right now?" I pull out my drawer as I rush around my room, looking for one of my burner phones.

"Aunt Maggie is with her. But they are yelling..." Ivy's voice trails off.

"Ivy, where are you? I need to call 911..." I start to ask her for her address as I grab my burner, about to call the police, but then I hear Cat's voice in the background.

"Ivy? You can come out now. He is gone, honey."

I breathe a sigh of relief at hearing her voice.

"Bye, Carter," Ivy says quietly before the line goes dead, and I am left staring at the phone, wondering what the hell is going on.

And hating myself for not being there to keep them safe.

24

CATHERINE

Even though my heart pounds and my stomach churns, I keep my head high as Maggie and I walk into the gym. I'm more committed to these classes now after my run-in with my dad. Knowing how to save myself and protect Ivy is my number one priority.

I tentatively look around, searching the faces. I know that Carter isn't here, but that doesn't lessen my nerves. Just being in his space is enough to give me unwarranted butterflies. It has been weeks since I saw him, but every time I enter the front door of his gym, it brings me right back to that night.

From what I can gather, he's still in New York, doing mob things. I don't even want to think about what he gets up to because I have enough of my own shit to worry about.

We walk up to the front desk, Benji on duty, like he is every week.

"Hey, ladies," he says with a smile, which evaporates as he inspects my face. Clearly, my makeup from today has worn off, and the bruising is more prominent than what I was hoping it would be.

"What happened to your face, Doc?" he asks, stepping around the front desk and walking up to me for a closer look.

"Oh, nothing, Benji. It's nothing." I swat him away, not wanting to get into the fact that I have nothing but asshole men in my life.

"You're Carter's girl. Of course, it is my business. Does he know?" Benji says in response, looking extremely unhappy that I am not more forthcoming. But what he says throws me totally off kilter.

"I am not Carter's *anything*." The words burn my throat. My body wants that to be a lie as much as I do.

"He is not going to be happy about this when I tell him," Benji says, shaking his head.

"Well just don't tell him, then," I huff out and grab Maggie by the arm, leading her past Benji and over to the mats to start our class.

I am exhausted after meeting my lawyer, Donovan, today. I worked from home this morning because a bruised face doesn't sit well with patients, then Donovan came over to talk through some specifics on the legal ramification of separating myself and Ivy from Daniel. So now, I feel drained.

Maggie and I met with him initially and both liked him immediately. He has fantastic credentials, a great track record, and although he admits it is going to be tough to get someone like Daniel away from Ivy and I permanently, he was willing to take my case.

Since then, we have been meeting regularly, either at

his office, a coffee shop, or my place, going through my history, which is long and intense. Every time he takes notes, asks more questions, and together we strategize and create a plan of action.

"How was your meeting with Donovan today?" Maggie asks as we both take a seat on the mats.

I rub my eyes, trying to will the exhaustion away. "It was fine. There is still so much to do. It's honestly really overwhelming. I just don't know how we're going to be able to get out of Dad and Daniel's clutches now with this politics mess." Maggie nods.

"You know what it is like. Media attention is not welcome in medicine. All senior doctors need to have a clear record, and as soon as Daniel and my father know I started legal proceedings to remove myself and Ivy from their lives forever, it is going to turn nasty. If what Dad says is true, and Daniel runs for senator, then the press will be all over it. There is a possibility that I will lose my job." I look at her, pained even from the thought.

"I know. But if that happens, there are so many other options for you. You know that, right? Isn't it better to be away from them, working somewhere else? I know medicine has been your life, but for the sake of your safety and happiness, you may have to give it away." It's true. I would give up my career in an instant to have a safe, happy life with Ivy.

"There's just so much happening at once. Dad wants me back with Daniel to help his political career, but removing myself from them both will be political suicide for them. They are not going to take it lightly. The sooner I can get the paperwork filed, the better it will be, because it will all be out in the open and then they can't stop it."

As we wait for the class to begin, I look over at Benji, drilling him with my eyes. What does he mean when he says I am Carter's girl? Carter threw me away so quickly my head spun. I mean nothing to him.

Carter. My eyes gaze upstairs to his office door, which has been shut for weeks. Unfortunately, the door to my thoughts about him has not. *That* door is open 24/7, regardless of how much I'd like to close it for even just a damn hour.

Maggie squeezes my hand, and my eyes flick to hers. She gives me a soft smile, already knowing what I am thinking.

"C'mon, let's get this class started." Maggie stands as our trainer comes out to begin. "Better than sitting around moping like a lost puppy," she teases.

"I am not," I grumble as I stand and join her. She looks at me, then up to the closed office door, and back to me.

"Gee, it must have been hot to still have your panties in a twist about this. I have never known you to be so caught up in a guy," Maggie says, shaking her head, half teasing, half in awe.

I roll my eyes. "Oh, please. I have the worst taste in men, and there's only been two. I think I need to stay single for the rest of my life."

Maggie chuckles when I huff, before glancing over at Benji again. He's now on the phone, but his eyes are locked in on me. "Looks like trouble is brewing over there," she says as she nods toward Benji, the two of us now assuming he must be speaking to Carter. I wonder if he even cares.

"I can't wait for the day when trouble doesn't follow me. It must be nice to have a stable, normal life," I say to her wistfully.

"Nah, what's the fun in that!" Maggie shoves me with her shoulder, and we both get started on the lesson.

God knows I need to learn to defend myself now more than ever.

25

CARTER

I hit the Philly outskirts after having cleaned things up in New York. There are two weeks left before I meet Big Dom, and after pushing myself and my anger out into my training day after day, I think I am the fittest I have ever been. It comes with sacrifice, of course, but the biggest sacrifice has been not seeing her.

Something I want to change.

And that's exactly why I'm back.

After my brief conversation with Ivy yesterday, I feel unsettled. I barely slept last night and want to get back to her as quickly as possible.

As I stop at a red light, my cell vibrates, and I take a quick look to see that it is a text from Benji. He doesn't know that I am back yet, and I purposely made it today because I know Cat is at the gym. I thought I would go straight there to feel her out and see how she is.

Benji: She's here

Cater: Good to know

Benji: Something happened

I bristle at that, and as the light remains red, I hit the call button, needing to know what the fuck Benji is talking about.

I don't even wait for him to answer. "What happened?" The traffic moves, and I am now impatient as I drive a little faster toward the gym.

"She said not to tell you," Benji says to me, speaking quietly.

"Well, you're sure as fuck gonna tell me now, Benji?" I know he has a soft spot for her, but how the hell did he expect me to react to that message?

"She came in for the class, and as I checked her and Maggie in, I noticed her face is bruised," Benji tells me with hesitation, and my stomach drops.

"What the fuck, Benji?" I grit out, barely hanging on to my anger as I speed up, now only twenty minutes from the gym.

"When I saw her, I thought her face looked a little odd on one side, so I walked around the front desk to get closer. Someone fucking hit her. There's no doubt about it," he grits out. He is as protective of her as I am.

"Who?" I bark as my temper rises.

"She didn't say. She waved me off. And when I told her you wouldn't be happy, she said not to tell you." Well, if that doesn't just piss me off and break my heart at the same time.

"Is she okay?" I can't help feeling like I am to blame. I should have been with her. I should have been there.

"She's seems fine. She is doing the class now," he replies, and I know he is watching her for me. I am glad to have someone like Benji in my corner.

"I will be there in fifteen mins."

"You're here?" he asks, sounding surprised, but happily so.

"Yeah, I came home to make things right," I admit to him.

"Good. About time. See you soon."

I end the call and continue speeding through the streets, itching to see her.

I walk into the gym just as her class finishes, and I wait at the front desk with Benji. As I watch her, I know she hasn't spotted me yet, not expecting me to be here. She looks beautiful, flushed from her class, immaculate in every way, and I hone in on her face. How I've gone weeks without being this close to her, I don't fucking know. Her glowing skin, sparkling brown eyes, pouty, cherry red lips... and then my gaze lands on her cheek and I see what Benji was talking about. Blue and purple marks her skin lightly, like it has been a few days, and it is starting to fade. Under makeup, you may not even notice, but tonight, when she is almost makeup-free, it's clear to see.

As she and Maggie head to the front of the gym, I step out in front of them. She looks up and gasps, stopping short, eyes wide. I notice Maggie giving me the death stare, and I look at her, remorse covering my face. I plead with my eyes for her to let me speak with her sister. Letting her know that I fucked up and will do better. Thankfully, she understands, nodding in acknowledgement, before I notice her squeezing Cat's hand.

"I'll just wait over here," she says, walking to the side to stand with Benji, giving us some privacy.

"Come to my office," I demand of her in the softest tone I can manage, not wanting any eyes on us.

"No," is all she says, quickly and confidently.

"No?" I ask her, tilting my head as I look around at prying eyes.

"No." She crosses her arms across her chest in defiance. "Whatever you want to say, you can say it right here. I am so sick of men telling me what to do."

I step toward her, asking the question before I can stop myself. "Cat, who the fuck did this to you?" My hand automatically reaches for her waist. I want to touch her, and I want her close to me. But before I can make contact, she takes a step back, and I still.

Even knowing she might react this way to me, that action sends a pang through my chest.

"Cat. Tell me who did this to you," I push on. Looking into her eyes, I see a mixture of emotions. None which I can decipher.

"Look, Carter, I appreciate the concern, but this really has nothing to do with you." Then, she's turning to leave.

"I need a name, Cat. The rest I will take care of," I say to her back, making sure she knows that I will take care of her problems. Any and all. I will eradicate them one by one until she can have a peaceful life.

Sighing, she turns to face me again. "Carter, it is fine. I am taking care of it."

"Let me take care of it for you... let me take care of you," I say, swallowing roughly, my heart thumping out of my chest.

"I think I'm okay on my own. Thanks, Carter." She

says the words with a bite, but her eyes look at me with confusion.

"Fuck, Cat, I'm trying here." I rub my eyes with my hand, fucking tired and frustrated and sad that she won't let me in, at least to help her with this. Although after what I did, I am not surprised. I just don't know how to grovel, how to beg, how to put things right, because I have never done it. I have never cared enough for someone to do it before now.

"Do you think running in here at my hour of need like Prince Charming, acting like you care about me, when really all you wanted was a quick fuck, is going to get me crawling back into your arms?" She huffs a laugh, but it's without humor. It's filled with hurt that I put there. When I don't say anything, she continues.

"Yeah... well, Carter, you need to try a little fucking harder than that," she spits out, spins away from me, and grabs Maggie's arm, pulling her along and out the door without a glance back in my direction.

"Fuck," I murmur, ready to punch someone, then chase after her and get on my knees.

I slam my fist into the nearby bag and look at Benji.

"What?" I bark out at him, seeing that he obviously wants to say something.

"She is never going to believe words, Carter. Show her with action. For once in your life, you are going to have to give yourself over to someone else and put your heart and soul on the line. Are you ready for that? It's a package deal with her and Ivy, so don't go fucking it up again," Benji says, looking at me like he is the expert in all things love and feelings.

"I have no idea what to fucking do," I say to him honestly.

"The wimpiest thing you did was run away from her. I don't know what she likes, but think about what you know about her, and make it right," Benji says, huffing as he shuffles papers at his desk.

"That's all you got, Doctor Love?" I ask him, teasing him for his interest in my personal life.

"I could charge you by the hour and let you know of my tales of seduction, but after I saw her with that lawyer guy the other day, you need much more help than I can give, brother." His solemn tone wipes the smile from my face.

Did she really move on so soon? We can't just explode together and have it be nothing. Right?

No, there are feelings involved; I could see it in her eyes today. I have got to make it right.

Starting tomorrow.

26

CATHERINE

As I sit at my desk, I can barely see the other side from the mountain of paperwork currently in front of me. Most of which I will need to take home and do at night once Ivy is asleep. My day is half over, and I am already exhausted, but I still have a long list of patients to check on before I can attempt anything else.

"Morning!" Ian sing-songs as he comes into my office, holding a nice hot coffee that he picked up on his way in.

"Oh, thank God!" I breathe, relieved to have both him and the coffee now in my office.

"Awe, how nice that you missed me so much." He places a hand over his heart sarcastically. "I have the stats from the overnights, and by the look of the ED, it is pretty quiet this morning. We should have a slightly easier day." Taking a seat opposite me, we both sip our coffees and begin talking about our day.

With thicker than normal makeup on, my face feels itchy, but it is hiding any discoloration well. Paired with bright red lipstick and my hair down in waves, I am doing a good job of covering up the decaying destruction that is my life at the moment, focusing instead on helping others. Which is why I became a doctor in the first place.

"Nice makeup. Hides it well," Ian comments, and I sigh.

"Unfortunately, I have had some practice, so I know what brand to buy and what works," I admit. The whole thing makes me feel sick to my stomach.

My dad is so different now. When my mom was alive, the two of them were madly in love, our family happy. But when she passed, his grief consumed him. Still does to this day. His resentment from that was placed on my shoulders as the eldest daughter, where it has remained ever since. When he pushed me to be with Daniel, I did it for him. I did it to keep him content, hoping and praying that his ongoing anger at the world would subside. And it did for a while. But then, when I first went to him to explain that Daniel wasn't the man for me, the anger was back stronger than ever, and he sided with Daniel instead of me.

"How can someone do that to their own fucking daughter?" Ian almost growls, which is so unlike him. He's been so upset for me since the second he saw the bruise.

"I wish I knew. I don't even know if we can ever come back from it," I whisper quietly, trying to keep my breathing steady and the tears at bay. The thoughts of Dad not ever going back to the kind, loving father he once was nearly breaks me from the inside out.

"Maybe Carter can fix him up?" Ian suggests, lifting

his eyebrows in question, fishing for something. I wonder if he has been chatting with my sister.

I roll my eyes. Yeah, Ian has definitely been gossiping with Maggie. The grin on his face tells me he already knows what went down at the gym last night.

"Enough of this chit-chat. Let's get to work, aye?" I say, standing, putting an end to any conversation about Carter. I need to try to stop thinking about him.

"Okay, I hear you, no more talking about the Adonis today," Ian says cheekily as we both step out of my office and into the hall. As I do, I slam into a body of rock, and Ian needs to catch me so I don't fall.

"Oh I'm so sor—" I start to say as I right myself and straighten my jacket, but the words get stuck on my lips as I look up to find it is Daniel's eyes staring back at me.

"A word with you please, Doctor Wakeford?" he asks, ever the professional in a medical environment, and I am sure seeing Ian standing tall and firm behind me squashes any thoughts he had of storming into my office unannounced. I'm sure that's exactly what he had intended to do.

Not only is he not meant to be within 200 yards of me, but he has never stepped foot into my workplace before. My heart races and my palms begin to sweat as I see his arm come up to grab my elbow out of my peripheral vision.

"Not today," Ian says forcefully as he positions his body at my side, standing between Daniel and I, effectively knocking his hand away from coming in contact with me.

"Oh, we will only be a moment," Daniel says with a

fake, placating smile, trying to be pleasant, but I can see the steam coming from his ears as the vein in his temple throbs.

"Daniel, you need to leave," I state, now having found my voice. Although it doesn't come out as confident as I had hoped.

"Will you stop being so stubborn? We need to discuss you coming back to New York. I am sure your father has told you of the plans." His hands now sit on his hips, and his eyes lock onto mine, fierce and filled with restrained rage.

"As Doctor Wakeford has said, you need to leave, otherwise I will call security," Ian says, and I can see Daniel visibly holding it together. I know he wants to explode at being told what to do, especially in a hospital, which is usually his domain.

He pauses for a moment, looking between Ian and I before his eyes land on me again. "Fine, I will leave, but, Catherine... I will come for you, and you will come back to New York with me. You have had your fun now, so it's time you be the good wife I know you can be." His voice drips with venom, and my grip on my clipboard tightens to prevent him from seeing the trembling working its way through my body.

He looks Ian up and down before turning on his heel and striding down the hallway. We watch him until he exits the building, and it is only then that I can breathe.

"Oh my God," I whisper, as full understanding washes over me. This is going to be a lot harder than I first thought. How naive was I to think that I could get a lawyer, draw up some papers, and go and live on my merry way? The first warning was my father and the hit that still marks my skin today. Daniel today was obviously a second warning, and by the look on his face, I will not get a third.

"What an absolute asshole," Ian grits out. "C'mon." He opens my office door and we both step back inside. I barely make it to the sofa before my legs give way and I start to panic.

"I need to get Ivy somewhere safe. There is nothing else I can do. They are going to come for me, and they are going to make sure I comply with everything they want. My life is no longer my own." The nightmarish possibilities of what this could turn into flick through my mind like a movie on fast forward.

"You can do this. He is an asshole, a very wealthy one, but I am a witness now, and I am sure you have other witnesses too. Other proof, documentation, voicemails, emails?" Ian says, and he is right. I have kept a log of everything for the past nine months since I moved, and even have some from before I left. Everything is in Donovan's hands now, with him and his team working through the details.

I nod to Ian, calming down a bit. "Donovan has it all."

"What does your lawyer say?" He now can't keep still, walking a path into the carpet, his adrenaline moving rapidly through his body too.

"He thinks I have a solid case. It won't be easy, but there is certainly good evidence of his financial and verbal abuse and intimidation tactics, all of which has been backed up in a variety of different places because we don't doubt that him and my father will stop at nothing to erase everything I have once they know I have a file on him," I say, the confidence I was lacking before now is beginning to bloom.

"You've got his, Cat. I know it. It is going to be tough, but be smart, stay away from him, and I know that your lawyer will make things happen for you," Ian says, coming to stop in front of me. "But I think you need to think about getting some security."

"I don't need—"

"If I wasn't here just now, what would have happened? He would have walked in here and done God knows what with you!" Ian implores me, and I have to admit, I don't like thinking of the what ifs.

"I'll think about it. Maybe my lawyer knows someone," I concede, looking at Ian with a small smile of satisfaction growing on his lips that I agreed to his suggestion.

"Your lawyer sounds like a good one?" Ian remarks before he sits down next to me.

My smile widens as I think about Donovan. "Is that because the two of you went on a hot date the other night?" I tease. After introducing them both last week when Donovan came past the hospital for me to sign some forms, they hit it off, and I am dying to hear how it went.

"Hmmm... maybe. He was the perfect gentleman," Ian says, his smile growing wider, and I laugh.

"So? Is there going to be a second date?" I pry. Even though my love life is in a flaming hole of doom doesn't mean I don't love hearing about the love others find. Because I still believe in love. Apparently, it is something that just doesn't happen to me.

"We are going out later this week, in fact." Picking up the files, he stands again. I push Daniel's visit to the back of my mind as I stand alongside him as Ian begins to tell me all about his romantic night, and we get back into work mode.

It is the only way I know how to survive.

27

CARTER

Standing at her front door, I roll my neck, nerves settling in the pit of my stomach. What if she won't see me? What if she tells me to walk away and not come back? I look around the outside of her place. Having never been here before, I didn't really know what to expect, but a warehouse conversion in the funky part of town wasn't it.

I pictured a large house, with a big garden for Ivy, and a whole lot of flowers behind a white picket fence. This is secure, locked up tight, and lit up like a fucking Christmas tree. As I press the doorbell, I wonder if she is even home.

I press the button again, but then I hear her.

"Carter?" she asks in surprise, and I turn and look up, eyeballing the camera where she is no doubt watching me from.

"Cat," I say, not removing my eyes. I hear her sigh in defeat, and the door clicks, signifying she has unlocked it.

So it is not all lost. Hope blooms in my chest.

I fucked up once, and I am not doing it again.

Walking into the large foyer, then across to a door, I get ready to knock. But before I can, she opens it.

"What are you doing here?" she asks as she opens it, and goddamn is she breathtaking. No makeup, hair in a topknot, jeans that hug her curves, and a white t-shirt that I want to rip off her body with my bare hands. But without makeup on, her bruise is more visible, and I am already feeling the anger at someone hitting her creeping up my back.

"I want to talk," I tell her, staying calm in my request.

"We really have nothing to talk about, Carter. You—" I cut her off before she can get too far, not willing to have a replay of yesterday.

"I know what I did, and it is something that I will regret for the rest of my life. Can we talk for a minute? Please?" I all but beg her, and I see her soften a little before she gives me a small nod and steps back from the door, holding it open for me.

"Ivy is asleep, so let's go to the kitchen," she says, and I follow her. Her space is nice, homey and refreshing, with lots of photos of Ivy, Maggie, and her. I spot Ivy's school bag and uniform near the table, the TV flickering in the living room. A stack of paperwork sits on the coffee table next to a glass of red wine, and I just know she was relaxing on the sofa, going through those papers, before I arrived. Clearly, she works all hours, and I admire her work ethic.

She walks into the kitchen, which is spotless and large, and I can imagine her and Ivy cooking together here as she leans her back against the counter, crossing her arms over her chest.

"What do you want?" she asks, not offering me a fucking inch.

"You," I answer, without any hesitation, as I slowly take steps to be closer to her.

She huffs and rolls her eyes, her hands unfolding and then perching on her hips.

"Carter..."

"Cat, I am an idiot."

"No truer words have ever been spoken," she bites back to me in a murmur, and I smile a little. I like her sass; it means she gives a shit, that there's still something inside her that wants me too. And at least she is not throwing things at me, or screaming to get out of her house.

"I want to try again." The statement feels foreign coming from my mouth, but I have practiced this all fucking day, and I want to get it right.

"Carter, I think you should go back to New York." Even though the words sting, I know that she doesn't really mean it. The heat we had before, it's still there, and we both know it.

"I ain't leaving, Cat. Not this time." At that, her eyes finally meet mine again.

"What I did was fucking deplorable." I shake my head, taking a deep breath. "You deserve more than that, better than that. Me just jumping up and running away from you, leaving you in the gym like that..." Rubbing my eyes, I try to erase the image, not liking having it in my memory bank.

"I want you, Cat. But I didn't think that I could be with anyone permanently. I didn't think I was wired that way. I have always run away from anyone who gets close." As I continue, she watches me, unmoving. "But I want to try. I want to try to be better and do better with you."

She remains still, staring at me, like she isn't sure what to say, so I slowly take a few steps closer until I'm within reach. She doesn't pull away as I wrap my arm around her waist, feeling the electricity as I feel her warmth under my palm as it settles on the small of her back. The pull I have for her still there, still present, her chest rising and falling quicker at my touch.

She stays with me as I run my thumb up and down against her skin, her soft body making me ache for her. She feels so good in my grip, my hand is large around her frame, and I resist the urge to pull her against me. I want to go slow with her this time.

"I think you should go," she whispers quietly to me, her mouth saying one thing, while her body tells me something totally different. But I nod. I know it isn't going to be easy to win her trust back, and although I will leave her tonight, I am going to keep trying.

"Cat," I start again, not sure what else to say, but I will say or do anything at this point so she knows how serious I am. "I don't expect you to forgive me right away, perhaps not even at all. Shit, I don't think I will ever forgive myself. But I would like to try again. We can take it day by day, hang out a bit..." My words drift off as I get caught in her gaze, her features soft, but still not giving me anything.

She doesn't speak for a moment, and my ears hone in

on a constant tapping sound I can hear in the background. My eyes divert from hers for a moment as I look around her spotless marble benchtop until they reach her kitchen sink. I see the tap dripping, in a constant rhythm that would drive me crazy. I remember her mentioning this.

"Carter, it's late..." she says, and my eyes whip back to hers. I only nod again.

"I understand." I give her waist a squeeze before I drop my hand and begin to walk backwards away from her, giving her a small smile.

"Lock your door after me, yeah?"

I still don't know who the fuck touched her. That's something I will pry from her at another time and then kill the man with my bare hands.

She nods, but remains still, standing in the kitchen, watching me walk away.

I may be walking away from her. But I'm not leaving her. Not again.

This time, I want to fight to keep the girl.

28

CATHERINE

I was surprised to have Carter turn up on my doorstep last week, and every day since then, the surprises kept coming.

The next day after his visit, a beautiful bouquet of white roses arrived for me, along with a smaller matching one for Ivy—which melted my heart a little. Her own father has never bought her a present, so she was super thrilled to receive something so special and immediately started asking when we can see Carter again. The colorful blooms are well suited to my interiors, and I wonder if he chose them specifically for that reason.

The following day, a box arrived addressed to Ivy. It turned out to be an ice cream subscription box, containing three different tubs with new flavors delivered each week until hundreds of flavors of ice cream have been tried. To say Ivy's eyes bugged out of her head would be an understatement. And as I saw the pure joy on her face as she scooped into the Belgian chocolate flavor, my heart melted just a little more.

In the following days, we received a stuffed toy lioness and its baby cub, then matching mom and daughter shirts with his gym logo on the front, and finally a brand-new soccer ball and pink cleats for Ivy.

So, not only has he been consistently spoiling me, but my daughter as well.

Lost in thought as Maggie and I walk into the gym for our class, I nearly run into her back when she stops suddenly in front of me.

"Oh my," she murmurs, and I look at her and then follow her eyes until they land on Carter.

He's training, shirt off, muscles sculpted even more than I remember, sweat coating his body and making it glisten. Every woman in the room is looking right at him, including my sister. Maggie is taking in his toned physique, and I wonder if I will need to wipe the drool from her chin in a moment. He looks good, *too* good. He always did, but now as I see him dancing in the ring, his muscles tensing and working as he fights with his opponent, it is clear he has been working hard. Really, really, hard.

The two of us stand there watching him, and he must sense me. Almost immediately, he looks around, spots me, then gives me a cheeky grin before winking at me, and calling five on his session. Breaking my stare, I glance around quickly, noticing everyone watching his every move, and my skin bristles. I don't particularly like the attention focused on him, and unexpected flames of jealousy lick at my skin. I look back up to where he is and watch him as he jumps out of the ring, making his way over to us, and so does everybody else.

He has captivated the entire gym. I have to nudge Maggie in the back with my shoulder so she can actually stop gawking at him.

"Hey, ladies, good to see you," he says to us both, but he's looking straight at me. His eyes are smoldering, burning into my core, and the remaining ice around my heart has now all but melted.

"Hey, Carter," Maggie says. "Getting a good workout in there?" she asks with a wide smile.

"I have a fight soon, so I need to make sure I am fit and ready for it," he says with a nod to her before he looks back at me.

"Hey," he says quieter, his hand coming to my waist. I don't step back, and instead I let him touch me, tired of depriving myself. His hand grips my skin lightly, his touch eager, his thumb caressing the bare skin between my tights and my crop top, making my skin prickle and my heart skip a beat.

"Hey," I say softly back to him as my hands grip onto my water bottle, afraid that if I let go, they will land on his chest, at which point he may as well scoop me up and take me home because I would be lost to him forever.

"When is your fight?" I ask. Now that I know he is stepping back in the ring and could get hurt, I am not liking the idea of him fighting at all.

"In under two weeks," he says, looking down at me from under his brow, his hand giving my waist a squeeze. My eyes flick down to his torso... how does he look even better up close? There is not an inch of fat on his chiseled body, and I swallow as I try to calm my racing heart. He is standing mere inches in front of me, my body almost shielded by his, and there is no question that he is trying to ensure everyone knows who I belong to.

"Thank you for the gifts. Ivy really loves them." His eyebrows rise and a smile forms on his lips.

"What about you?"

"What about me?"

"Do you love them?" he asks, his cheeky smile contagious. I like that he isn't pushing me, trying actively to make things right.

"They are very sweet, Carter. Thank you," I say with a small smile appearing. His gaze drops to my lips when he sees it, and when he meets my eyes again, my whole body heats.

"Okay, ladies, are we ready?" Cliff calls out to us all.

"I gotta go," I say to him as Maggie starts walking over to the mats.

"I will catch you before you leave," he tells me, and with a final small squeeze, he walks back to the ring to his training, and I try to tear my eyes away.

As I join Maggie on the mat and begin listening to Cliff about defensive poses, I can't help my thoughts from drifting to Daniel and my father. I think about Daniel's visit to the hospital, rubbing my cheek, not forgetting the hard slap my father landed not too long ago. I have to admit, I'm not feeling as confident now with the situation. I feel like I am on a timeline, and at any moment, they will pounce, and I have no idea when, where, or how.

"It's okay, Cat. Take a breath for me. Everything will be okay," Maggie says, nudging me with her shoulder. My face must portray everything I am feeling. I hear her words, but they don't stop the fear and hopelessness that suddenly washes through my body. My breathing doesn't slow after my deep breath, it quickens, along with my heartbeat. Flicking my eyes from her to the rest of the women here, I become slightly dizzy.

"I think I need the bathroom." I quickly jump up and walk swiftly to the nearby ladies' room, before running into a stall and emptying the contents of my stomach in the toilet.

"Cat!" I hear Maggie say, and then she's right behind me, pulling my ponytail back as I continue to heave until nothing is left. Sinking onto the floor, I lower my head in my hands and try to catch my breath, to stem the tears that I know are about to escape.

"Are you all right?" Maggie asks gently, and I look at her quickly and nod.

"Just give me a minute. I will come back out. I just need a moment to gather myself," I say to her through rough breaths, and she nods reluctantly, leaving the bathroom and giving me the privacy I need.

It is all becoming too much, and I am not sure how much more I can handle. It is like I am lost out at sea, and I can see the big wave coming, knowing that there is no way I can survive it, yet there is nothing I can do to stop it from crashing into me and pushing me to the depths of the ocean floor where there is no chance I will surface again.

The fear is now suffocating.

I stand gingerly and walk slowly toward the sink, running the cold water, before dipping my hands into it and splashing it on my face. As I look back up in the mirror, I gasp as Carter stands right behind me, sweat dripping from his forehead, his eyes latching right onto mine.

"You know, I met this woman," he says, and I look up at him, my heart pounding. "And for some reason, she saw good in me when I couldn't see it for myself." My chest warms as I wait, remaining silent, watching him through the mirror, hooked on his words.

"I told her that I lived in the darkness and had no idea how to step into the light..." My nerves from moments ago are left behind as he takes a step closer to me, slowly, like I am a hurt animal that will scurry away.

"But do you know what she said?" he asks me, his voice so beautifully vulnerable, his face becomes blurry from the tears glazing over my eyes.

"She told me that it was easy. I just had to do it one step at a time." His hand connects with my waist, and I turn around to face him. As I look up at him, a lone tear runs down my cheek, my lips trembling with emotion I'm holding back.

"I got you, Cat," he assures me, as his other hand comes up and cups my cheek, his thumb brushing away my tears. "Let's take those steps together, yeah?"

And at his declaration, I take a big breath, leaning into his chest where he holds me tight.

My arms wrap around his sweaty body, and I squeeze my eyes shut, tears overflowing onto his bare skin.

He remains quiet, letting me be, holding me strongly with one arm around my waist, the other softly squeezing the back of my neck.

I have never felt as safe as I do right now in his arms.

And I never want him to let me go.

29

CARTER

After holding her for over an hour last night, I did the right thing and let her leave with Maggie. But only because Maggie told me that both Cat and Ivy have a day off from work and school today. As I look up and see the bright morning sun, I am glad something is going right for me for once.

I ring the doorbell and wait.

"Carter?" I hear her voice and look at the camera. I didn't tell her I was coming; I wanted it to be a surprise.

"I brought coffee and donuts," I say as I lift the paper bag up.

"But you don't eat donuts, Carter!" Ivy's voice yells across the intercom, and I smile as the familiar click of the door latch tells me to come in.

Walking through the foyer, her front door opens, and there both my girls stand. Beautiful and breathtaking, both in denim cut-offs and fresh white shirts, hair shining to perfection like they are from a luxury goods commercial.

"What flavor?" Ivy asks, and I hand her the bag, which she takes and runs of with.

"Morning," Cat says, a small blush coming to her cheeks.

"Morning, Cat. Here. This is for you," I say as I pass her a coffee, and at the same time, I lean in and kiss her cheek. I really want to strip her down and worship every inch of her, but I am taking this slow, trying to do the right thing this time, showing restraint for the first time in my life.

"Thanks. Come in," she says as she steps back from the door, and I follow her inside. In the brightness of the day, I get another look at her immaculate home, now even more inviting. The sun beams in from the skylights that run the length of the room, and in the kitchen, Ivy sits up at the bench, a donut already half eaten.

"They any good?" I ask her as I lean against the bench next to her.

"Mmmhmmm," she says with a mouthful of the tasty treat, sugary speckles now covering her chin and lips.

"So, are you ready?" I ask, looking between them both as I take a sip of my coffee, trying to act cool and collected.

"Ready for what?" Cat asks, furrowing her brows, and I smile.

"The zoo." Ivy's eyes widen.

"The zoo?! Are you taking us TO THE ZOO!" she screams in delight, jumping off the stool, her donut all but forgotten.

"Well, it's a beautiful day, and I have it on good authority that you both have today free, so..." My words drift off as I shrug innocently and look at Cat who is standing in complete shock.

"Mom, can we go? Pleeeeease?" Ivy says, hopping from one foot.

"Oh my God, Carter! Look what you've done," Cat says, her smile wide, as she laughs at her daughter, and it is the best fucking sound in the world. One I wasn't sure I would get to hear again.

"I'm taking that as a yes?" I ask, to which Cat nods, before squatting down to Ivy's height.

"Go get ready. Comfy shoes, okay? We're gonna be walking a lot today." Instead of running down the hall to her room, she runs straight into me, slamming her small body into mine. The force shocks me a bit, the little thing having some power in her, which makes me laugh. Luckily, I have enough time to grab her before we both topple onto the floor on impact.

"Thank you, Carter! You can spend every day with us from now on, as long as you bring donuts and we go to the zoo!! This is the best day ever!" She jumps out of my arms and runs to her mother.

"Mom, I think we need to keep Carter around. I like him." She's attempting to whisper, but I can hear every word, my smile now plastered on my face.

"We'll see, honey. Why don't you go and get ready," Cat says, her smile matching mine, and we both watch as Ivy runs down the hall to her room.

"How did you know that we were home today?" Cat asks me as I stand and walk toward her.

"I spoke to Maggie last night. I decided that you both

probably need a little bit of fun in your life, and you're safe with me to do just that."

"About last night..." she starts to say, running her hand through her hair. We haven't talked about what happened. She cried, I held her, and then I delivered her back to Maggie who took her home.

"We can talk about it later. As I said, I am not going anywhere this time. You're stuck with me, if you'll still have me." I put my cards out again, needing her to really understand where I stand. Even though she fell into my embrace last night, there were a lot of emotions going on, and I want to make sure she wants me for me and every-thing that I bring with me.

Once I'm in front of her, I grab her around the waist and pull her to me. She doesn't hesitate, her arms running up my chest and looping around my head. I lean my forehead onto hers.

"You feel good," I groan. I feel like I have waited a life-time to have her in my arms again.

"So do you," she whispers, and I lean in, taking her lips softly, tentatively. When she kisses me back, I'm a goner.

"DO I NEED A HAT?" Ivy screams from down the hall, jarring us both and making me chuckle. Her excitement levels are sky high, and as Cat and I pull away, she giggles.

"Let me go and help Ivy. We will be out in a minute. Make yourself at home." She waves her arms around the kitchen, stepping around me and walking down the hall.

I decide to be helpful and clean up the donuts and empty coffee cups, placing them in the trash I find under her kitchen sink. As I survey the room, I notice the water still dripping from the tap, so I start to play with the taps, seeing if I can fix it. Realizing I will need a few tools to do so, I walk out of the kitchen and move into the sitting room, saving that project for another time.

The sofa looks way too inviting after my fitness session early this morning. I had to get it in early today, knowing I wanted the freedom to spend the day with the girls. Turning away from it, I walk over to the open fire-place, looking at her trinkets and photos spread across the mantle.

Photos of her and Ivy line the bench, from when Ivy was a baby until now. There are a few with Maggie, and one of an older woman with what looks like a teenage Cat, and I assume that is her mother. But there are no men in any of these photos. None of Ivy's dad, no broth-ers, not a male of any kind. Unusual.

"Okay, we're ready," Cat says from behind me, and I spin around, seeing them both with jackets and their bags.

"Great, let's go!" Letting them lead the way, I make sure I lock up behind us.

Walking through the animal exhibits, I feel like I am having an out-of-body experience. This day couldn't be further from my usual routine if I tried. I've never been to the zoo before; it wasn't somewhere that my mother ever brought me. In fact, she never really took me anywhere. Not for lack of love, but because of lack of money. Today, as the sun shines down, and I hold Cat's hand, we stroll behind Ivy, watching her excitement with rapt attention. We laugh at her as she recites everything she knows about each animal we approach, and I wonder if this family moment could ever become my life.

"You've done an awesome job, Cat," I say, nodding toward Ivy. "She's a great kid, and so damn smart."

"She is. She has been through so much in her short life, yet constantly astounds me with her kindness and intelligence," Cat says with a grateful smile, looking up at me.

"What about her dad? Is he in the picture?"

"Her dad is the man you saw in the grocery store, Carter. He is not a nice man," Cat tells me honestly but with a bit of hesitation, and I squeeze her hand in reassurance. I thought it might be. Ivy doesn't look anything like him, but from the way he was looking at Cat, I could tell he was infatuated with her. And not in a healthy way. I don't want to push her or pry, but I continue.

"Is that who bruised your cheek?" I ask, and she huffs. My eyes flick to hers again, and I watch her with interest.

"Oh no, he didn't do that. Not this time, anyway. My father was responsible for that one." I stop mid-stride, muscles tensing, and I can already feel the smoke coming from my ears.

"What the fuck?" I say to her as we turn to face each other. If I heard correctly, she has two men in her life, who are meant to love and cherish her, but instead are now on my most wanted list. I will kill them both.

Pulling my hand, she has us moving forward again, and whether it is the sunlight, the joy at seeing Ivy happy, or the fact that I am here and can protect her, she is relaxed. So, I let it go for the moment, willing myself to calm down with her and soak in this time with them.

When a few minutes pass of silence, she begins to open up. I listen intently, wanting to know every detail she'll give me.

"It started years ago, Carter. It has only been this last twelve months, though, that I have had the confidence..." I watch her throat as she swallows hard, taking a breath. "...and the money to get out." She looks at me knowingly, and the penny drops.

"Dante," I say, and she nods.

"Him and Annie were thrust into my life at just the right time and to be honest, I didn't really have to think too hard about it. I wanted an out and the universe gave me one, and so I took it." My thumb rubs her hand as she stares off into the distance, lost in thought.

"My father changed after my mom died. He became angry and cold, and to make him happy, I tried to do everything he wanted me to. I worked hard at school, then became a successful doctor. He also wanted me to date Daniel, and with both of us doctors, I think it was all about appearances for my dad. He never asked me what I wanted, but I wanted him to be like he was before my mom died, so I did everything he asked of me."

"Did you ever actually want to be with him, before it got bad?"

"Yes and no. In the very beginning, everything was okay. Not that my feelings for him were ever as strong as his were for me, though. But then when it wasn't, when things started getting worse, I just distracted myself. Working in medicine is demanding. I barely saw Daniel or my father, and I lost myself to my job. I guess I felt that

I could continue the relationship without ever really being in it, just to keep them happy."

I nod, letting her continue. This situation is so messed up.

"One night, Daniel had a few drinks and I happened to be home. At that stage, we were living together, but given our schedules at the hospital, we rarely saw each other. I always made sure whenever I had a day off, he was rostered to work, because I just didn't want to be around him... But on this night, I was home and so was he, and he got aggressive." When she pauses, her grip on my hand gets tighter.

I can feel my heart rate increase a little as I clench my jaw, knowing I am not going to like what comes next.

"He was really angry and forced himself on me. That was the night that Ivy was conceived," she admits quietly as she looks lovingly at her daughter. Meanwhile, I am trying to hold myself together, wanting to demand his address.

I am astounded at hearing it all. I totally misjudged her all those months ago at the hospital, and I feel sick for calling her a daddy's girl, knowing now that he pushed her into an abusive relationship. I feel glad that Dante crossed her path. If it wasn't for him and Annie, then who knows if she would have gotten away like she did.

"You're a good mom, Cat, and Ivy is a fantastic kid. You should be really proud. I'm just sorry you had to go through all of that to get here."

I can see nothing but love in her eyes for her daughter, and I'm in awe of her strength as I stare at her. She's truly an incredible woman.

"So, what about you? How did you meet Sebastian?" she asks, and I can see her hesitancy, hear it in her voice, that this is her way of learning more about me. About what I do and what it all means. It's kind of terrifying, but I want to share, want her to get to know the real me.

"I didn't have a great upbringing," I start, not exactly sure how much to share. She squeezes my hand in response, and I keep going.

"I don't know my father and was raised by my mom. We lived in a trailer on the edge of town. I skipped school a lot, got into a bit of trouble here and there," I say, each bit dragging out of me. She remains quiet, letting me talk.

"When Mom died, I went out on the streets, trying to pickpocket to get some money for food. I didn't realize it at the time, but one of the men I attempted to pickpocket was Sebastian." That has her looking at me, wide-eyed.

"No way..." she says in a hushed tone.

"From that night onward, he and Dante took me in, taught me everything, and made me a part of their family. I will never be able to repay them. Ever." She simply nods in acceptance, and for some reason, it's a comfort to me.

"Hey, guys! Over here!" Ivy yells, our moment over. Cat smiles, and the three of us enter a new exhibit called the *Arachnid Adventures* and both girls shiver.

"I hate spiders," Cat says with a shake of her head, and I lift an eyebrow.

"What?" she asks.

"You are a doctor. You peer into human bodies and see blood and guts and all sorts of things, yet you are scared of a small eight-legged insect?" I mock her, grabbing her and skating my fingers across her back, mimicking a spider crawling. She jumps away from me and laughs, slapping my chest.

"They are not insects, Carter!" Ivy says to me with her hands on her hips. "They are Arachnids. Did you read the sign?" she adds with sass before marching into the small room containing what are some of the world's deadliest spiders.

Inside, it is darker, and the walls all house sealed glass aquariums filled with different materials to make for natural habitats. Peering into each one, some of them look colourful and others downright ugly.

"Ahhh, the Redback Spider. Native to Australia," Ivy says, her face right up against the glass.

"Not surprising, all animals are deadly in Australia," I grunt out before we walk to the next one and then the next one. My hand wraps around Cat, keeping her close, Ivy right in front of us where we can both see her. The dim lights are not the best for seeing people, although each aquarium is lit up like the Fourth of July.

"Here's one that's different," Ivy says, stopping to read the small plaque next to the exhibit.

"Stegodyphus lineatus." I have no idea if she is pronouncing it correctly. "From Europe!" she exclaims, and I pay little attention to what is on the plaque, leaving it to the girls to read. But looking at the spider, I can see it is a white and grey, ugly motherfucker.

I spot the exit up ahead. "Let's get out of here, back into the sun," I say to the girls who turn and smile. "Are you scared, Carter?" Ivy asks with a lifted brow.

"No, I am not scared of anything," I say to her, and she nods in approval. Though, I have to say, I'm not a fan of spiders now.

"C'mon, giraffes are next!" Then she's leading the way as I grab Cat's hand again and we continue on the journey.

Once we are outside, Cat stops beside me.

"Thanks, Carter. This is really special and very thoughtful," she says with a big smile, and not one to waste an opportunity, I wrap my hands around her waist and bring her in tight against me. Her arms rest on my chest, and I look into her eyes.

"I'm glad you could come," I say, as my hand rubs up and down her back, touching her curves as best I can in this G-rated environment.

"When do you have to leave to go back to New York?"

"I'm not going back any time soon." I brush a fly away strand of hair and tuck it behind her ear.

"Really? Why is that?" She seems genuinely surprised, but in the happiest way, and that has me smiling.

"Sebastian told me to come here and make things right with you, and that is what I am doing," I state, matter of factly, her eyes widening as she gasps.

"Sebastian? As in Sebastian Romano?" she asks, and I continue rubbing her back. I know she is not sure about him, about that part of my life.

"Yep," I reply, watching her mind work overtime.

"How does he know about me?" she asks warily.

"Because I told him how special you are, and he told

me to come here and make sure you knew it," I tell her frankly. Her eyebrows rise then, so I continue.

"He is my brother. I know many people hear different things about him, about what we do. Some are right, some are wrong. He is decent. He took me in, gave me a home when I had nothing, gave me guidance when I had no direction. He made me into the man that stands here before you today." She nods slowly, and I decide to say the one thing that might have her running.

"He is going to be wanting to meet you soon." Sebastian has to meet everyone we bring into the family. It's just how it is done.

"Me? He wants to meet me?" she almost squeaks out, and I chuckle.

"I'm sure his wife, Goldie, will be there too. Actually, I think the two of you would hit it off. Plus, you already know Dante and Annie sooo..." I drift off, letting her take it all in. Waiting to see if she jumps out of my hold, runs a mile, or looks apprehensive in any way.

Is it presumptuous of me? Absolutely. But this is my life, and I need to lay it all out for her so she can make an informed decision about being with me or not.

Her eyes move from my chest, to my face, back to my chest again. I know she is deep in thought. I can almost hear the wheels turning in her brain, and if she pulls away from me now, I know it will be the end. I know there is nothing else I can do.

"What does it mean... being in the mob? I mean, what do you do? No, you know what. Don't tell me that," she rambles, obviously full of questions and not sure what to ask.

"Ask me anything. I will be honest."

"I just need to know one thing," she says firmly.

"Okay, what's that?" I ask, intrigued, though my palms sweat a little.

"Will we be safe? Will Ivy and I really be safe with you? Considering what you do and all..."

I look at her seriously as her eyes search mine, wanting her to know what is about to come out of my mouth is honest and will never change.

"You will be safer with me than anywhere else on this earth. I know you and Ivy are a package deal. I know that you'll both have different needs, and as she grows, things will change. You work a demanding job too, so there is a lot to consider. But the one thing I know with absolutely certainty is that you and Ivy will be safe, secure, and protected with me. I will never let anything happen to you. Either of you. Ever." My hands grip her tight as she stares up at me, and as I wait for her final say, my stomach does an unpleasant flip.

"Okay..." she whispers tentatively.

"Okay?" I ask her, ensuring that I heard right because it could've gone either way. I am a little shocked that this could ever go in my favor.

"Yes, Carter. Okay. Let's try again. Let's do this, together," she says, with more determination this time, and I don't hesitate. My hands cup her cheeks, and I slam my lips into hers and kiss the ever-loving fuck out of her.

"Ewww! You two are disgusting," I hear Ivy say, and she better get used to it, because I will be kissing her mom every day from now on.

30

CATHERINE

Carter dropped Ivy and I off at home earlier and after a wash in the bath and early dinner, she is now passed out in bed, fast asleep. I can't blame her; she walked for miles today and didn't come down from the high she experienced at seeing all those animals. I am kicking myself for not taking her to the zoo earlier.

Now, as I stand in the kitchen, wiping the benches and tidying up, my cell phone buzzes. Grabbing it, I see that it is Carter. A smile reaches my lips at just the sight of his name.

"Hey, front door," he murmurs as soon as I answer it, and I go to the security screen and look through the camera. This security system was one of the main reasons I leased this place. It is locked up tight and the feeling of safety I have being here is one of my few comforts.

I see him standing there at the door, carrying a large basket that looks heavy, and I immediately buzz him in. Throwing the dishcloth in the sink, willing the tap to stop dripping, I walk swiftly to the front door to open it for him.

"Hey, what have you got—" I don't get to finish my sentence before he's pressing his lips against mine, and although the basket looks heavy, he leaves it in one hand as his other wraps around the nape of my neck, pulling me closer, deepening the kiss.

My desire for him is growing, even more than it was ever before, and I know letting him back in was the right decision.

As his tongue swirls with mine, I moan into his mouth. I love the way he feels, the way that he doesn't care who is around. Like he can't wait another moment to touch me any time we're together.

Pulling away, we are both panting.

"I brought over a few things," he says as I step back and let him in, locking the door behind him.

We walk to the kitchen, and he places the basket on the bench.

"Where is your little cub?" he asks, looking around for Ivy.

"She was wrecked, so she's sound asleep down the hall," I explain, and he smiles.

"Ahh, yeah, it was a big day. That's why I called you instead of buzzing the door. I wasn't sure what time she goes to bed, and I didn't want to wake her. How are you feeling?" He is so attentive of me and my needs now, clearly very attuned to the fact that how he treated me before is not something that either of us want a repeat of. In fact, I have never had a man so willing to please me. It feels really nice.

"I'm doing just fine. I guess I am used to being on my feet, with the hours I do at the hospital." He nods.

"I brought over some supplies. Tomorrow night is movie night, right?" he says as he lifts the lid on the massive basket, and I get a flash of bright rainbow colors which hit me all at once. The basket is full to the brim with all different types of candy.

"Carter! This is insane!" I dig through the stash, giggling as I imagine him emptying every supermarket shelf between my place and the gym.

"Well, I know you and Ivy have your special nights, so I want you to be prepared." He shrugs, and I need to bite my lip at how considerate he is. Being around kids is totally new to him, I think, but he is really hitting it out of the park.

As I look at him, I know that although we have shared a few kisses, I need to be the one to make the first move. He is trying to hold back, letting me lead, only touching me when he absolutely knows I want it. But it's my turn now.

And boy, do I want it.

I take a small step closer to him, and he grabs my waist, pulling me all the way to his body, his hard chest firm and solid against mine.

"Carter..." I say, his name on my lips drifting as I get lost in his deep blues.

He leans in, pressing his lips to mine, before he runs his nose across my cheeks, placing small kisses along the path to my ear. "Tell me, Cat. Tell me what you want," he whispers, causing shivers to skate the length of my body, my nipples peaking underneath my clothes.

"Carter... I want you..." I say quietly, almost needy, my hands smoothing up his chest and circling around his neck.

"You sure about that? Because like I said, I'm not running this time. If you want me, you will get me. You will be mine," he says, still waiting for me to be 100 percent sure that I want to be with him. And I am. I'm all in.

His hands run up and down my back, slowly, almost teasingly, as his lips continue to trail along my neck. I feel my heart beating out of my chest, my breathing has quickened, and the throbbing down below aches for him to satisfy.

I don't say anything. Pulling away from him, and I hear him take a breath in, waiting for the words, but instead I grab his hand and lead him behind me as I make my way down the hall. I walk quietly past Ivy's bedroom, but I needn't have worried; she is snoring and out cold. I walk us farther, to the end of the hall, and into my bedroom, closing the door behind us.

Leaning against the back of the door, I turn to face him. He stares at me hungrily, but there's still an unsurety there as his eyebrows pull together.

"Carter..." I bite my lip, walking toward him. "Make me yours." As soon as the last word leaves my lips, the hesitation he had disappears in an instant. He's meeting me in the middle in two big strides, grabbing my hips, and pushing me back against my bedroom door.

The movement makes me gasp, and that quickly turns to a moan when his hands grip my jaw and his lips slam onto mine. Our tongues clash as he lowers one hand, lifting me up by my ass, and my legs automatically wrap around his waist. His effortless strength is such a damn turn on.

"You were mine the minute I saw you in the hospital. I let you go once, and I am never fucking making that mistake again," he growls against my lips. I arch into him, my need for him obvious. His claim on me warms my body from the inside out. He grinds his hips into mine, my back still firm against the door, and I whimper at the friction.

"Carter," I say breathlessly. "Too many clothes." I'm panting as I pull at his top, desperate to feel his skin.

He chuckles. "Not so fast, baby. I want to take my time with you. I want to taste every inch of your body. Mark ever curve as mine." He captures my mouth in his again, the endearment *baby* making me feel wanton. With my legs still firmly wrapped around his waist, he leans back from me for a second, just enough to lift his top over his head before he's kissing me again and sending me into a spiral.

My hands grab onto his shoulders as he swivels us around, stalking us to my bed, then tossing me onto the mattress with a bounce that makes me giggle. Leaning over me, he takes my shirt in his hands and rips it from my body, clean down the middle. My breath leaves my lungs in shock, but my arousal skyrockets, completely enraptured by this man. There's no questioning how much this man wants me.

Standing at the side of the bed, he grabs my legs and tugs me toward him, my body sliding across the sheets. I watch his muscles flex with the action, and my pussy clenches in response.

His hands reach for my jeans, and he undoes them swiftly, pulling them right off my legs, my hands gripping onto the bed underneath me to keep me in place. I'm now left in only in my underwear, my chest heaving with pants as my mind tries to catch up with my body. Carter throws my jeans across the room, joining my t-shirt on the floor, and then his hands are back on my legs, gliding up to my thighs.

He's making me crazy with his touch. One minute, he's savage, the next, he's light and languid. I'm basically squirming beneath him for more.

"You're so fucking beautiful," he growls, his eyes unfocused as they roam my near naked body, my skin prickling with goosebumps under his stare.

"We need to be quiet because of Ivy," I say softly, reminding him that there is a little girl in the house.

"Oh, I will be quiet, Cat. It will be you who will need to hush your screaming," he taunts with a small grin, and my stomach flips in anticipation. Then I watch in awe as this big man falls to his knees onto the floor before me.

Leaning back on my elbows, my eyes follow him as he begins to kiss the inside of my thighs, alternating from one to the other, and my head falls back on a sigh. I haven't had a man's mouth on me in a very long time, and even then, it was lackluster. My legs tremble as his fingers caress my skin, his face edging closer to where I want him.

His hands come up to my waist, fingers grabbing

either side of my underwear before he pulls them slowly down my legs.

"Fucking beautiful. I could look at you like this all day. Bare and completely at my mercy." His hand runs across my pelvic bone, his thumb brushing over my center gently, openly admiring me.

"Carter, please," I beg him, needing him to touch me, my voice quivering with need.

"Please what?" he asks with a curve to his lip, his eyes still taking me in, his thumb now rubbing me slowly, deliberately.

"Oh, God. Carter, pleaseee. I'm- I need-" I can't even form a full sentence when he runs his fingers through my wetness, then swirls them around my clit again. My senses are overloaded, my head is swimming in desire, my heart pumping out of my chest.

"Tell me what you want, Cat. Tell me what you want me to do to you." His restraint is admirable because I am about to combust.

"I want... Oh God, I want you. Right now. I want you... so bad... and I want it hard. I need it... Please." I'm a babbling mess, barely able to draw in a breath, as he continues toying with me.

"Hmmmm... I want you to tell me *exactly* what you want. Keep going," he says, as his touch sends ripples through my body, his other hand squeezing my ass, hard, like he himself is nearly at breaking point.

"Do you want me here?" he asks, pressing a small kiss to the inside of my thigh. I have to throw my arm over my face to muffle my moan.

"Or do you want me here?" He kisses up my hips

toward my chest. He is teasing me, and I hate it and love it in equal measures, and I don't want him to stop.

I have never told a man what I want before. I have never had anyone ask me what I wanted in the bedroom. Daniel always took; what I wanted or what I needed was insignificant. I realize that even after everything we have been through, Carter is still letting me lead, even here, with me bare beneath him, still letting what we do be my choice.

It is empowering.

So I finally tell him exactly what's on my mind.

"I want you everywhere... all over me. I want your hands and mouth on my body, leaving no spot untouched. I... I want you to pull my hair, bite my skin. I want you to take all that I have and give me everything of you in return," I say, panting, feeling my body on the edge with a sprinkle of nerves at my honesty.

His fingers touch my clit, and my breath hitches. I continue.

"I want you to put your mouth on me now, Carter. I want you to fuck my pussy with your tongue until I come for you." The dirty words are new to me, but I feel another surge of power run through me as I say them, and his eyes alight.

"Fuck, Cat. You are so damn sexy...." He groans as he lowers his face, those magical lips of his connecting with my throbbing clit, and I almost jump right off the bed.

"Yesssss. Oh. My... God. Yes," I whimper, my head falling back again as Carter feasts upon me. His tongue massages my clit with precision, his lips sucking on my flesh like he is famished. My hands grasp the sheets below me again, as his grab onto my waist, pulling me closer to him, making my back hit the cool sheets underneath me.

"You're gonna have me addicted to you, baby."

Moaning, I reach up and delve my fingers through his hair, feeling Carter growl against me. The vibration crawls up my skin, driving another moan from my chest that I try to quiet. But he doesn't stop; he is needy, greedy, and everything I have been missing.

One of his hands skims across my hip and down my inner thigh, pushing my legs wider, before he slides his hand up to my center and pushes a finger inside of me. I want to thank him, but I whimper his name instead.

My hips begin to rock in rhythm with his pressure, his finger grazing a special spot inside me that has my body shaking, withering to pieces on the bed.

It has never felt like this for me. I have never enjoyed sex this much in my life.

"I want you to come, Cat. Give me your perfect pussy and come on my tongue," he growls, and his words ignite something in me. My fingers grip onto his hair, my hips still, and before I know what is happening, I do as he asks. I let go.

As my mouth opens to scream out my release, his hand shoots up and covers it. The sound of my ecstasy is muffled by his palm, as my body convulses against him, the single most intense orgasm of my life ripping through me.

As I come down from the high, Carter slowly removes his hand from my mouth, brushing it across my jaw and down to rest on my neck as his lips remain on my skin and travel up my body. His lips kiss up my torso, across my breasts, before they meet my face. He looks over my face, a cheeky glint in his eyes, and I smile.

"Tell me what else you want, Cat, because I am not finished with you yet."

31

CARTER

"I want to taste you," she says breathily, and I am glad I was hovering over her on the bed, otherwise I would have fallen over.

"I want to focus on you tonight, Cat. I want to please you." I don't want her to feel like she needs to look after me. But she cuts me off.

"You told me to tell you what I want, Carter... and that is what I want." She gets a little snip to her tone that makes me smirk, looking at me like I am meat, and she is a bear that has woken up from hibernation. I wasn't sure she would appreciate my dirty talk, but judging by her just-fucked hair and the sultry look in her eyes, I think I may have only begun to scratch the surface of her desires. And I have no plans on stopping.

"Whatever you want, I will give it to you. Including my cock in that beautiful mouth of yours," I grit out as my lips take hers again, my hand smoothing down her body until I cup her breasts. They're the only things still covered in clothing, and I immediately reach around her back and unclip her bra. I want them in my mouth. Now.

"Tell me," I whisper to her as my mouth travels down her chest and I circle her nipple with my tongue. I'm not sure how I will ever let her out from underneath me.

"Tell me how you want to taste me."

"I want you to stand." Her breath hitches as I suck on her nipple, before circling it with my tongue again.

I move across to her other breast, repeating the action, humming my agreeance.

"I want to kneel in front of you..." she whispers, watching me as I lavish her other nipple.

"You want to get on your knees for me, Cat?" I ask her cheekily, and she smiles.

"I have dreamt of having you naked and on your knees for me. Are you going to turn my dreams into reality, baby?" My lips leave a trail back up her chest until I stop and look into her eyes, our noses nearly touching. Not quite believing that she is wanting this, wanting me.

She nods lazily, biting her lip through her smile. "Mmmm. Yes, Carter. I want to make your dreams our reality."

There is something about the way she says *our reality* that hits me in the chest. Hard. I pause, staring down at her in awe, wondering if she was made just for me. At this moment in time, I have no doubt that she was the exact reason I have survived this long.

Because she was meant to me mine.

Standing up then, and with my eyes trained on hers, I undo my jeans, my cock pressing painfully hard against the zipper. I lower them down my legs and throw them to join the rest of the clothes across the room. Grabbing myself, I am hard and heavy in my hand, and I am not sure how I am going to last long enough to enjoy this experience. Her eyes spark at the sight of my hands on myself, and my knees nearly buckle from the desire.

"Come here, baby. Come and get on your knees for me." My muscles tense as I watch her beautiful naked body slip off the sheets, coming to kneel in front of me, her hair flowing down back as she looks up at me.

Her hands meet my shins, and she runs them up my bare legs as she lifts up on her knees, her face now mere inches from my dick.

"Fuck me, this is a sight," I grit out, as her hands skim up my thighs and replace mine on my cock.

"Is this better?" she asks with doe eyes, her gaze remaining on mine as she leans in, her tongue coming out and licking me from my balls to the tip, like a fucking lollipop.

"Are you teasing me, baby?" I ask her, loving this sexy minx that has appeared in the bedroom. It's reminding me of what she mentioned wanting... wanting it *hard*, wanting her *hair pulled*, wanting to be *bitten*...

"Hmmm... maybe... It would only be fair," she says as she does the same thing again. Before I can reply, she takes the tip of me in her mouth, and when her tongue swirls around me, I see stars.

My hand falls to her head as she begins to bob up and down on my cock, moaning around me when I grip her hair.

"Fuck, that feels good," I groan, wanting to close my

eyes and lose myself to the sensation, but enjoying the view too much.

"Touch yourself Cat. I want you to put your fingers inside of your sweet pussy."

I don't miss her eyes ignite with passion, and she immediately does what I tell her. I watch her delicate hand travel across her hip and her fingers disappear inside of her.

She moans around my cock again, this one louder, the noise vibrating to my balls. I am now in control, her hair wrapped around my fist, moving my hips in and out, trying to hang on, never wanting this to end.

She moans again, and so I tug her hair a little more.

"You like that baby? You like me pulling your hair and taking control?"

She nods once, and I pull her hair even tighter, which enlists another moan, so I know she enjoys it. I look down and watch her as her eyes close for a moment, her jaw relaxing around me as a long, drawn-out moan vibrates my cock, her hand coming up to grip my thigh as her body shakes with her orgasm.

"You're fucking beautiful when you come," I pant, sweat now beading on my forehead. I am about to explode right along with her. I start to pull out of her mouth, but her other hand flies up to my ass and pull me forward.

"Fuck, Fuck, Fuck." I grip her hair and push myself in and out of her mouth with more force, now at the point of no return. I let go then, shoving to the back of her throat, and she takes all of me eagerly. At the last minute, I remember Ivy down the hall, so I swallow down my shouts of pleasure, and it comes out as a deep growl as I grind my teeth with every drop of my release. The fucking beauty of what we did makes me want to do it again and again, over and over, for the rest of my fucking life.

"Fuck, Cat," I breathe, leaning over and picking her up off the floor, lifting her into my arms and kissing her with everything I have.

Her bare legs wrap around my waist as she basically climbs me, my palms squeezing her ass and massaging her muscles, wanting to feel her underneath my hands, branding her as mine.

"I want to do that again..." she whispers out against my lips, and I laugh.

"Fuck, baby, we can do that every fucking day," I say with a wide ass grin.

That was heaven.

I walk us back to the bed, lowering her down, before I lie next to her, my hands running across her naked body, wanting to cover every inch, to feel every dip and curve, committing her body to my memory.

"Carter?" she says, her eyes piercing mine.

"Yeah?" My hand finds her breast, and I mold to it, pulling her nipple, seeing them peak, and I hear her breath catch.

"There is something else I want." I watch her as my hand lowers, until I find her clit and start circling it. A small moan leaves her throat, and even after what we have just done, I am as horny as a teenager and ready to go again.

"Tell me what you want, Cat." She hisses through her teeth as I suck her nipple into my mouth.

"Carter, I want you to stay the night," she says, and I pull back to look at her. She is watching me, waiting for my answer, and any tension I had is leaving my body as I take in the sight of this beauty underneath me.

I never put any thought into staying the night; I just knew I would if things escalated. Now she is asking me to, and I feel the trust she is placing in me. Trusting me not to run, trusting me with not just her body but her heart.

"I'm not going anywhere, Cat. I will stay right here, because it's exactly where I want to be. With you," I say, my hand coming to stroke her face, wanting to live in this moment forever.

I lie on my side, my eyes unable to leave her as my hand rubs up and down her bare curves. Her hands find my chest, where one rests before the other caresses up my neck to cup my jaw.

"I've never felt as safe and protected as I do when I'm with you, Carter," she whispers, and my breath catches in my throat a little. Her hand smooths around my neck, gently squeezing, massaging my muscles, looking after me just as much as I am with her. It is nice. And as safe as she feels with me, I realize that being here, in her bed, in her arms, for the first time ever, she's created a safe place for me too.

32

CARTER

I rub my eyes as they adjust to the light streaming through the window. Groaning, I roll over to pull Cat toward me, but as I do, I hit an empty mattress. As I start to wake, I wonder what the time is, our nighttime activities obviously making me more tired than usual. I had her another two times last night in the darkness of the early morning, and each time she met me with fervor. I lean back, my eyes remaining closed, as I think about how fucking beautiful she is.

She is sweet, delicate, and smart during the day, but at night, my girl is a fucking sex maniac, and I love it. Already sporting morning wood just thinking about her, I growl because she isn't beside me.

"Carter, did you know the Salt Water Crocodile is the largest reptile in the world?" a little voice asks from next to me and as my eyes pop open, I see Ivy standing right next to the bed, looking down at me. I jump a little, startled, and wonder how long she has been watching me.

"Good morning, Little Cub. It's a bit early for animal facts, isn't it?" I grumble, rubbing my eyes and sitting up, before realizing that I am naked and ensuring I stay hidden under the covers. I look at her, her hair in two little braids, wearing a cute purple dress, seemingly all ready for the day. *Shit, I must have slept in.*

"Ivy!" I hear Cat call out to her. "Breakfast is ready!" Ivy runs out of the bedroom like her pants are on fire, and I wonder if she was meant to be in here.

Too late now, as she has seen me in her mom's bed and didn't seem concerned, so I am taking that for a win.

Grabbing my phone, I see the usual missed calls, mainly from Benji, and am shocked that it is nearly 9am. I never sleep that late.

With Ivy and her innocent eyes now gone, I slip from the bed and pull on my jeans, then make my way to the bathroom and splash some water on my face. I see the half-moon dents of Cat's nails on my shoulders and grin. Fuck, she was incredible last night.

Pulling my t-shirt on as I walk down the hall, I hear morning cartoons on the TV so assume that Ivy is in the sitting room. As I get closer to the kitchen, my step falters a little when I hear Cat talking quietly to a man. I am now fully awake, strutting down the hall, and as I step around the corner, I see Cat in the kitchen, looking like she should be underneath me in bed with her hair in a messy bun and daisy dukes on that give me far too much leg for just anyone to be looking at.

Then I spot the guy she's talking to. Fully suited up, dark hair slicked back, drinking a coffee and sitting up at the bench like he lives here. I recognize him as the lawyer that Benji said he met with her at the coffee shop. Donovan something-or-other.

"Hey," she greets me as I approach. "Sorry, I didn't want to wake you." She gives me a small smile, lifting up the coffeepot. "Coffee?"

All I want is her, so I walk over to her in the kitchen and stand behind her, wrapping my arms around her, letting this dickhead know who she belongs to. I feel more settled as she leans back into me.

"Donovan, this is Carter Grange," she introduces us, and I nod to him, not wanting my hands to leave her body to shake his hand.

"Carter," he says with a nod, clearly knowing exactly who I am. He eyes me for a moment before looking back at Cat, lifting an eyebrow at her.

"It is fine, Donovan. Anything you need to say, you can say in front of Carter." She sighs, and I rub her hip with my thumb as I kiss her softly in the crook of her shoulder, peering at Donovan from behind her.

Donovan clears his throat. "As I was saying, you have every right to get your money. From what I can pull from the records, there are millions that you are entitled to and that is before we take Ivy into consideration for parental support, which he hasn't supplied at all." I remain quiet, listening to the conversation as understanding washes over me that he is in fact *her* lawyer, not a lawyer she was dating.

Cat moves from me then, turning to grab a mug from the cupboard and filling it with coffee before passing it to me.

"I don't want anything. All I want is for him to leave

me alone," she replies, and I look at him over the brim of the cup as I take a sip, and see him sigh.

"It is easier to get the money. It is going to be hard to remove yourself from him entirely. Are you sure you want to press ahead?" he asks, and my gaze swings to Cat in time to see her swallow nervously. Her eyes flick to me, and I can see the concern in them. I remain tight-lipped, but my nostrils flare, because no one is going to be touching a hair on her head ever again.

"I want to press ahead. I want him to leave me and Ivy alone, and I want to live a simple, safe life," she says to Donovan while looking directly at me, and my jaw clenches. Fuck, I cannot wait to get my hands on this asshole.

"What about your father?" Donovan asks, and both Cat and I turn our attention back to him.

"What about him?" she asks, obviously surprised by Donovan's questioning.

"I sent you the paperwork to sign for a restraining order after he hit you, but you haven't returned it. I assume you don't want to put that in place?" He looks at me, and I nod in agreement, because she needs to ensure she is safe from her father too.

"I don't think so," she says quietly, rubbing her eyes.

"Okay," Donovan concedes, seeing her defeat, and he stands, grabbing his briefcase. "I will see you later in the week. Let me know if anything changes in the meantime."

"Thanks, Donovan, I appreciate it," Cat says, giving him a brief smile.

"Carter." He looks at me and nods, which I return, before he turns and walks out the door. I wait until I hear the click, knowing that he has left, locking the door on the way out.

Smart man.

Cat stands near the kitchen sink, her back to me, as she starts cleaning up the dishes. I put my coffee down and go to her, standing behind her. Resting my hands on her shoulders, I run them up and down her arms before I settle them on her waist and hold her tight.

"I will look after you. You don't need a single penny from him. I got you Cat. You and Ivy are safe with me," I say into her ear, wanting her to understand she's not alone. No matter how down she might be feeling about this situation.

She spins in my arms and looks up at me, her eyes glistening, and as I pull her tighter, she buries her head into my chest.

"Thanks, Carter. I appreciate it." She pulls back from me a little, but my hands remain around her waist, not wanting to let her go. "So... last night..." she says, and I see a hint of blush come to her rosy cheeks.

"Hmmm. What was your favorite part?" I ask her, my hands now all over her body, running up and down her back, keeping her close to me.

The blush on her cheeks deepens.

"Was it when I kissed you here?" I ask her as I dip my head and kiss her on the neck, inhaling her scent as I do.

"Was it when I had you sit on my face and I tasted your sweet, sweet—"

"Carter!" she whispers a growl to me, which turns into a giggle when she realizes Ivy can't hear us.

"You took my cock well last night, baby. Did you like that?"

"I liked it all. I also liked that you woke up in my bed," she says, smiling softly, and I lean forward and press a gentle kiss on her plush lips.

"Best fucking night of my life."

"Mine too."

"You look cute when you blush," I say to her, my smile wide before I lean down to her ear. "You look even better with my cock in your mouth." She gasps, and her cheeks go ever redder, making me chuckle.

"So, I have my fight this weekend..." I say, changing the topic, knowing I'll be training hard for the rest of the week. Though I'll be making time to see her, regardless.

"Don't remind me. I hate to see you black and blue," she grumbles, looking at me with concern.

"I know it isn't your thing, but I would really like you to come." I pause and wait for her to wrap her head around my request. "Benji will bring you and be with you the whole time. Dante, Nico, and Sebastian will be there too, and I would like them to meet you, officially, as mine."

She chews her bottom lip as she thinks it over. "Carter, it isn't really my thing..." She starts to say, and disappointment wells inside of me. "...but, I will come if you really want me to. I want to support you." Her hands circle my neck and she lifts up on her toes to kiss me. When she pulls away, I'm smiling like a fool.

"I like it when you come..." I can't help but tease her, wanting that flush to reappear.

"I like it when you make me come..." she murmurs, and my mouth attacks hers as my fingers find her bare skin underneath her t-shirt.

"Why don't you go and have a shower, and I'll clean up and look after Ivy," I say to her, and she pulls back and looks at me in disbelief.

"Seriously?"

I sour at the fact that she is so shocked that a man would step up and help her.

"Go, baby. I got this." I give her a quick peck on the lips before I smack her on the ass.

"Carter!" she squeals with a smile, and that is exactly what I want to see on her face from now on. She giggles a little before giving me another kiss.

"I won't be long. Thank you!" Then she's scurrying off down the hall.

I finish washing our cups as Ivy walks into the room.

"Why do you call me Little Cub?" she asks, taking me by surprise.

"Because you are your mom's little cub. She is a lioness, and you are her cub." I lean against the kitchen bench and watch her as she mulls that over. She is just like her mom.

"Okay, wait here," she says before running to her room, coming straight back.

"We need to have a meeting," she says seriously as she sits at the dining table with a small pink fluffy notebook and glitter pink pen in her hand.

"A meeting?" I ask, my eyebrow raised. This kid is something else.

"Yes. A business meeting. Please, take a seat," she explains as she sits up taller, trying to be professional, so I entertain her. I walk over and sit down in the chair opposite her.

"Okay, hit me with it," I say as I sit up straighter in my chair too, straightening my imaginary tie, matching her demeanor. I can see her trying not to laugh, wanting to remain serious, yet obviously finding it funny that we are now acting like two businessmen in the city.

"So, now that you and my mom are... *dating*," she says, drawing out the word in question and looking at me for confirmation. I nod to her in agreement, and see the smile cracking through for a moment before she tries to school it again. My heart beats a little faster, liking that she is happy that I am around, and her mother and I are together. I remain quiet, waiting to see where she is going with this.

"Then it's time we had an agreement," she states, steepling her hands and reminding me of Sebastian. That almost has me breaking character.

"An agreement?" I ask her, tilting my head.

"Yes. An agreement," she confirms.

"Okay, what is this agreement?"

"You need to agree to be our best friend, always and forever. To protect us, to laugh with us, and to always bring candy or donuts whenever you come over," she says with a completely straight face, and I struggle to not smile, not wanting to insult her when she is taking this so seriously. I want to show her that I will listen to her, whenever she needs me. I never want her to feel like I am dismissing her.

"Okay, I will protect you, laugh with you, and always bring candy or donuts when I come over," I repeat back to her.

"AND be our best friend," she reminds me, and I need to take a breath. This kid is accepting me, bringing me into her heart. This moment is significant for the both of us. I never thought I would ever have kids. I never thought they were going to be part of my future, yet here I am, making a deal that is one of the most important of my life.

"And be your best friend," I agree, watching her dig into a small pouch she has inside of her notebook.

"Here, you need to put this on to signify that our agreement is confirmed," she says, handing over a small silver chain.

"What's this?" I ask as I grab it from her and dangle it in my hand so I can see it clearly. It is one half of a heart with the letter ST and ENDS on it. My eyes flick back to Ivy.

"I have the other half. See!" She pulls out the other half of the heart from under her top, showing the letters BE and FRI on it. When put together, it spells out *Best Friends*. My chest constricts with pride.

I take the dainty necklace in my big hands, but I can't open the clasp. So, jumping off her chair, she walks around to me, plucks it from my hand, opens it up, drapes it around my neck, and clasps it together.

"There. Best friends forever," she exclaims, giving me her hand to shake.

"Best friends forever, Little Cub," I grunt out, trying to keep my emotions in check. I shake her hand, sealing the deal.

As she runs off back down to her room, I lift the half heart in my hands, knowing that even though it is pink and glittery that I will never take it off.

33

CATHERINE

I am a nervous wreck when Benji finally pulls up to the front of my place, and I jump into his big black Escalade. Carter has been training like a madman, and I have been busy at work, so I haven't seen a lot of him the past few days. But he spends every night with me, and holds me until morning. With Ivy staying with Maggie tonight, I continue to fidget in the front seat, trying to not have a panic attack about watching Carter's fight and also potentially meeting Sebastian Romano.

If anyone had told me that this was the turn my life was going to take, I would have laughed in their face. I should be worried about bringing Ivy into this life, but she is happy, healthy, and has a bigger smile on her face than she ever has. Carter continues to bring us joy, and we haven't laughed so much before in our lives.

"Are you okay?" Benji asks, turning to look at me as we drive down the street.

"Fine. Why?" I reply too quickly, looking out the

window to where we are headed. A side of town that I am not familiar with and have never been to before.

"Ahhh... because your leg is bouncing, you're wringing your hands together, and I feel like you are about to take off the minute the car stops," he says honestly, and I pause.

"Sorry," I say with a wince, taking another breath to calm my racing heart. "I'm just nervous."

"Nothing to be nervous about. Carter will be fine. You might actually enjoy it!" Benji says, trying to encourage my excitement.

"Have you met Sebastian before?" I might as well try to get to know the man who I am so scared to meet.

"Yep. He's cool. No need to worry. And Carter is not going to let anything happen to you. Neither will I." His face grows serious, giving me a look that tells me that there is no question he would protect me with his life.

I nod in response, appreciating this new friend I have made, as I look back out the window and get lost in my thoughts.

Before long, we drive down a dark street in what looks to be an industrial district. I wore jeans and combat boots with a black jacket, so at least I *look* badass. There is warehouse after warehouse, roller doors, and even though there are streetlights, they seem few and far between, a light glow the only indication they are even on. There are cars around, a few people standing in small groups smoking, and we park and make our way inside. I keep my head low, not that I expect to see anyone, but if this ever got out, I would definitely need to explain it to the medical board.

"This way." Benji leads me, putting his hand on my back and moving me through the small industrial door and into the warehouse, where I nearly trip over myself as I try to take it all in.

It's big, really big and full of people. Mainly men, many scary looking, but some in suits, which is surprising. I stand on a cement floor, and I look beyond the crowd to see a ring marked out with ropes, surrounded by rows and rows of plastic chairs and people standing, talking, and yelling at a fight that is currently happening in front of them. There appears to be a makeshift bar over on one wall, and I see a man waving money nearby, calling out bets, the hundred-dollar bills flapping as he speaks with his hands.

"Keep moving, Doc," Benji grits out, his head down but his eyes wide, so I follow him as we move in tandem to the side of the large space and down a corridor. There are less people in this area, but a few still milling around, with more females who are scantily clad, looking me up and down.

"Here," Benji says and bangs on the door, which opens swiftly, and Dante Luciano stands solidly in front of us.

I gulp as he shakes hands with Benji.

"Hey, Doctor Wakeford," he says, a small smile appearing on his face, and I feel a little more at ease.

"Hi, Dante. Just Cat, please," I say, probably needing to be less formal now. I watch as he smiles as he stands back and opens the door for us to enter. I can't say that we are friends, more like acquaintances, but I feel better that there is a familiar face.

"Good to see you."

"Thanks. How's Annie?"

"She's doing good, thanks to you," he tells me, his compliment taking me by surprise.

"I'm glad she is doing well," I say, expertly dodging the compliment. It is my job, after all. I am not a miracle worker and don't claim to be.

I take a few steps in, and I spot Carter over in the far corner, his back to me, sitting on a table, Nico in front of him, wrapping his hands with white tape. Then I see who I assume is Sebastian Romano standing next to him, talking to him in hushed tones, and as he does he eyes flick to me, and there is no facial expression. Not a smile, not a scowl. Nothing. Before his eyes look back at Carter, ignoring me entirely.

I gulp. This is not my idea of a good time.

"Cat?" Carter calls out to me, turning. "Come here." I don't hesitate. I leave Benji's side and go to Carter, wanting to be next to him.

"Hey," I say with a smile, trying to appear happy to be here, the heat from Sebastian's stare drilling into the side of my face.

He jumps off the bed and pulls me close, giving me a chaste kiss on the lips.

"Cat, this is Sebastian. Sebastian, this is Cat." My heart is thumping so fast in my chest, I think the whole neighborhood can hear it.

"Doctor Wakeford, nice to meet you," Sebastian says, extending his hand for me to shake, which I accept. It all feels a little too formal and not the warm greeting I was expecting.

"Likewise, Sebastian. Please, call me Cat." As his hand grips mine, I feel like he is assessing me. I wonder if this is what it was like for Annie when she first met Dante. My eyes flick to Carter, and I see him looking at Sebastian curiously.

Carter wraps his arm around my waist, keeping me in tight as I pull my hand away from Sebastian's grip, but he continues to stare at me.

"Hey, Doc," Nico says as he joins us, and I let go of the breath I was holding as Nico gives everyone a grin. Then I finally start to relax.

"Hi, Nico, good to see you," I say, feeling better now that the introductions are out of the way, and Sebastian steps over to stand next to Dante. My eyes flick to him again, and he is still eyeing me warily. My blood runs cold for a moment as I begin to think that perhaps he doesn't like me.

"How are you feeling?" I ask Carter once Nico leaves his side, looking at the beast of a man in front of me, questioning how I am going to survive watching this fight. He looks amazing, his muscles on full display, glistening in the lights. I hope it doesn't take too much of a beating.

"I'm fine now that you're here. Can you hold this and keep it safe for me?" he asks, and I look down to his open palm. I see a small silver necklace, and I grab it from him before lifting and studying it. It is a half heart; a best friend necklace.

"Where did this come from?" I ask, looking up at him, surprised that he has such a thing.

"Your little cub. We have made a business deal, her

and I. I need to wear this every day, but I don't want to lose it tonight, so I will grab it from you at home later."

Home. He is now referring to my place as home, and I quite like the new love bubble we have created. And Ivy gave him this? If I wasn't a ball of nerves, I'd be melting at his feet.

"Ready, Carter?" Nico shouts from across the room, and Carter looks at him and nods.

"Time to go. Don't worry, I got this. Go with Benji straight home after the fight, and I will see you there, okay?" he says, his hand giving my waist a squeeze in reassurance. I am glad he is okay, because I feel like I need to vomit.

"Okay. Good luck," I offer him with a small smile, and he pulls me close. His lips meet mine and his hands wrap my waist tight as I hook mine behind his head. My fingers grip into his hair, never able to get enough of this man.

A throat clears behinds us, and we pull apart, me wiping the gloss from Carter's mouth.

"Good luck," I whisper again before I step away from him and go back to Benji.

"Good luck, Carter!" Benji hollers, and then the two of us make a quick exit out the door. Sebastian Romano's eyes don't leave me the entire time.

Benji and I start to make our way through the crowd of people to find our seats. We are not sitting up the front, as I didn't want to distract Carter with my gulps of fear or panicking breaths. I also wanted to remain as inconspicuous as possible, not wanting the fact that I attended an underground MMA fight to be reported back to work, or my father, which is exactly what would happen if I sit at the front row next to someone like Sebastian Romano.

We find our two seats a few rows back and settle in.

"What did you do to piss Sebastian off so much?" Benji grumbles to me, and my head whips around to look at him so fast, I make myself dizzy.

"I've never met him before... I've never even spoken to him before," I stutter out, wide-eyed, looking at Benji for support.

"He was sure looking at you intensely. I thought perhaps you already had a run-in with him."

"No, nothing. I could see he didn't look overly welcoming, but I wasn't sure if that is just the way he is or if it was me." Benji shakes his head.

"No, I only see Sebastian like that when he is wary of people, and he was certainly wary of you for some reason," Benji says, looking at me seriously. "Don't worry. Carter will sort him out." He gives me a small smile that does absolutely nothing to reassure me.

Before I can ask any more questions, the lights dim, some music comes on, and I hear a man with a microphone introduce Carter's opponent. Fear creeps up my throat, and I shiver as the man they call Big Dom walks in with his team. He is huge and, like Carter, extremely fit. I watch him for a moment but get slightly distracted as I see Sebastian and Dante walk down the aisle at the same time Big Dom is jumping into the ring, obviously timing it so they don't have as many eyes on them. They are fully clothed and not as broad as Big Dom, yet I find Sebastian more frightening. A thought that is cemented when Sebastian turns and looks at me again, his eyes finding mine immediately with a hard, penetrating gaze. It makes me still, before he takes a seat in the front row.

The music stops then, and another tune starts, the bass thumping heavily, the beats vibrating up my shins and through my body, and the crowd begins to cheer.

"He's coming," Benji says, before he stands and starts clapping. I jump up too, trying to see Carter between the heads and bodies in front of me, and I do. If I didn't know him, I would be fearing for my life because he looks extremely dangerous, angry, his eyes laser-focused as they stay on his opponent. Nico is walking with him, as is his training partner, and I am sure Benji would be too if he wasn't babysitting me.

"Wow, he looks so intense," I say to Benji, my eyes not leaving Carter for a second.

"I know, right. Who would think that he is such a cute teddy bear around you?" Benji teases with a grin, his pleasure at seeing his friend obvious.

I smile then, happy that I get to have a side of Carter that no one else does. The music dies down and we all take our seats as the referee in the ring yells out instructions. My heart rate rises again, wanting this fight to be over. I clench my hands and my knee bobs up and down at a rapid rate as Benji cheers next to me.

Grown men all around us yell and scream at Carter and Big Dom as they begin to dance around each other in the ring. I thank God I am with Benji because I am so far out of my comfort zone, I don't even know what to do.

My hands are clenched so tight, I feel my nails digging into my palms, and as Big Dom makes a few small punches in Carter's direction, my head ducks and weaves to see through the crowd to follow their movements.

Big Dom lashes out, but Carter is quick, and before too long, they get in a tussle. I have to cover my face with my hands. Benji doesn't even notice me as he sits on the edge of his seat, screaming at the top of his lungs, and I peek through my fingers to get a glimpse of what is happening.

My heart rate is so elevated that I think I might pass out. I force myself to watch again, my eyes glued to Carter as he remains light on his feet, moving around the cage. But something changes. Big Dom says something, and Carter's face completely morphs with a rage unlike anything I've ever seen on him before. He looks murderous, and my stomach drops.

It is then all hell breaks loose.

34

CARTER

The lights are bright and Big Dom and I are only minutes into the first round, when he drops his hands and leans in. He is known for talking smack, so I entertain him and listen.

"Nice piece of ass you are seeing at the moment," he says to rile me up. Obviously talking about Cat. Given that I have been open with her at the gym, I'm not surprised he has heard about her.

"You watch your fucking mouth," I spit at him, my hackles rising because I want to end him for even mentioning her name in this cage.

"I look forward to fucking her once I beat your ass to the floor tonight. She looks like the type I can hold down easily; take what I want and give you the leftovers." And then, it's like a match has been lit. Fire wells in my chest. I stare at him for a beat and see his face change, because he knows he went one step too far.

And then, I lose it.

Before he even realizes, my fist comes up and

connects with his chin, and I hit him so hard I am sure I heard his jaw crack over the roar of the crowd. The referee jumps in between us for a moment, but I can't stop.

I step even closer to Big Dom, pushing the referee out of the way, and hit him a second time, this time with my left hand, across the other side of the head, watching as his jaw wobbles right off his face. He falls to one knee and screams in pain, his hands rushing to support his chin. The referee steps in again, putting his hands on my shoulders, and trying to push me back. But I push him to the side, seeing only red.

I kick Big Dom in the ribs, the noise in the warehouse so loud it is going to lift the roof, but it is not loud enough to drown out the words in my head of him insulting Cat. So I keep going.

Big Dom doubles over, his hands wrap around his torso as his head hangs low, trying to limit the damage I am inflicting. I heave air into my lungs and see people entering the cage from the corner of my eye to stop me. But I can't stop. I kick him again, straight across his head, which bounces around on his shoulders like a newborn baby before and he falls back with a loud thud.

Out cold and in dire need of an ambulance.

Dante and Nico are next to me in an instant, everyone else too scared to get close to me. I am breathing heavy like a raging bull as I wait for Big Dom to get up so I can keep going. But he isn't moving. He isn't getting back up. The boys pull me away, and I shake my head, trying to center myself. The crowd in the warehouse is going nuts. Everyone is screaming, the music pumping, and the crowd starts to chant my name, pleased they got their money's worth tonight.

I try to look in the crowd for Cat, but the lights are too bright, and I can see only darkness. A team of medics steps into the ring and surrounds Big Dom, and I shrug off the boys, now eager to leave.

As I walk out of the cage, I am immediately surrounded by grown men back slapping me, cheering and hollering. But I don't want any of it. I put my head down and walk, Dante and Nico on either side, keeping everyone at a distance.

I want to grab Cat, see if she is okay, and get the fuck out of here.

***

Sitting in the backseat of the car next to Sebastian, I can't help but feel like something is off. Not with the fight, though that was crazy, but at least it went my way.

The energy from the packed crowd was intense, my need to end it quickly even more so. I was so focused on being with Cat, that when Big Dom spit out his remark, I needed to end him quickly so I could get to her sooner. He knows nothing of her history, but those words were more than taunting, they dug deep.

Usually, I like to dance around a bit, play with my prey, but I had no hesitation tonight after he went there. The shock of the early knockout was evident as once Big Dom hit the floor, the room totally erupted. The promoters may not have got a long fight, but everyone sure got what they paid for. Unfortunately, for Big Dom, he will have a sore head for some time.

It was good having Cat there, and the fact that she came, even though it was really not her thing, cements to me that she is as into me as I am her.

I got a text from Benji half an hour ago to say she was home safe and sound, and so now I can focus on what happened earlier. Sebastian has been odd all night, and I didn't like the way he was when he met Cat. It was extremely unusual, very intimidating for her, and it makes me think that he won't accept her into the family. I just have no idea why.

"Good fight tonight, Carter. You made me a cool 100k," Dante says from the passenger seat as he fans out the hundred-dollar bills and waves them in front of his face like he is trying to cool down. "Quickest 100k I have ever made."

"What are you going to do with it?" I ask him, already knowing the answer.

"Spoil my woman," he says confidently, a smile on his face, his love for Annie still burning bright.

"You killed it. It was like you had extra energy about you. The crowd went nuts when you knocked him out!" Nico says enthusiastically, his eyes remaining on the road, a big, proud grin on his face. "Big Dom hit the floor so hard. He will be seeing double for a week!" I can already see the wheels turning in his head, his business brain in motion.

I look over at Sebastian, but he remains quiet, looking away from me and out the window, deep in thought.

"I think it might be my last fight for a while..." I say to

them as I rub the back of my neck, and they all turn in unison to look at me.

"What? Why?" Nico asks, shock evident on his face.

I shrug. "I have been thinking about it for a while. It feels like it is the right time. I'm not getting any younger, the competition is becoming more fierce..."

"You still have years left in front of you. You proved that tonight with Big Dom. They promoted this as the fight that would have you on your knees, but you knocked him out in the first round!" Nico exclaims, clearly not wanting me to stop.

"Is it the girl?" Sebastian asks, and it is the first words he has spoken since we got in the car. I don't want to lie to him, and if I am perfectly honest, she is a big part of it.

"She's not the whole reason, but a part of it," I say to him and as I do, I see his jaw clench.

"Fuck," Nico says in quiet awe from the front.

"Carter is finally whipped," Dante says with a smirk, happy that he can now pick on me for once. I ignore the banter being aimed at me as I look at Sebastian's narrowing gaze. What the hell is up his ass tonight?

"What's going on?" I ask him, feeling like I am missing something and starting to feel very fucking uncomfortable. Dante and Nico quiet down, but neither of them have said anything. We don't keep secrets in this family, so I know whatever it is about, Sebastian hasn't shared it with anyone yet.

"You fought well. It was quick," Sebastian says, and I can see the gloss over his face that appears like he is trying to be nice, when all he really wants to do is act out.

"Is there something you are not telling me?"

"There are a lot of things I don't tell you boys." He expertly dodges the question, turning his head again to look out the window at the passing buildings like he can't look me in the eye.

"Sebastian," I say, but he turns suddenly, his face tense, his eyes serious.

"Go home to her, Carter. Spend the night. I need you back in New York tomorrow," he states, leaving no room for further questions, and I nod to him, my lips pursed. I'm pretty pissed about that, but I will do as he asks. Maybe in New York, he will be more forthcoming with whatever it is he is withholding.

35

CATHERINE

I look at him and swallow roughly. That was intense. I knew it would be, but the fight tonight seemed to go from zero to 100 in a second. As he stands in my kitchen, I let my eyes canvas his body, and in my honest, professional opinion, I actually don't think he needs any medical attention.

"Are you all right?" I ask him, my heart pounding at the memory of him hitting Big Dom with such force; I don't even know how to process it all.

"I feel like I need to ask you that question," he says, as his hand comes up and caresses my cheek. The same hand that smashed Big Dom's face almost clear off his head merely hours ago.

"I'm fine," I lie, not sounding very convincing.

"Cat. I lost it tonight. I wasn't planning to get that aggressive. I know it isn't your thing. I should have tried to go a little easier. I'm sorry you had to see that." As the words rush out of him, I look up and see the panic on his face.

"It was a lot," I whisper to him. "The crowd was nuts." I say, remembering how grown men clambered over seats to cheer for Carter as Benji tried his best to shelter me from the mayhem.

"Yeah, well... Big Dom said some things that got under my skin, and I lost it for a moment," Carter tries to explain, and I grab his hand and hold it in mine.

"As long as you are okay?" I ask him again, looking over his hands that are red and a little bruised but otherwise uninjured.

"I'm fine, just worried about you. About us," he says quietly, and my eyes flick back to his face.

"No, you don't need to be worried about us. It's okay. We're okay. I knew it would be tough tonight. I was prepared, perhaps not as prepared as I should have been, but I'll get over it," I try to reassure him, but his eyes still search my face, so I ask him something that's been on my mind since I got home.

"Is that what usually happens? Because the night we met, you were black and blue." Carter wraps his arms around my waist, holding me like I'm precious cargo, like he didn't just finish a fight in a dark warehouse on the outskirts of town.

"I wanted to knock him out quick tonight, Cat. I didn't want to play with him too much," he says before leaning in and kissing me softly. The difference in him now from the man I watched walk into that ring tonight is astounding, but I am glad this is the Carter I get.

I pull back a little and look at him. "So you mean, the night we met, you were playing around and deliberately got hit for crowd entertainment?" I quiz him, astounded at how this works.

"Pretty much. That guy got lucky that night and got a few good hits in. Now I know it was the universe leading me to you, though." He walks me backwards through the house, kissing my neck, making me shiver in desire. And with that comment and these kisses, I'm completely lost to him.

"Very smooth, Mr. Fighter. But seriously, there isn't a mark on you. Are you sore anywhere?" I ask again, not sure if I missed any hits to his torso, and wanting to make sure he is really okay and not just saying that to appease me.

"Yeah, I'm a little swollen, though..." he mumbles, his lips not leaving my neck as he pulls at my t-shirt, his intentions clear. But now my mind has snapped into doctor mode.

"Where?' I press, knowing I have prepared ice packs in the freezer and a solid supply of pain relief at the ready, all of which I put together before I left while thinking the worst. My back hits the wall in the hallway as his hands come up and rest on either side of my face. He looks down at me and smiles before kissing me again.

"Down here," he murmurs as his lips slide down my jaw at the same time as he grinds his hips into mine, and I can feel exactly where he is swollen. I laugh, a loud one that has him chuckling against my skin.

"Ivy's at Maggie's tonight, right?" he asks me as my hands run up his back.

"Yes, she is," I answer, now slightly out of breath, as his lips dragging along my skin makes me quiver.

"Good, because I am going to make you scream so loudly your neighbors will come knocking." He pulls away, lifts me up by the waist, and throws me over his shoulder like I weigh nothing, slapping my ass in the process.

"Ahhhh! Carter!" I squeal in surprise as he marches us to the bedroom, throwing me on the bed.

"Clothes off, Cat," he orders as he rips off his top and starts unbuttoning his jeans. "I've been waiting all damn night to have my cock inside of you."

I sit up on my knees and pull my top over my head, and as I do, I feel his hands on my bare waist and the bed dip a little as he kneels next to me.

"On second thought, I want to undress you myself," he murmurs, as his lips meet mine, and his hands roam my torso. His tongue swirls into my mouth, his hands reaching my shoulders and pulling at my bra straps.

His lips leave mine then, trailing down my jaw and neck, until they reach my bare shoulders.

"God, I want you naked," he growls, and I shiver.

"Your body is carved from stone, I swear," I say to him in a whisper as my hands run up his naked torso, feeling his chiseled chest, eager to see him naked too, a sight I will never tire of.

"Your tits are fucking amazing," he says between kisses as his mouth now moves farther south across my flushed skin, his hand pulling down the cup of my bra, as his mouth covers one nipple and sucks hard.

"Your mouth is everything..." I say as my head falls back, just as his jeans drop to the floor.

"Mmmm. Fuck, I could suck these tits all night," he

murmurs as he continues to suck on my breast, one of his hands moving around my back to unclip my bra.

"I want you on your knees for me tonight," I pant in reply, my bra now tossed across the bedroom.

His hands and mouth and praise feel like they are caressing me everywhere, and I can't get enough.

"I fucking love having my mouth on your pussy," he says cheekily, his hands now moving to the waist of my jeans and deftly opening the button, lips trailing up my chest.

"I want every last inch of this, then I want it again and again until morning," I say to him slowly as I reach down and wrap my hand around his swollen cock, feeling him throbbing underneath my grip.

He is now face to face with me, the two of us kneeling on the bed, and his eyes ignite as I massage him. I love how hard and ready he is. It turns me on to know he desires me like this.

"Anything you say," he says with a sly grin as he grabs me around the waist, lifting me off the bed before lying me on my back onto the mattress.

"These need to go." He whips the jeans right off my legs, and I bite down on my bottom lip as I see him standing fully naked in front of me.

"There are so many different ways I want to fuck you right now." Groaning, he looks at me as he pumps himself, his eyes hungry as his tongue flicks out and swipes his bottom lip.

"I will take everything you give." And I will. Carter makes me feel wanted, safe, beautiful. He can't keep his hands off me whenever we are together, and my feelings for him are growing exponentially every day.

He comes back to the bed then, leaning over me, with one hand at the side of my face, his other hand trailing over my body. As he gazes over me again, he looks like he is weighing up options, and I begin to squirm underneath him, my need for him strong. I am already throbbing for him.

His hand skims across my hip bone before he grazes my center, my hips automatically rocking into his touch.

"You are so wet for me, Cat."

"Only for you," I say on a moan, and his eyes widen, arousal evident, as he grabs himself and rubs the tip of his cock against me.

"You want every inch?" he questions me again as he now hovers above me, and I feel him hot and heavy at my entrance.

"All of you."

He doesn't hesitate as he pushes inside of me, his eyes on mine as he moves all the way in, slowly, deliberately.

"Carter..." I breathe. God, he is big, but it feels so good.

"You look so good full of my cock, Cat," he grits out, our faces almost flush, as he watches me. Before he starts to move.

I grab onto the back of his neck, my fingers digging into his skin as we move together. Carter takes me with hard thrusts, looking me over, watching my breasts as they move. Reaching down with one hand, he lifts up my thigh, and I wrap my leg around his waist as he pushes in deeper.

"This feels so good. Bite me, Carter. Mark me," I plead, my eyes closing in pleasure. He owns this, he owns me. My body reacts to his like we were made for only each other.

"Fuck, Cat, you are perfect," he grits out, and I let his compliment wash over me, like sunshine, filling my confidence further, my chest rising and falling with quick breaths as I feel my orgasm building.

"So." *Thrust.* "Fucking." *Thrust.* "Perfect." His mouth drops to my neck, where I feel his teeth nip my skin, the small flick of pain igniting my soul, before he does it again, then sucks the spot, no doubt leaving a mark, just like I wanted.

"Carter..." I say, my hands gripping onto him as his flex on my hips, pressing into me.

"What do you want, baby?" he asks, still pumping, his muscles flexing and clenching, just that image of him enough to make me wetter. I know what I want from him, want his strong hands to do to me... but I'm not sure I can say it.

"Tell me," he demands, and I know he wants to please me. His pace increases, my breasts jiggling with every thrust.

"I want your hands on my neck." He watches me intently, slight concern on his face, and I move my hand to grab his.

"I feel safe with you. I love your hands on my body. I want you to hold my neck." He still looks a little wary, so I grip his hand and move it up my body, placing it on my neck, showing him exactly what I want.

"You want me to choke you, baby? You want me to

wrap my hand around your neck and fuck you hard until you come all over my cock?" I nod, moaning as my pussy clenches around him from the look in his eyes. Also relieved that he's just as into the idea.

It isn't something I have ever thought about before. The way my life has been, you would think that this is the last thing I would want, but with Carter, I want it all.

His big hands owning my body is what I want.

"Yes... Please. Hold me tighter, Carter. Fuck me hard. I want everything. Pleaseeee," I whimper my plea, feeling my orgasm nearing closer.

"Fuck, Cat, you are so pretty when you beg," Carter groans as his hand rests on my neck, and he grips on, his other moving south to my clit. His hold isn't too tight; it's perfect. I can still breathe, but the move pins me to the mattress, and I spread my legs wider, encouraging him to fuck me harder.

"You're perfect Cat. Fucking perfect." Looking down at me, his hips thrust faster, his hand massaging my clit with every powerful movement of his hips.

My hands grip onto his wrist at my neck, and I begin to moan and writhe in pleasure.

"Carter," I whisper, his eyes watching me closely. "You're going to make me—" is all I get out before I arch my back and his pace quickens, and fall over the edge and into euphoria. His hold on my neck loosens as his name leaves my mouth, and I scream it out to the room, over and over again.

I barely have time to register anything before I feel his hands leave my throat and grab onto my hips. Sitting back, he pumps into me, his thrusts vicious and everything I've ever wanted as he growls my name, his climax overtaking him.

"Fuck! Cat!" he roars, before exploding, gripping my skin tight, the pain of his hold searing my skin as thrusts through his release. In this moment, he looks exactly like the Adonis he is.

We are both panting, and sweat coats Carter's body, making it shimmer. He lies next to me, pulling me in close, holding me as his fingers slowly caress my skin.

"You're perfect for me, Cat... fucking perfect in every way," he says, his lips kissing mine softly. I look into his bright blues and smile.

"We're perfect, Carter," I state, knowing that I have finally met my match.

36

CARTER

I wake from my slumber, feeling warmth at my side, and I look to see soft deep brown hair in my vision. Cat is still asleep, and I watch her. I could watch her all day, every day, and never get bored. The morning light catches her hair softly, making it shine against her complexion, her eyes and lips relaxed.

Drugs were never my thing; I've always worked too hard for my money to shove it up my nose, but I imagine the hit I get from her, the constant need I have to be with her, is a feeling similar to getting high. She makes me feel like I can't get enough.

It must be early, because the sun is starting to peek through the curtains, and knowing I have to leave her today, I want to make the most of my time with her. Peeling away from her slightly, I slide down the mattress and position myself between her legs, because I need another hit.

I run my nose along the soft skin of her upper thigh, before I put my lips on her.

"Carter..." she murmurs, sleepily.

I don't answer her with words, instead I lick her, my favorite flavor, and begin to circle her clit with my tongue.

"Oh. Carter, that feels so good..." I feel her body relax into the bed as her hands settle on my scalp and dig into my hair.

She is the best I have ever had, and I don't know how I will cope being away from her. The way she makes me feel, the way we fit together, the way her and Ivy have accepted me with no questions, no demands, no assumptions. I can be myself with her, and she wants me that way.

Her legs open wider for me, and I know she is enjoying this wakeup call, so I put my hands on her hips, keeping her steady as I can feel her starting to rock, wanting more.

"Oh God, Carter. Pleaseeee... Oh yes, right there..." she moans, and I really want to record the sounds she makes for my ringtone. Her saying my name like that is everything.

As I suck on her clit, I flick my eyes up to her and see her pushing her head back, back arching, breasts pushing out, nipples peaked. I love how she comes undone at my touch.

I pull away for a moment and bring my hand down, sliding one finger inside of her, and her hips buck against me. She is wet and warm, and I'm rock hard already, my cock throbbing from watching her.

"Carter, please, please. I need more of you, Carter, please..." I can feel myself getting harder with every noise she makes, with every move, every moan, my cock twitches into the mattress.

"Let me look after you, baby," I say softly, wanting her to wake up to me nice and slow, enjoying every second of my time with her.

I lower my lips again, sucking on her clit as my fingers move inside of her slowly, but deliberately. I curl them a little, and I know when I hit her spot because her hips convulse under my other hand, and her breathing becomes rapid.

I move my fingers and tongue faster, in tandem, as her grip in my hair gets tighter, and if I had to pick my dream location in the world, it wouldn't be the Bahamas or the tropics, it would be right here, in between her legs, savoring every drop of her on my tongue.

"Carter! Carter! YES!" Her climax overtakes her, and I slow my pace, dragging out her orgasm with matching circles against her G-spot and clit until she's whimpering and boneless, easing back into the mattress. And only then do I come up for air.

I kiss my way back up her beautiful naked body, trying to memorize it so I can imagine her underneath me while I am away. Making my way to her face, I see her smile, her bright white, perfect teeth glistening, her arm is thrown over her eyes, and a soft blush taints her cheeks.

"That was a great way to wake up," she says softly, as she moves her hand from her face and looks at me. The just-fucked flushed look suits her well. Another image for my memory bank.

"Hmmm, best breakfast I ever had," I tell her gruffly, having not really used my voice yet this morning as I continue to kiss her body, never wanting to stop.

I sidle up to her, and pull her close, my nose in her hair, filling up my lungs with her scent, knowing it will be a while before I can do it again. I like that we are up early enough not to be rushed, but the heaviness of leaving her today hangs over me like a storm cloud.

"I need to be back in New York today. Sebastian was on edge for some reason last night and needs me back." Her body stiffens a little in my arms.

"Okay," she whispers, tracing small circles with her fingers on my chest. I wait for something more, but she remains quiet, her head resting on my heart.

"I'm not sure when I will be back. Maybe a week or two. I will have Benji come by each day and check on you two," I say to her, wanting her to know that I am not leaving her like last time. I rub her arm, her bare skin is soft under my touch, and it makes my chest ache. I don't want to leave.

"Don't worry about us, we will be fine," she says, trying to sound reassuring. "I have a hectic week at work with the building assessors coming in for the redevelopment. Plus, Ivy has school and soccer, so we will both be busy," I feel a bit more settled knowing that she will be busy with lots of people around her.

"Any news from your ex? Has Donovan progressed anything?" I ask for the first time, wanting to know if that's something I should be concerned about while I'm gone. She seems open with her affairs, but we haven't spent a lot of time talking about it.

"Donovan said the paperwork is all ready to be filed. I hope to look over everything with him tomorrow and then he will submit it all. From what I know, it may take some time, but he will be served, as will my father." I have so many more questions about the men in her life and what they have done, but I don't want to spend more time naked, in her bed, talking about them.

"You're the strongest woman I know, Cat."

Turning her head to look up at me, she presses a kiss to my chest. And we don't have to say anything else. As I brush my hand through her hair and cup her face, her eyes gazing into mine, I know she believes me. That she feels like that woman right now.

"Let's have a shower. I want my hands all over your body again." Moving my hands down her curves, I squeeze her ass. "Plus, I have a swollen appendage that I think needs your medical attention," I add with a smile, and she laughs.

Sitting up from the bed, I take her with me. I am a little stiff from the fight last night, but nothing like I usually am, so I lift her up into my arms. Her naked body wraps around mine, and I carry her with me to the bathroom, placing her on the floor near the shower.

As she leans in and turns on the hot water, I admire her body. Sure, I have seen it multiple times now, but it has always been in the heat of passion, and I have to say that Cat is by far the sexiest woman I have ever seen.

"Hmmm, what are you looking at?" she murmurs to me, as she steps under the water.

"I'm looking at you and wondering how good you are going to look when you are bouncing up and down on my cock in just a minute," I answer her honestly, and I see her eyes flash in surprise.

I don't hesitate. I stalk into the shower and back her up against the tiled wall.

"Carter?"

I don't reply. Instead, I let my hands do the talking as I grip her around the thighs and hoist her up, positioning myself at her entrance.

"Fuck, you are beautiful, Doctor Wakeford." As I slowly push into her, her head falls back against the tiles and her hands loop around my neck.

She moans my name, her hands digging into my skin, and I watch the water stream down her breasts before I take one of them in my mouth and suck. Hard. Biting a little, knowing that she likes it.

I start to move then, my hands gripping onto her ass as I thrust into her. Hitting deep, her legs tighten around my waist, hanging on for dear life because I can't get enough.

The intensity I feel with her makes me lose control, the need I have to ravish her running strong. This is going to be hard and fast because if this is the last time we are together for a week, then I want her to remember me for those entire seven days. Every time she moves, every time she showers, every time she fucking breathes, I want her to know that she is mine.

"You feel so good, Carter," she pants out, her hips moving in rhythm with my thrusts. Her bouncing tits look fucking edible, and I move my face lower to suck the other one into my mouth, biting and mauling her sensitive flesh, not able to get close enough, not able to get enough of her, full stop.

Lifting my head, I take in her wanton expression, her head back, eyes hooded, pouty lips parted on small whimpers. My need for her grows with every show of her desire, and I grip onto her even tighter, no doubt leaving marks behind.

"Are you going to come for me, Cat? Are you going to let go and show me exactly what I do to you?" I grit out, the heat's building up within me, my balls getting tight as I continue to slam into her over and over again. Her fingernails are leaving marks of her own, tearing me up, as I lift her up and down my cock at a vicious pace.

"Carter, yes, I'm going to... I'm going to..." she pants, and I can feel her pulsing around me, so close to the finish line, and bringing me with her.

"Look at me, baby."

And she does. Those gorgeous brown eyes gaze right into mine as she comes undone for me, my name leaving her lips on a breathless scream, face contorted in her pleasure. She looks amazing.

There is not much that I do right in my life, but right here, right now, if I can make her smile, laugh, and feel this good every day for the rest of my days, then I will die a very happy man.

As her body moves under my thrusts, I don't have much time to enjoy it, as watching her sends me over the edge. My muscle clench, and I yell her name, emptying myself inside of her, burying my head into the crook of her neck, kissing her, biting her, not ever able to get enough of her.

As we catch our breath, I slowly lower her back down

onto her feet and grab the soap, lathering her up, not waiting for her, the dreamy look in her eye telling me that she had a very good time just now. I want to look after her before she leaves to go to work, which will no doubt be a twelve-hour shift before backing it up day after day for the next week while I am gone.

"That was amazing," she says, looking up at me, a big grin on her face that is contagious.

"It was. I look forward to a lot more showers like that from now on, if that is all right with you?" Leaning over, I kiss her, swallowing her murmur of approval. Her hands travel up my chest, before they loop around the back of my neck, and she holds me in the kiss as my hands cup round her hips, feeling the water cascade down her curves. Her soft body I know is all mine.

I never knew it could be like this. The boys call me pussy-whipped, and Benji thinks it is hilarious that I have actually found a woman who wants to be with me, but if I am truly honest with myself, I did not expect this and did not think my life would ever be filled with this type of sexual appetite for one person. I am permanently hungry only for her.

We finish up in the shower, and I walk out to the kitchen to get the coffee going while Cat gets ready for work. As I do, there is a knock at the front door.

"That's Maggie!" Cat yells out from the bedroom.

"I'll get it!" I say before moving to the front door and opening it.

"Hey, Cat, I just have to—" Maggie starts, not expecting me to be the one at the door.

"Sorry! Hey, Carter," she corrects herself, looking a bit embarrassed.

"Hey, Mags, you coming in?" I ask her as I grab Ivy and hoist her up for a hug.

"Hey, Little Cub."

"Hey, Carter!" Ivy says in glee, her little arms wrapping around my neck, squeezing me tight.

"Sorry, Carter, tell Cat I will catch her later. I am late for my morning meeting. Bye, Ivy! I'll see you at soccer practice later!" Maggie waves to us, and I hold Ivy in my arms as we close the door and go back for breakfast.

"Hey, sweetheart," Cat says to Ivy as she takes her from my arms, giving her a big hug before planting her on the kitchen stool.

"Breakfast?" Cat asks me as I sit on a stool next to Ivy.

I shake my head, knowing that I need to go home and pack. I have barely been in my apartment since coming back to Philly, my life firmly revolving around the gym and my fight, and then being here with the girls. My mood sours as I'm reminded I'll be away from them, as I watch Cat get busy in the kitchen, grabbing a coffee.

"I've gotta leave this morning, Little Cub, but I will be back," I say to Ivy quickly and notice Cat watching the exchange from the other side of the bench.

"You promise you're coming back, Carter? We had an agreement."

"I promise, Ivy, you can't get rid of me that easily. Besides, we're best friends, right?" I say as I pull the necklace out from under my top, and her eyes light up with a smile.

My face falls for a second, and I look at Cat quickly before looking back at Ivy.

"You call me Ivy, for anything. Even just to tell me a random animal fact you learned at school or something. Doesn't matter what it's about, you can always call."

"Okay, Carter. I will," she agrees, and even though she doesn't say it, I know she is sad that I am going. I watch Ivy for a moment, and she looks at me. "Carter, did you know that hummingbirds are the only birds that can fly backwards?"

"No, Ivy, I did not know that," I reply with a smirk as I shake my head. This kid is a walking internet search.

When I look at Cat, her face says it all. She is scared, and I know she doesn't want me to go, but like the amazing woman she is, she is not asking me to stay because that is a decision I am not sure I am ready to make yet. Choosing her over Sebastian is not something I have thought about a lot, but when Sebastian calls, I go. That is the way it has always been. But she is becoming a very big part of my life, one I hope only grows, so what that means for the future, I can't yet determine. For right now, I need to live life like I always have, and that means working between two cities for a while.

I catch her eye, and she gives me a smile, again trying to reassure me she will be all right. It's the doctor in her, always looking after everyone else, and pushing herself to the side. I see her do it, with Ivy, with me. Something else I hope to remedy in time. I want to show her that she matters more than anything.

"Okay, I gotta head out," I say reluctantly, standing, which prompts Ivy to jump up and give me a big hug.

"Bye, Little Cub." I hug her back tightly.

"Bye, Bear," she says, and I grin, looking at her in question.

"Bear?" I ask.

"Yeah, you're like a big cuddly teddy bear," she says with a smile, and I hear Cat laugh behind her. I can't say anyone has ever called me a teddy bear before.

"Be good for your mom, okay?" She nods, and I walk over to Cat.

"Bye, baby. You call me, for anything." I say, wrapping my arms around her. "Don't hesitate, not for a second, okay?" I take a serious tone, looking her in the eye, wanting to ensure she understands I am still here for her, even though I will be miles away.

"Okay, but don't worry, we will be fine." I tighten my grip around her and kiss the ever-loving fuck out of her.

"Ew! You guys!" Ivy says from next to us, and Cat laughs. I grab her ass, where her daughter can't see, seeing her eyes light up in response to my manhandling. She loves it.

"Lock up behind me, yeah?" I say to the girls, who both follow me to the door and stand there watching me as I step out.

I turn and take one last look at them both. Cat looking like sex on legs at the door, waving goodbye. Wearing her work attire, the same navy dress and black heels she was in when we first met. I stifle a groan, because I still need to fuck her with those sexy as sin black heels on. I have lost count on the number of times I have imagined her naked underneath me, her legs over my shoulders, those black heels near my ears since the day we met at the hospital. I decide then and there that is exactly what I will do with her as soon as I get back.

37

CARTER

I sit in our meeting room at the compound, perplexed. Sebastian has been eyeing me from across the table since the moment he walked in five minutes ago, and I don't like it one bit.

"What the fuck is going on?" I finally ask, cutting through the general chit-chat from Dante and Nico.

"What do you know about her?" Sebastian quizzes me. Pulling his head back and looking at me down his nose, and my eyes crinkle in question. Where he is going with this?

"She's a doctor, a very fucking good one," I say as my eyes flick to Dante quickly, and he nods in agreement. "She is a mom to a little girl named Ivy. She moved to Philly almost a year ago to get away from her ex here in New York. I saw him once at the grocery store, trying to intimidate her. He is a prick who looks like he has plenty of money. But she is scared of him. I'm sure he's hit her, as her father has too. She is trying to legally separate from the both of them at the moment. She also takes self-defense classes at my gym." I watch for Sebastian's response.

"So he is a woman beater, then?" Sebastian grits out. He hates violence against women. We all do. "What else?" Sebastian prods, and I am beginning to feel unnerved.

"She has a sister, Maggie, a nice woman, with a family of her own. Their mother died when she was younger. And as I said, her dad is an asshole, from what I can tell."

"Anything else?" I need to take a breath because this is really starting to piss me off. Dante didn't get this treatment about Annie, and so what the hell has gotten into Sebastian.

"She looked scared when I left her this morning. Her house is secured with cameras, intercoms, and double doors. She has a lawyer who is working on the paperwork to extract her and Ivy from the ex. She seems hesitant with her father, as I said, he hit her, Ivy is scared of him too. She hasn't signed off on the intervention order for him yet, though. I have Benji keeping an eye on them while I am out of town." I look at Dante and Nico before looking back at Sebastian, and they seem as confused as I am.

Sebastian nods. "Could she be faking it?" he asks, and for the first time in my life, I don't like what Sebastian is proposing here.

"You think she makes up the bruises on her face?" I ask with a bite, my voice getting louder, fists clenching. "You think I can't see the fear in her eyes, the tears that run down her cheeks when she thinks I am not looking?"

"You're in love, Carter. You're blind to it if it is there,"

Sebastian says to me simply, like he is discussing the weather.

"She is not a liar," I grit out, ignoring the love comment.

"She seems all kosher to me, Sebastian. She is a great doctor, has even spoken to Annie about leaving New York and wanting to get away from her ex," Dante offers, and I thank God I have back-up because I am starting to feel like I am missing something.

"You know I need to be 100% sure about people before they can come into the fold. Just because she is special to you, Carter, doesn't mean I don't investigate," Sebastian says, his face still not giving away anything. "I checked out Annie just as closely." He looks at Dante, and I see shock on Dante's face, none of us knowing what lengths he goes to, but assuming he is pretty thorough.

Sebastian throws a file onto the table, and it slides across the polished timber surface, stopping right in front of me.

"What the hell is this?" I grab the file and start flicking through the contents.

"This is information I gleaned a few days ago from my sources. It appears that her ex-boyfriend is a Mr. Daniel Cole, and is going to be up against our man Roy, running for senator. He has huge money behind him from his own father and his pals. One of which is a doctor named Thomas Wakeford," Sebastian says as I start to look at the information in front of me.

"Apparently, at the City Gala Dinner tonight, he will be not only announcing his run for senator, but also their engagement," Sebastian spits out, and my world implodes.

I sit in shock. Reeling. My chest tightening, lungs seizing.

I'm quiet as I study a photograph in my hand. It is her, with him by her side, but it looks to be a few years old. She looks beautiful, there is no denying it, but her smile doesn't reach her eyes. No, this can't be true. She's been honest... I know it.

I raise my eyes and look at Sebastian, giving nothing away. "Go on," I say, asking him for further information.

"They want Daniel in as senator so they can run drugs," Sebastian says, steepling his hands together under his chin.

"Brian Cole is using his son to get ownership of the docks and influence over the city police. Essentially, he wants what we have got, and I am not planning on giving it to him." Leaning back in his chair, he continues to watch me, waiting for my reaction.

"Her father is a retired heart surgeon, and wealthy beyond measure. He is funding 50% of Daniel's campaign." I lean over and pick up the photo.

"What is his stake in the game, then?" Dante asks, as we all try to piece together the players.

"Well, it seems like he is a significant investor in Cole Logistics, so he will benefit greatly from the increased access to supplies from the docks," Sebastian answer, having already done his homework on a lot of this.

"So he is making his eldest daughter marry this asshole, who treats her like shit, to then have him run for senator, all to line his own pockets?" I surmise, and I can already feel the anger swelling inside of me. These men have money. A lot of money. They are also well known and well liked in the elite New York community. This whole issue is getting bigger and more entangled as we talk.

"No way," Nico says. "Did she play you?" he asks, gaping at me. "Did she play all of us?" he repeats, looking around the table.

Sebastian is livid, Dante is confused, and I am gripping white-knuckled onto the table, about to fucking explode.

If she is engaged, I have never seen a sparkling diamond on her finger. I don't believe it.

"Daniel Cole is a white male, mid-thirties, heart surgeon in New York. Son of Brian Cole, the boss of Cole Logistics and many other businesses, who is currently using his son as a puppet to get his way with the supply chain running in and out of New York," Dante says, reading what we already know from the file. I remain silent, trying to work through the jumbled mess in my head.

She couldn't have played me...

I knew something was up with Sebastian, but I was not prepared for this. Staring down at the photo of Cat that remains in my hand.

I pull my phone from my pocket and dial her number. It goes to voicemail straight away, so it must be off.

"She isn't answering, but you have got this all wrong, Sebastian," I mutter, but Sebastian looks at me questioningly. I don't care what he thinks, she hasn't lied.

Love, as Sebastian pointed out.

I am in love with her. There is no doubt, there has never been any doubt. She is it for me.

Throwing the papers across the table, I get up and storm out the room. I need air, need to get out of the confines of this space, and hit something or someone.

I pace down the hall and run down the stairs to the only place I know that will help me. The gym. Walking through the massive room, I tear off my shirt and remain in my jeans before getting to the bag and throwing punches. One after the other, my fists hit the vinyl, smashing into the bag.

I hit until my arms feel numb, sweat pouring from my body, and I slump on the floor to catch my breath. I am a mix of emotions. I don't know what to feel or who to believe.

Grabbing my cell, I try to call her again, but she still isn't answering. My head fills with scenarios... she could be in surgery, she could be busy with Ivy, or is she with her new fiancé, and they're all having a laugh behind my back.

I decide to call the hospital and ask to speak with Ian.

"Hi, Carter," Ian says, being professional.

"Where is she?" I grit out, barely able to contain my anger at the situation at this point.

"What do you mean? Cat? She didn't come in today. It is unusual, and I have been trying to call her cell, but no answer," he says, and I don't even say goodbye before I hang up the phone.

I look at the clock, noticing it is late afternoon. I make one more call, hitting the number to Maggie.

"Hello," she says, her voice rushed and panting like she is running.

"It's Carter. Where is she?" I growl, no longer playing Mr. Nice Guy.

"Oh my God, Carter. She has gone! Her and Ivy have disappeared. Ivy didn't turn up to school today, and Cat didn't show to work. I only noticed when they were both supposed to be at soccer, but they weren't there. I have been calling everyone, but no one has seen her. Something is wrong, Carter. My dad, Daniel, I don't know, but I have been calling them, and no one is answering."

"Fuck," I spit out and end the call, my head not even functioning right. My blood has turned to ice. She has either played me or been taken, and either option is not the one I want to hear.

I need to find her. Now.

It's a good thing that Sebastian has tickets to the Gala tonight, because I already know she will be there.

38

CATHERINE

Ivy sits on my lap, burying her head into my chest, her eyes screwed up tight and body shaking with fear. I am frightened, but I am also livid.

How can they do this to such a little girl? How can they do this to me?

I watch as Daniel and my father walk into the opulent space of my father's living room. We're in his high-rise penthouse apartment, one I haven't been in for a very long time. It hasn't changed except for the photos that are now gone. Every image of my mother has now vanished. What was once a shrine to her on the side table is now a bar cart full of expensive whiskey.

My father comes toward us, and all I see is extreme disappointment on his face. Yet as I look up at him, I realize that I am the one that is disappointed. Disappointed and now very, very angry. I'm disappointed in myself for not seeing him for who he really is before now. Disappointed that I couldn't protect Ivy from them all. But angry, so very angry, that these men in my life are using me as a pawn in whatever game they are trying to play.

"Still a fucking disappointment," my father's voice drips with disgust, and I don't know how I have never seen it before. He has no love for me. No love for Ivy or Maggie, and I begin to wonder if he ever even loved my mom.

"We let you go off and have your fun, flirting yourself through Philly while we waited patiently for you to come back," he continues, and I squint my eyes, trying to understand what he is saying.

My eyes flick to Daniel, his gaze fiery and hands on his hips. "Did you fuck him?" he spits out at me, and I pull Ivy closer to me. This conversation is jumping around so much I am getting whiplash.

"Carter Grange... Did you FUCK HIM?!" Daniel screams, stepping closer to me with every word.

"You've been watching me?" I ask in shock as it sets in, looking between him and my father. My father rolls his eyes, like I am a stupid girl, and perhaps I am. I should have known they would never have just let me leave New York that easily. I have always been part of their plan; it has just taken me until now to see it.

"Fucking whore!" Daniel yells out to the room, the anger at someone else having me when I won't give myself to him evident. Ivy curls herself closer to me, whimpering. This conversation is not for little ears, so I hug her tighter, hoping to muffle the words that slice like knives through me.

It all happened so fast this morning. One minute, we were saying goodbye to Carter and getting ready for work and school, then the next, I turn and see both Daniel and my father in my kitchen, along with some goons who were not interested in being gentle as they grabbed me and my daughter and threw us into a blackened car, racing us to a private airfield.

We were in a private jet and in New York within an hour.

Now as we cling together, my father paces the floor in front of us, and Daniel looks like he is on the verge of violence.

"Fuck it," my dad says as he comes to a stop in front of me. Leaning down, he grabs Ivy, who immediately starts screaming and reaching for me. I follow suit.

"No! NO! Leave her alone!! Give her to me!" I scream so loud my throat burns as he peels Ivy away from my hands, carrying her out in front of him, like she is infected with a virus. Daniel steps in front of me when I go to chase after them, halting my attempts with a firm grip that I fight with all my might.

"Mommy!!!" Ivy screams, tears running down her face as my father walks her out of the room.

"IVY!!!!" Daniel pulls me away from her, farther into the room and around the corner, slamming my body back onto the sofa as my screaming daughter is taken out of my sight, to somewhere I don't know.

"Where is he taking her?" I demand as I stand back up again, looking at Daniel, who is mere inches in front of me.

"Play by our rules, and she will be safe. You will see her tonight. Go rogue, and you will never see her again." He's speaking in a voice I haven't heard him use before, and a shiver runs up my spine. I look at him with tears in my eyes, my breathing labored, and watch as he brings his arm up slowly and strokes my cheek with the back of his hand.

My father walks back into the room, straightening his clothes, and running his hand through his hair. Walking up to us, he looks at me like I am filth. I would do anything for my daughter, and as I look at my father, I know for certain that he was never the man I thought he was. He is pure evil, money and status the only things that matter to him.

"Now, are you willing to start playing by our rules, because quite frankly, dear, your little tantrum of running off to Philly and the adolescent way you are conducting yourself down there with a known associate of the mob makes me question your worth," my father says in his most condescending tone, as he goes to the bar cart and pours himself a tumbler of whiskey.

"If you touch a hair on her head, I swear to God—" I start to say, but before I finish, Daniel's fist flies forward into my stomach, and I double over in pain.

Gasping for air, I keel over, my arms wrapping around my middle as Daniel leans over me. "I can't go smashing that pretty face before the photos of our engagement tonight, but I can and I will make you fall into line. You belong to me now, so don't you forget it," he sneers, and I throw up all over his shoes.

"Fucking bitch!" he yells, punching me in the side, and I crumble onto the floor. The burn through my torso is intense, I have no idea how Carter does this for fun. My breath leaves me, my lungs stalled. I'm winded and try not to panic as I can't expand my chest for a few moments.

If I ever make it out of here, I will be upping my self-defense training. I didn't push myself as much as I should have to be prepared for this. I couldn't feel any more pathetic right now.

My eyes water as I look up and see my father standing back, looking at us, taking a sip of his whiskey like he is watching his favorite sitcom for entertainment.

I already know I am going to be bruised black and blue, but it doesn't compare to my broken heart at having Ivy ripped away from me, and at having my father stare at me like I am nothing.

Carter.

If only I could call him, my cell phone now in pieces on the side of the road somewhere between my house and the private airfield.

"We have been watching you. We know who you have been spending time with. Really, Catherine, I expected more from you than a low life criminal," my Father says, taking another sip of his whiskey, not at all concerned that his daughter is on her knees, in pain and struggling to breathe.

"Your little Philly boyfriend can't save you now. We will be engaged tonight, and he is not going to come near you again," Daniel spits.

Evil. That's what they are. Powerful rich men who will stop at nothing to get what they want. More money, more networks, more, more, more. My thoughts spiral with every throb of pain running through me... If I never meant anything to either of them, then maybe I really have probably been a pawn for them since the beginning. Since I graduated from med school, or even earlier. No wonder Daniel never took to Ivy, and no wonder my dad never showed Maggie or I any affection. I always thought he changed after mom died, but If I really think back, he was never home before then either. The love in our house all came from our mother. My dad was never the caring, loving type. We were always a nuisance to him.

I shake myself out of it.

"He will kill you. Both of you." And I hope he does. Because now I know that if and when it comes down to it, if we become a liability, they'll kill me and Ivy. There's no question about that.

"Ha, I don't think so. Daniel will win the senator role, and the city will be ours. Your little soldier and his boss, Sebastian, will run back to Italy with their tails between their legs while the big boys come to own the city," my father says as Brian Cole, Daniel's father, walks in. A tall chubby man, his chest puffs out, and he commands all the attention in the room. One of the wealthiest men in New York, he runs a logistics business, I think, although he has his fingers in so many things these days, I really have no idea what he does for a living.

Like my mother, his wife died in a car accident years ago, and now he has a scantily clad woman half his age gripping onto his forearm with her red-polished fingers. I look at him, then Daniel and back again. They look alike, their mannerisms similar, and I can only hope that his daughter and Daniel's sister, Emilia, is far, far away from them because like me, she deserves so much better.

"Gents," he greets as he leaves the woman with my

father and comes to stand beside Daniel, looking down at me like I'm a piece of rubbish.

"Are we all sorted for tonight, then? Will she get into line?" He talks about me like I am not even in the room, and I can't believe this is the man who expects me to be his daughter-in-law.

"She will because we have the girl, and she won't see the girl again unless she does," my father says, eyeing me, and I can't believe he is calling Ivy *"the girl."* She is his goddamn granddaughter!

"Ahhh... yes, my granddaughter, pretty little thing she is," Brian Cole says, walking back toward my father, no longer interested in me.

"You have a role to play, Daniel. Don't fuck it up." Daniel nods to him, tight-lipped and serious.

"Who's this?" my father asks, looking at the blonde woman who now stands between the two of them, again talking like she isn't in the room, and I notice that she is looking everywhere except at me.

"She took the edge off. You can have her later," Brian says, as if she's a possession. But that is all they want— possessions. They want people to do as they say, not as they do. They want ownership of everything and everyone.

And now they have me and Ivy, and I will do *anything* for my little girl. So as the three men tower above me, I know there is no escape for me.

I need to do what they tell me to.

I need to do it for Ivy.

39

CATHERINE

My feet are squished into sparkling strappy high heels, my hair blow dried within an inch of its life, and as the makeup artist finishes applying the gloss to my lips, I begin to feel woozy.

"Darling, you look so beautiful," Daniel says to me in front of the team doing my hair, makeup, and styling, that he hired to get me ready for the gala tonight. He walks up to me, placing a kiss on my cheek, giving me a knowing look before I take a deep breath in.

"Thank you," I say graciously, when all I really want to do is rip his eyes out of their sockets so he never looks at me again.

"Awe, you two are such a cute couple," the makeup artist comments innocently as he starts packing up his kit, and I want to vomit all over again.

I look at my appearance in the large mirror and although my insides are full of turmoil, on the outside, I look like the perfect fiancée to an upcoming senator.

Impeccable makeup that hides any minute flaw, sleek hair flowing over my shoulders, sparkling jewels coating my neck, wrists, and now finger, the large 6-carat emerald cut weighing me down into the pits of despair. A gorgeous red gown sticking to my body, showing off my shape and falling to the floor. I am a real-life pretty woman.

I haven't seen Ivy since they ripped her from my arms this afternoon. They have locked her up in a room on the opposite side of my father's large penthouse, with the promise that I can see her as soon as we get home, provided that I play the part and don't do anything to jeopardize the evening.

So even though I want to run, want to scream and fight, I can't. I will not do anything that may harm Ivy, and I will do everything they ask. I have no other choice.

"It's time to go, sweetheart. Here is your bag," Daniel prompts me, and my eyes leave the mirror and look at him, his lips tight, and shoulders stiff. I nod my head slowly, taking the bag, and I grip onto his elbow that he offers. We walk out of the room like a beautiful, happily in love couple.

I try to keep it together as we make our way down the hall into the front foyer, and as we step into the elevator, I can't help but glance down the hall, hoping to see my daughter, to hear her or get any type of signal that she is all right.

"She is fine, but won't be if you do anything stupid," Daniel mumbles to me, as he pulls me into the elevator.

Tonight is a big night for Daniel and my father. The stakes are high, a perfect image needs to be presented, and I am part of that arrangement. If I act properly in public, then Ivy and I can be together in private. That is the deal.

Once the voting public love us and Daniel becomes senator, I hope the pressure can ease off me a little, but the more I think about it, I wonder if I will be relieved of my duties some other way. No longer needed, a widowed senator would be well regarded, especially if his wife and daughter are killed in an "accident." Perhaps a car accident, just like my mother. It would be very poetic.

The drive is short, and as the limo pulls up, I look out the window and see crowds of people, journalists, paparazzi, and I have to take a deep breath.

"Remember to smile. We are in love, darling, so let's show the people what we are all about," Daniel says, a mask slipping into place as he smiles broadly and the driver opens his door.

Do it for Ivy. Do it for Ivy.

My mantra repeats in my head as I step out of the car and paste a large smile on my face, taking Daniel's hand and letting him lead the way.

Daniel smiles and waves, and as we walk in, lights are flashing, blinding me. I lift my hand to push my hair back, and the crowd goes wild, more flashes appearing, and I realize it is because they all want a photo of the ring. My heart rate increases as the media scrum starts shouting questions, and I am bewildered as I see Daniel laugh in glee, confirming to everyone that, yes, we are, in fact, engaged. His hand leaves mine and then wraps around my middle, pulling me tight, and the pain from the earlier hits jolts through my body. I suck in my breath as my eyes water slightly.

"Smile for the cameras, darling," Daniel grits into my ear, although it looks more like he is kissing my cheek. I smile softly, not meeting anyone's eyes as I look around at the crowd.

Do it for Ivy. Do it for Ivy.

As we step into the venue, Daniel greets a few more men in suits, and then grabs me a champagne from a passing waiter. I don't drink it, I just carry it around, not wanting to drop my guard, needing to be alert to every-thing and everyone.

My father and Brian come up to greet us, and soon a photographer is in front of the four of us, snapping away. My father stands next to me, his smile wide as his hand comes around my middle, and I take another sharp breath in as the pain from my beating earlier today pulsates through my muscles again. In this tight dress, it continues to radiate around my torso like a python grip-ping me into a death hold.

I know how these photos will look. My father will appear like the proud, doting parent, next to his beautiful daughter. I have seen photos like it in the past, but now with an inside view, I know they are all fake. All for show, never for genuine love.

Before too long, we are asked to take our seats and the formalities begin. I smile and nod at the appropriate times, making small talk around the table with the other ladies, all of them admiring my ring and passing on their best wishes.

The night progresses in equal parts slow motion and

high speed, and the speeches go on forever until Daniel grabs my elbow, and I escort him to the side of the stage.

"Now, ladies and gentlemen, we are proud to officially announce Daniel Cole will be running for New York Senator!" The announcement is made, and holding hands, we walk onto the stage, like a happy couple. Flashes go off, and the crowd cheer, all the while my stomach curls in on itself. As Daniel takes the podium, I stand like a supportive partner to the side, looking at him like he is my everything, when all I really want to do is run.

Do it for Ivy. Do it for Ivy.

Daniel talks for ten minutes about the city, his plans if elected, and all the hopeful dreams he has, none of which are his own or that he will even implement.

"I would also like to take this opportunity to introduce my beautiful fiancée, Catherine Wakeford," he says with hearts in his wicked eyes, looking over his shoulder at me. The crowd cheers like I am a celebrity, and not currently in a hostage situation, and I smile and wave like a good politician's wife-to-be.

"Without her constant love and support, I would not be the man I am today, and together we look forward to leading the great state of New York and becoming your senator elect," he finishes, and I clap along with the rest of the crowd, trying to smile while bile rises in my throat.

As we step off the stage, Daniel receives many pats on the back and handshakes, my father giving me a kiss on the cheek and smiling for everyone as the bright lights beam down on us from above.

I feel overheated, overwhelmed, and I need some space. Grabbing Daniel's arm, I lean into his ear.

"I need a refreshment break. I will be right back," I say to him, and his head whips around, nostrils flaring.

"Five minutes," he says quietly, and I nod, agreeing to the time limit. I smile to everyone and step away from the crowd, making my way to find the bathroom.

Being stopped every three steps for people to shake my hand and offer their best wishes is suffocating me even more, but I smile broadly, thanking them and playing my part.

I see the bathroom and put my head down to avoid any more attention, lifting my gown a little to make a quick dash for it as.

I push through the door and look around, pleased to see it entirely empty, as my walls feel like they are closing in. Leaning over the sink with my head down, I close my eyes and try to concentrate on my breathing, counting to slow down my racing heart.

Do it for Ivy. Do it for Ivy. Do it for Ivy.

40

CARTER

I am going to fucking end this motherfucker because as I stand in the room, looking at the grandeur, my eyes hone in on one person and one person only. Cat. Standing right by his side.

She is fucking breathtaking as the lights dance off her face, her hair, her dress, looking sexy as sin and fucking smiling as she stands on the stage, supporting her fucking fiancé.

I watch them from the dark corner of the room, Sebastian and Dante and Nico placed nearby as I survey what is happening. Pulling at the collar of my navy three-piece suit, my black shiny shoes show the reflection of my clear dislike for the man. Us four boys looked like a menacing but well-dressed sight as we walked in tonight. All ticket holders, Sebastian has been working the room quietly, us others hiding in the shadows. We caught the attention of a few people when we walked in, most who looked the other way, and some even hot-footed it to the other side of the room.

And they should run. Because my anger is palatable, and as I watch him up on stage, looking lovingly at her, I decide then and there if I could kill him right now, I would.

No hesitation.

But then my eyes flick around the room to see the hundreds of people who would witness my attack. No expense has been spared for this event. The room overflows with flowers, the scent running up my nostrils every time I turn my head. People are dressed to the nines in ball gowns and tuxedos while black-tied waiters scurry around, ensuring everyone is looked after and every demand is met for our senator wannabe. The opulence is repugnant; the money these people have is obscene. We are wealthy, probably just as wealthy as these people, but we share our wealth with many, we invest, and we don't flaunt.

It is called having class, and these people have none.

"She looks pretty happy to me, Carter," Sebastian grits out from behind me. I can feel his anger at the situation pouring out of him, but it is no match for my own.

I watch her closely, and my gut churns. Her playing me is what a man like me should expect. That is what I deserve. After everything I have done, all the lives I have ended. And even though Sebastian's voice is a constant in my mind, I know she didn't do anything. Deep down, I know she is still my safe place.

"Something isn't right. She wouldn't play me like this," I say to him as my eyes remain fixed on her. I see her step off the stage and greet her father, a crowd swarming them.

"It could all have been to get intel on us," he grits out, wanting me to determine by looking at her from across the room if his suspicions are right. I shake my head in disbelief.

I thought what we had was real. It felt more real than anything else I have ever had in my life.

As she grabs Daniel's upper arm to get his attention, I spot the large diamond sparkler on her finger. It is new, and I haven't seen it before. Not on her hand, not on her dresser at home, not on her bedside table, not anywhere.

Something isn't right; she is smiling, a big, bright smile that's beautiful and contagious to everyone around her. But it isn't reaching her eyes. I see how she moves away from her father and whispers something to Daniel, and then she steps away.

I stalk her, sticking to the outer rim of the room, watching her interact with people, playing the role of dutiful fiancée, carrying champagne, yet noticing that she doesn't take a sip. She hasn't all night.

She puts her head down and walks quickly then, and as I spot where she is going, my legs are moving before I even know what I am about to do. I see the bathrooms and I wait for her to enter, then a few more moments to ensure no one else follows her.

Stepping into the bathroom, I spot her leaning over the sink, her head down.

"Cat," I grit out, my anger at the situation palpable as I watch her. She's so fucking beautiful, and she's so fucking mine. Why is she here?

"Carter!" she says in surprise as she stands up, her head whipping around in shock.

"Oh my God. No, you can't be here. I can't be seen with you," she whispers fiercely, now panicking, grabbing her purse, her hands fidgeting. I know something isn't right.

"What the fuck are you doing here with him?" I spit out, harsher than I mean to.

"Keep your voice down," she reprimands me as she comes close, her hands cupping my jaw, her eyes glassy.

"Carter," she says my name breathily as she puts her lips to mine, and every small but nagging negative thought I had melts away in that instant, my hands coming to hold her face, wanting to keep her close. But as quick as she kissed me, she pulls away.

"What the hell is going on?" I ask her in a grating whisper, my eyes searching hers for the answer I don't think she'll give me.

"I love you, Carter. So much." She says the words that fill my soul like it is goodbye, and my stomach falls to my feet as I watch a lone tear fall from her eye.

"Cat, tell me what the hell is going on?" I press, but she is shaking her head, her eyes looking around the bathroom, and she starts to walk toward the bathroom door. I grip her arm as she goes, trying to stop her.

"I need to go. Please, Carter, please let me go." Her voice becomes more desperate as she tries to free herself of my grip. The sheer fear in her face has me releasing her arm as I look at her in shock, raising my eyebrows.

"Cat, just talk to me. I can help." I know deep down something is going on. Taking a breath, she stares into my eyes, and I can see the internal battle there. I can't not hold her for another moment. Grabbing her around the waist, she yelps out in pain, and I pause, lifting my hands away like I touched fire.

"What did—" I start, looking at her wide-eyed. My gaze travels up and down her body, assessing her, and I notice the way she hugs herself, the way she seems pained to breathe.

"What did they fucking do to you?" I grit out, wanting to kill every last motherfucker in this room.

"Please, Carter, please, I need to go.. They are watching me..." she begs me, and I don't know what to fucking do.

"Someone will come looking for me... someone can probably hear our entire conversation, Carter! I need to go..." she whispers harshly, her hands now trembling and voice coming out choked. Fear is painted all over her face.

She starts to walk away from me again, backwards toward the bathroom door, and out of my grip. I stand in total shock and watch her, before she stops, looking up at me with a glimmer of determination.

"Stegodyphus lineatus," she says, her eyes pleading with mine, and I have no idea what she is talking about.

"From the zoo, Carter. The spider. Stegodyphus lineatus," she repeats, like I'm supposed to know what the fuck she is talking about. And I'm so beyond confused and filled with anger, I can't even move or respond. I see her eyes begin to water before she spins and walks out the door.

The bang of the door has me jolting, and I get a grip on myself. Fuck my girls and their animal references. I haven't yet had the heart to tell them I didn't finish school and have no idea what they talk about half the time.

Their knowledge is one of their most incredible qualities to me.

I wait a moment and walk out after her, watching as she greets Daniel, him grabbing her arm and then parading around for a moment longer, talking to people and shaking hands before he whisks her out the door, leaving for the night with daddy dearest following suit.

I pull out my phone and start to research this fucking spider. She mentioned we saw it at the zoo, so I go straight to the zoo's website, but I can't remember a fucking thing about it. Where is Ivy when you need her?

"What the fuck is going on?" Sebastian barks as he, Dante, and Nico crowd around me, and we make ourselves inconspicuous at the back of the room.

"Stegodyphus lineatus. She said something about a Stegodyphus lineatus... It was a spider we saw at the zoo a while ago," I say, my head down, searching the zoo website, but finding nothing.

"Let me search it," Dante says, grabbing his cell. I continue to look through the information from the zoo in the hopes something comes to mind.

"The Stegodyphus lineatus is a spider from the southern Mediterranean," Dante says after finding it on an internet search.

"A spider? What the fuck has a spider got to do with anything?" Sebastian says, angrier because I know none of this is making any sense.

"The male is known to exhibit infanticide, by killing the offspring of already-mated females..." Dante says out loud before looking at me.

I roll the information over in my brain as Dante reads

on. "Infanticide increases the male's ability to force females who have already mated to mate again with them."

It comes to me then. "Fucking asshole. I am going to kill him. I am going to fucking gut him, then strangle him with his own fucking intestines," I grit out, looking at the boys who all look confused.

"They have Ivy and are baiting Cat with her own daughter to play the part," I say to the boys, everything now locking into place and Cat's scared face etched into my mind.

"I am going to slice him from fucking belly to throat and watch him bleed out!" I all but yell, trying to keep it contained, given the amount of people in the room.

"What the fuck?" Sebastian pulls back, looking at me in astonishment.

"In the bathroom, Cat told me about this animal we saw at the zoo the other day. She told me that they are watching her, was thinking they were listening in too, so she wouldn't answer my questions directly. It all makes sense now. They grabbed her and Ivy and now are forcing Cat to play a part so that Daniel can portray a happy, successful doctor to help him win the Senator seat," I say quickly, trying to get them all up to speed.

"So that they can win, and then get full control of the city," Dante finishes for me, everyone now fully understanding that she didn't play us at all.

"Fucking hell," Nico says in awe.

"We need to find out where they are holding her." My eyes flick around the room, hoping something or someone jumps out that may give us a clue.

"I put a tracker on their car. Our boys in the valet sorted us out," Nico says, and the three of us all look at him.

"Smart move, Nico," Sebastian says with a nod, approving his initiative before his eyes land on me. "She is smart, after all, your girl," Sebastian says to me, but I feel little pleasure in his observations, already murderous and out for blood.

We walk out of the room, moving as quickly as we can, weaving in between the guests and the staff and making our way outside. Our car is already out front and waiting, and as the four of us get in, Nico grabs his cell to see where they are.

"Straight ahead, then make a left. They are going down Fifth Avenue," Nico says, watching the blue dot of the car tracker on his map.

"Her father has a penthouse on Fifth on the Upper East Side," Sebastian adds, and Dante nods from the driver's seat, already knowing exactly where we need to go.

A penthouse is going to be hard to penetrate, so any ideas I had of walking into a house and grabbing her and Ivy and leaving are pushed from my mind. I try and work out ways for us to enter the building and get to the top floor. Whatever scenarios I think of will take time. A fire drill, walking in fully armed, all of the options will take too long... I need to get her tonight.

"Jesus..." Dante murmurs from the front, and I look up as we park across the street. It is an older apartment building, one of New York's finest, most established. Where the 'old-monied' residents live. Whilst it may not have all the mod cons, we are under no illusion that it will be any easier to enter. Some of New York's richest people live in this building, and they take their security very seriously.

"I need to get in there tonight," I grit out, my hear thumping, my skin crawling with tension as I try not to jump out of the car and do something really stupid.

"Fuck, let me think," Nico says, looking around the streets.

"What the fuck!" Sebastian barks out, leaning forward in his seat, his eyes looking into the brightly lit foyer.

We all follow his gaze, and I see a few men in the foyer, maintenance men, along with a guy who looks to be barking orders. He looks familiar, but I can't place him.

"Boys, we might have just been given a golden key," Dante whispers out as Sebastian pulls out his phone.

"William, walk out the front of the building and come across to the dark escalade, I need something from you," Sebastian says and then ends the call as abruptly as he made it, and it is then I remember the man.

It's William Walters, one of the lead Art Curators from the Maddison Miller Gallery. The gallery Sebastian's wife, Goldie, owns, and he is now my new best friend.

41

CATHERINE

The car ride home from the Gala was silent, but I get the eerie feeling that Daniel is not happy, and I know that the night is far from over. The only thing getting me through this is the need to see my daughter and the hope that Carter will be able to decipher my clue.

As the elevator opens to the penthouse, we walk into the living area and my body is racked with nerves. Pain radiates from my cheeks from the constant fake smiles I had to deliver, and the muscles around my torso continue to push and pull against each other, stinging and burning from the hard punches I endured this afternoon. My body was red earlier when I put on this stupid red dress, and I have a feeling it will be purple when I unzip it.

"I want to see Ivy," I demand as I throw my purse down on the armchair as soon as we enter the room. "I did as you said, I acted the part. Now I want to see my daughter." Daniel and my father both act aloof.

"I had to sedate her. She is sleeping," my father

replies, and my eyes shoot to him as my stomach drops. *He gave her medication without me knowing?*

My mother lioness is now alert.

"A sedative? What for? Which one?" I demand, infuriated they touched my daughter when they told me they wouldn't.

"To calm her down. She is just as painful as her mother, it would seem," he says as he takes a sip from his fresh glass of whiskey, not really caring for what I have to say. The arrogance of the man is astounding.

"You do not get to medicate my daughter! You do not touch her, you hear me! Do not touch Ivy!" I all but scream, fear for myself absent, but fear for my daughter overwhelming.

I am too busy looking at my father in anger to notice Daniel's hand rise and slam against the side of my face. I yelp as I fall down onto the plush carpet, and my forehead hits the coffee table on the way down.

Pain radiates through my head, my hand instinctively coming to source of pain, and feeling the wetness underneath. Blood now coats my hand, and there's no doubt a gash running across my forehead from the impact. I'm in too much shock to do anything about it, though.

"Stop Daniel." My father's commanding tone vibrates around the room, and I look at him, my gaze hazy, but I'm surprised he is coming to my defense.

Is he finally coming to his senses?

"You want me to become senator, then I will fucking treat her how I fucking want!" Daniel yells at him, and my father smirks.

"I don't care about her, but don't get any blood on my

new Egyptian rug. It came in from overseas last week, for fuck's sake." My blood runs cold as I stare at my father's back and watch him walk out of the room and down the hall.

"I WANT TO SEE IVY!" I scream from the floor, tears now overflowing onto my cheeks, defeat building in my bones. Daniel's foot lands on my side under my breast-bone, and I gasp for air at the shock of being kicked.

"I am not finished with you yet. You did well tonight, my love, but there is more I need from you before I can let you go for the evening." I look up at him, my body heaving, trying to get oxygen into my lungs, and I see desire pooling in his eyes. I also don't miss the way he rubs his crotch with his hand.

He can't be serious. How can you hit a woman and then fuck her? I did not agree to this; I agreed to present a united front in the eye of the public. If I did that, then I was promised I would get to see Ivy when we got home.

Now my daughter is on who knows what drugs, God knows where, and I am slowly giving up hope that this will end in our favor.

"I want to see Ivy," I say again, calmer, more of an ask this time rather than a demand.

"First, I want you to suck my cock." He says ,slowly undoing his belt buckle, and I scamper away, trying to run, but these stupidly high heels are preventing my quick getaway.

"Not so fast, my love." His hands land in my hair, yanking me back toward him. He lowers his head to my ear before whispering, "I want you on your knees here, in your father's living room, because I want him to know that while he may be funding this fucking expedition, it is me who is the face of it all. I will always get what I want." His voice drips with venom, and chills overtake my body, making me tremble.

"No... No, Daniel," I say, determined that this man will not be winning this war.

"I know where Ivy is, Catherine, and I may or may not have some more potent sedatives on hand to ensure she doesn't wake up for a very long time." His threat trails along my bare shoulder, before his tongue comes out and he licks along neck. It feels disgusting, like I need a long hot shower, and I stiffen, trying to remain calm.

Do it for Ivy. Do it for Ivy.

"Now, get on your fucking knees and open wide, my love. You know that I don't like to be kept waiting," he says with a sadistic grin. His hand runs up my arm from my wrist before eloping my shoulder. His grip becomes hard, biting into my skin as he forces me down onto my knees. I am running out of ideas, so I decide to play along with his little game, and then pray I can flee when he is relaxed.

"No, Daniel, please. Don't do this. Please, if you loved me, if any part of you ever loved me, please, I beg of you, don't make me do this." The pleading tone of my voice makes me feel even sicker. I am not succumbing to him. I would rather die. But I play the part, now down on my knees, looking up at him, tears streaming down my cheeks.

"You look like such a good little slut with your tears

already running down your cheeks..." he groans out as he lowers his zipper, opening his trousers.

"No, Daniel. Stop!" I say trying to be more forceful since begging is now out of the question.

"You are so fucking sexy with your mascara smudged under your eyes and your red lipstick smeared. Now bring those glossy red lips forward, my love, and wrap them around my cock." He pulls himself out of his underwear, gripping himself hard.

"No. No. No..." I say and start to shuffle back on my knees, trying again to get away from him while he is so enraptured with himself.

"Fuck!" he yells, clearly agitated that I won't do as he says, and he grabs my hair, rougher this time, yanking me back in front of him.

I scream out as it feels like he has ripped my hair from my scalp, and as he holds my head firm in one hand, his other flies across the other side of my face.

"Do as you are fucking told, or so help me God, I will walk down that hallway and have your daughter take her last fucking breath right in front of you," he grits out, spit flying from his mouth, sweat pouring from his forehead, bearing his teeth as pure evil runs over his face. And my heart stutters.

He is at breaking point, and I have no doubt that he will kill Ivy to get to me. I don't miss that he calls her *my* daughter, even though he helped create her.

"Now get on your fucking knees and open that fucking mouth." Letting go of my head, he pushes his pants down to his knees, baring himself to me.

With disgust clearly written on my face, I lean away from him, my back hitting the sofa. I feel trapped.

I have no one to help me. I have nowhere to go.

Do it for Ivy. Do it for Ivy.

42

CARTER

The boys and I make quick work of the building maintenance team and now don their uniforms. It is better than the monkey suit from earlier, but I still itch to get it off. After disabling the cameras and paying off a few of the key security team—who knew exactly who we were and are now on their way home with enough money in their banks to buy a house —we are following William through to the rear of the foyer to the private elevator reserved for the penthouse.

"Here, take this," he says, handing a swipe card to Sebastian. "It will give you full access to the top floor. I only had access for today; it will expire at midnight, so you don't have much time."

As an art curator, William is often hired by the wealthy of New York to purchase and hang art in their homes and buildings, and tonight is our lucky night. After he saw us outside, he told us that he is currently redesigning the interiors of the building, and doing so at night to avoid interrupting too many residents.

"Go to the compound and see Goldie. Don't leave before I get back," Sebastian says by way of instructions. Although I appreciate the favor, it means that William will have to lay low for a while, staying out of sight and not talking to anyone, so we can make this disappear with the authorities, which we know will take some time.

We are not dealing with low level thugs here; we are dealing with some of the wealthiest men in New York.

"Good luck," William says as he nods to us, then runs back to one of our cars, our men waiting to take him to the compound. The boys and I jump in the elevator, heading up to the top floor. Nico remains in the car outside, our other soldiers now also on the scene, walking the perimeter. Others are stationed in the streets nearby to block traffic if we need a quick getaway.

"We need to jump on them early," Dante says, giving us instructions, and with every second that passes, I get increasingly anxious to get to my girls. I know we have come up with a plan. But whether we have a plan or not, I am fucking getting my girls, and I will die trying.

As the elevator moves, I check my weapons for the tenth time tonight. A gun in my hand, a gun at my back, a knife in my boot, a switchblade in my pocket, and my fists are ready too, if needed.

I watch the levels light up as we progress, and before long, **PH** lights up.

"Fucking showtime," I grit out and step forward the minute the doors open, with my gun raised. As is typical in these places, the elevator opens right into the main living room, the wealth of it all hitting me in the face.

"What the fuck?" a man's voice barks, and I look

sharply toward him. It is just who we wanted to see, standing with his pants down right in front of Cat.

She is on her knees, tears streaming down her face, blood covering one side, her hair disheveled, and I see red.

"Get the fuck away from her," I seethe, my finger twitching to pull the trigger, but not yet sure if he is packing or if anyone else is here. He stands looking at me in shock for a moment. "I said, GET THE FUCK AWAY FROM HER!" I scream at him, my anger now exploding.

Gritting my teeth together, I walk slowly toward him with my gun raised, aimed at his head.

"Oh, thank God!" I hear Cat breathe in relief, and out of my peripheral vision, I see her scramble in her long red gown and move toward me. She looks at Sebastian and Dante who stand behind me, their guns also raised. "My father went that way," she says, and Dante walks down the hall in search of the man.

"Anyone else here?" Sebastian asks her.

"No..." she starts to say, whipping around to Daniel.

"Where is Ivy?" she demands of him now that she is standing by my side, like the mother lioness she is.

"You have some nerve." He looks right at me with his bottom half still uncovered, and there is something to be said about a man who is overcompensating with his wallet. Now I know it's true.

I move another step closer, because I am about to kill this motherfucker, but it is Cat that retaliates. She walks up to him and stares him down.

"Where is IVY!" she screams at him, and even though he is outnumbered, he only smirks.

"Asshole!" she screams before her fist flies out, and she punches him across the nose.

He doesn't fall, but he staggers backward, his pants wrapping around his legs, causing him to be unbalanced. There is some damage, and I can tell it surprised him. He looks at her wide-eyed, his eyes now watering, so I know she got him good.

"Fucking bitch!" he yells, and I have had enough.

Throwing my gun to Sebastian, I take two steps forward and punch him square in the face. He falls back, and I don't stop. I can't. My fists fly out, landing on his face a few times before I take my anger out on his body. Blood pours from his nose, which is now broken and on an angle that is going to be hard to repair. His eyes are squeezed shut, his cheeks red and blue, and his jaw is tight as he grunts and groans every time my fists connects with his flesh.

Deep, unnerving rage fires in the pit of my stomach, and I continue to thump my fist into his torso until I hear his ribs snap. I break each of them, one by one, until I feel her soft touch on my shoulder and stop abruptly.

"Carter... we need to find Ivy," she says, and I look back at her and see her panicked face. I stand back up quickly and pull her to me, suffocating her to my chest, the desire to have her in my arms again all-encompassing. I hear her gasp, and when I pull back suddenly, I see how hurt she is.

"Fuck, Cat..."

"Carter!" Dante yells from down the hall. I grab her hand and we run, leaving an unconscious Daniel lying in a pool of his own blood, with Sebastian looking over him like he will take his last breath from him. Sebastian throws my gun back to me, and even though I am quick, Cat is keeping up with me in her heels. I know she is in pain, but unless we have Ivy, she will never be complete.

I see Dante down the end of the hallway, and I wonder how big this fucking penthouse is because it feels like it goes for miles.

"She's here!" he yells out from an open doorway, and I grip Cat's hand tight as we approach.

"What the hell is going on!" a voice booms as a man steps out in front of us, between Dante and I, from one of the doorways in the hall.

"Dad!" Cat yells in surprise as we both stop dead in our tracks, and I see Dante behind him slink quietly back into the room to protect Ivy, unnoticed.

"You are such a stupid girl," he sneers at her. There is no love in his eyes for his daughter, only rage and disgust, and he must be insane if he thinks Cat is anything other than the beautiful, smart woman she is.

"Please, Dad, please, let me get Ivy and leave," she begs, her tears falling freely, and I want to end this motherfucker right here and now for ever making her feel less than.

"Leave? You are not LEAVING!" I am about to step in when he produces a gun and aims it right at his daughter.

"You look just like your mother the night I killed her too. Stupid fucking women," he says and pulls the trigger.

My heart leaps from my chest as my hand flies out to Cat, pushing her hard out of the way. It all happens in slow motion as I hear her screams echo through the apartment, and then she falls to the floor in a haze of red from her dress.

Lifting my hand, I fire back at her father, my aim straight as it pierces his chest, right where his heart would be if he had one. His body falls back, his white shirt now tainted red, and it isn't until I empty my gun into him that I feel the familiar burn in my arm and have never been more grateful for the pain.

"Cat?" I grunt, as Dante and Sebastian come running out, but I fall to my knees next to her, needing to know she is okay.

"Cat!" I shout, my hands gripping the sides of her face, looking her over, my heart pounding as I do.

"Carter?" she whispers, her eyes wide, looking over my face and body, her hands immediately finding my wound.

"Oh My God! Carter!" she yells as the red liquid coats my arm, and her hands rush to cover it.

"It's all right, baby. It's nothing serious," I say, trying to comfort her as I brush her cheek with my thumb, so fucking glad she is in one piece.

"Where's Ivy? Did we find her?" I stand quickly, pulling her up with me, and we continue down the hallway to the room Dante was guarding. Cat rushes inside, and I follow her, and then we finally see her.

Little Ivy, lying tucked in bed. She is still, not moving, and Cat is on her in a second, feeling for her pulse.

"Is she okay??" I ask, panicking as I step up beside her, my stomach lurching into my throat.

"They gave her a sedation earlier. I think she has slept through the whole thing." She tries to pull her up and cuddle her to her chest, but can't because she is shaking too much, weak from stress.

"Here, let me," I say, leaning over and grabbing Ivy, holding her to my chest. Cat's hands wrap around my bicep, and she sticks to me like glue as we walk out the door.

"Tony is downstairs with the car running," Dante says to me as he walks us down the hallway to the elevator where Sebastian is waiting for us.

"Nico is on his way up to help us clean up this mess. Doctors are already at the compound, waiting for you," Sebastian tells me as the elevator chimes, and Nico plus eight others come inside.

"Thanks," I grit out, my arm killing where the bullet grazed me, but I could care less. I just need to get my girls out of this place as quickly as possible.

Sebastian holds the elevator door and looks directly at Cat.

"Cat, whatever you need, you have it. Welcome to the family," he says before stepping back and beginning to bark orders at the others.

The doors close, leaving me with my girls. Where they belong.

43

CATHERINE

We step into Carter's New York City apartment, which I have learned is part of the compound, a large, connected fortress taking up an entire block of the city where Sebastian and his mob family live. After spending some time in the very modern and well-stocked medical ward downstairs, checking Ivy's stats, and cleaning up mine and Carter's wounds, I am grateful for the quiet that his apartment brings us. He has carried Ivy the whole way and now as he lays her on his bed, we wrap her up in the blankets. She is still fast asleep, blissfully unaware of what happened.

Although I don't like that they drugged her, I am glad she didn't witness anything about tonight. Flashes of seeing my father's bloody, lifeless body fill my mind, and I take a deep breath to try to keep my nerves in check. But they are totally shot, and I don't know how to calm myself down.

"Sit with her a bit. I will be back in a minute," Carter

says as he leans down and gives me a peck on the cheek. I have never been more thankful for a man before in my life.

He has been the only man to look after me, love me, support me, be there for me, and now he saved me. Not only from my own family, but literally saved my life by pushing me out of the way of the bullet and taking it himself.

He is right; it is only a scratch, but it could have been worse. So much worse.

I pay no attention to where he has gone or what he is doing as I sit on the bed, totally enamoured with my daughter. I slowly brush her hair from her forehead, taking in her peacefulness, knowing that we have a steep road ahead of us to heal, but a lifetime of happiness coming our way because we are free. We are finally free of the restraints that the men of our family placed on us.

She will be frightened when she wakes up in a strange bed, with memories of being ripped from me earlier today. But I will sleep with her, hold her in my arms, and will never let her go.

"Okay, your turn," Carter says to me as he comes and stands by my side, and I look up at him in question. He gives me a small smile, and I gasp as he leans over the bed and picks me up, bridal style, my arms flinging around his neck and hanging on tight.

"Where are you taking me?" I ask as he steps away from the bed. Not worried, but not keen to leave Ivy at all.

"Don't worry, just in here," he says, knowing what I am feeling as he takes me into his bathroom and places my feet back down on the floor.

The bathroom is steamy, and I notice that he has filled the tub with warm water and some bubbles too. Walking around to my back, he slowly lowers the zip of my dress.

I want to burn this dress. I have wanted to rip it from my body all night, not because it is horrible or uncomfortable, but for what it represents and the cage it became, keeping me held in tight, reminding me who owned me earlier.

"Shit," he grits out as the zip lowers, and I assume it's because my skin is purple now. But I don't care. Now, I can finally breathe, for the first time in what feels like years.

"Baby," he says quietly, his voice deep in concern. His hand skims down my back before he gently grabs my shoulders and turns me to face him, looking me over.

"Who did this?" he asks me, anger burning in his eyes.

"Daniel," I say honestly. I don't care anymore. My father is dead, and I have no idea about Daniel. If he is still breathing, he is as good as dead anyway.

Carter nods in understanding as his hands wander softly around to my back, and he unclips my strapless bra, before grabbing my underwear around my waist and lowering them to the floor. My hands lean on his shoulders as I step out of them.

I have never had a man to look after me like this before, but I can depend on Carter. He has proven tonight that I can always depend on him.

Standing up before me again, he runs his hands back

up over my shoulders and up my neck before cupping my cheeks softly.

"You're the strongest woman I know," he says, admiration in his eyes. It's not the first time he says it, but right now I sure don't feel that way.

I huff, and rolling my eyes. "Look at me, Carter. I am hardly a tough soldier," I say, as I lean my face into his cupped hands.

"You're also beautiful and sexy as sin," he says with a small grin, which I return, my hands grabbing him around the middle. I lean against him, hugging him to me.

"I never want you to let me go," I say honestly, feeling more vulnerable than I ever have.

"Good, because I never will. I don't plan on ever leaving you or Ivy. Ever." As he kisses the top of my head, I smile against his chest and squeeze my eyes tight, wanting to bury myself into him and never come out.

"Let me help you get in the bath. You relax, and I will go and sit with Ivy. I will keep the door ajar in case she wakes up," he says, as he guides me into the tub, holding my hand as I step in and sink into the water and close my eyes.

As he leaves the room, I see he has a candle lit to create ambiance, the door remaining open a little, and for the first time in the last twenty-four hours, I am alone. I take a deep breath, then release the tears I have been holding, letting the stress go.

***

"Where are you going?" I ask Carter in the morning as I see him up and dressed. He slept holding Ivy and I all night. Ivy woke up in the earlier hours, and after a few tears, she went back to sleep in my arms. Carter never left. But now, in the bright light of the day, I watch him as he sits on the armchair and ties his boots.

"I need to go and sort a few things out. But the girls are here," he says as he stands and walks over to the bed.

"I won't be long. Annie has brought over some food. Her and Goldie are downstairs, and Maggie and Ian just arrived," he says, cupping my cheek with his hand.

"Maggie and Ian?" I say, startled, because I haven't thought about Maggie. I was too busy concentrating on Ivy.

"Sebastian sent the private jet to pick them up early this morning. They know most of what happened, but both are keen to see you. It was hard to keep Maggie out of my room all morning, to be honest." He smiles, eyes glistening, and my heart booms in my chest.

"What time is it?" I ask, sitting up, careful not to wake Ivy, although she is stirring.

"It is 11am."

"11am!" I almost screech in shock. "Why didn't you wake me earlier?" I start to move out of the bed, wrapping a blanket around myself.

"I wanted you to get some sleep; it was a rough night. Maggie brought you some fresh clothes, the bag is in the bathroom. There are fresh towels in there too, so take a shower and relax for a minute. I will send Maggie up when I leave," he says, standing in front of me, gripping my waist, as he likes to do.

I rub my face. "Carter, I don't know how to..." I begin to try to thank him for everything, knowing that words are not possible, but he cuts me off.

"Don't. Don't say it." I can't just not address it.

"But, Carter, you literally took a bullet for me!" I gape up at him, then look at his arm, seeing no signs of any damage under his top. Yet, I still feel remorseful for the wound that I caused.

"I would do it all over again for you in a heartbeat," he says gently as his hands brush my cheek. "Seeing you next to him last night at the gala, seeing you in the penthouse last night, and seeing your body purple today, there is nothing I wouldn't do to make sure you are safe, make sure Ivy is safe." His expression is pained, his eyes flicking over to my daughter who is still sleeping.

"I promised you I wasn't leaving you again and I am not. I promised you I would keep you safe and protected, and I didn't. That is going to eat at me for the rest of my life. But I love you, Cat. I'm in love with you."

"I love you, Carter!" I blurt out, needing him to understand that he means the world to me. When I told him I loved him at the gala, I thought I might not ever see him again. Now, to be here with him, to hear those words from his lips, I can't contain my emotions. I watch him as he takes a breath, relaxing into my embrace. "I love you too, Carter, so much." I repeat, a little quieter, my eyes watering.

He looks at me seriously, the most serious I think I have ever seen him, before he moves suddenly, pulling me to him and smashing his lips into mine. Licking my bottom lip, I open for him, his tongue darting to tangle with mine. My body melts into his as he holds me up, the feeling of knowing I can always lean on him, sending butterflies through my stomach. His hands wrap gently around me, giving me the comfort to know I am always safe and loved with him.

"Gee, what a sight to wake up too..." Ivy says groggily but sarcastically from the bed beside us, and we both pull away and look at her. Her smile is wide and bright, and Carter leans over and gives her a peck on the nose. "Love you too, Little Cub," he says with a grin as she rubs her eyes.

"You girls freshen up. I will let everyone know you will be downstairs in a bit and to get the coffee and donuts organized," he says as he starts to turn from us, clearly on a mission for whatever he needs to do this morning.

"Carter?" Ivy asks, and he turns swiftly to look at her, as do I, because we both hear concern in her voice.

"Yeah, Little Cub?"

"I love you too," she whispers, a soft pink blush coming to her cheeks, and my eyes water again because this is the first man she has ever uttered those words to. A lone tear finally escapes my eye and runs down my cheek. Carter stands still, in shock for a moment, before looking at me and then back to Ivy. He walks to her, sitting on the bed beside her, and she jumps up and into his arms, his holding her tight.

"I got you, Ivy. I will look after you and your mom from now on, okay?" he says quietly to her, and I see her nod against his shoulder.

***

Ivy and I spent our entire morning and afternoon lying under blankets with Annie, Goldie, Ian, and Maggie as we dissected the night. Ivy has slept on and off, the drugs still making their way through her system, and after eating three donuts, she passed out from a food coma, barely stirring since.

Annie is an amazing cook, and she and Goldie have made me feel so welcomed into this new apartment and new life, of which I continue to uncover more about Carter as the day goes on.

"So..." Maggie says, looking quickly at Ivy to ensure she is still asleep. "You mentioned Dad before, but do we know anything about Daniel? Is he... I mean, is he still..." Her voice tapers off, not knowing how to ask the question. Is he is dead or alive?

"If he is not, he should be..." Ian says, still very protective of me, which I adore.

I take in a deep breath and shrug because I have no words, and I have no idea.

"The boys do what they need to do," Goldie says to us. "They are fair, but they are firm, and from what I know, Daniel," she pauses, looking at me before progressing, "your father, and Brian Cole have all been trying to take business and many other things from us. So this fight is not just for you, Cat; they are fighting for the family on this as well. While I know Carter is angry, Sebastian, Dante, and Nico are equally angry, so you should in no way feel any guilt about what happens to him."

"After everything they have done to you, I can't

imagine Carter will go easy on them, though..." Annie pipes up. "If it was Dante and I, then Dante would rip the world apart to avenge me." Whilst I don't like talking about it, not ever wanting to cause anyone harm, it is new for me to have a man who will burn the world down to protect me. It makes me feel strong, secure, like I am his everything.

"He is an asshole who deserves everything he gets," Ian murmurs, and as I look at him, I know he is firmly team Carter all the way.

Not really wanting to talk about it anymore, I remain silent and continue to stroke Ivy's hair. What do I want Carter to be doing to Daniel? What do the mob do exactly? Can I be with a man who killed my father? Who might kill Ivy's father? It all feels overwhelming as I think about it. As a medical professional, I am taught from an early age to do anything I can to save a life, so the idea of being the reason someone loses theirs doesn't sit well with me.

But they weren't really fathers and having the same blood does not equal a family. They didn't care. About me, about Ivy, about anyone other than themselves. They only care about their bank account and their status. Whether death comes to Daniel or not, I know that I am always safe, always protected and that makes me calm and brings me peace. So I trust Carter. I trust him to make the decision for me and I will live with the decision he makes just fine.

As we all continue to chatter, Annie giving me cooking tips and Goldie helping fill in the gaps I have about mob family lifestyles, the door opens, and Carter comes in. I watch him from the moment he enters, his clothes straight and clean, his eyes tired but focused. He walks into the room and bends down, kissing Ivy on the forehead and nodding to the ladies before he comes to embrace me. Kissing me on the lips, taking his time, and I hear the girls shuffle and start the conversation again, obviously not wanting to see our display of affection.

Pulling away slightly, our noses nearly touching, he whispers to me, "You don't have to worry about him anymore, Cat." And I know Daniel's life is now over. I remain silent, but nod, and then search his eyes. "What about his father?" Brian Cole is a man who will not stand to see his son and best friend now gone.

"Sebastian and Nico are dealing with him. You don't have to worry anymore. You are free, your fight is over, baby." As he presses his lips to mine again, the remaining weight lifts from my shoulders.

My fight is now over.

CATHERINE - SIX MONTHS LATER

With Ivy concentrating on her schoolwork at my desk, I wrap the hands of a young fighter in the medical clinic at the gym.

"There, you should be all good to go!" I say as I snap off the tape and make sure it is secured.

"Thanks, Doc," the kid says, giving me a half smile as he jumps off the bed and saunters out the door.

I watch him go. He is new, and a little quiet, but Carter has been working with him. Apparently, he has a lot of aggression and a lot of fighting potential. No doubt another boy who Carter will take under his wing, his list of kids now growing every day. Carter has changed a lot over the past few months. He helps every single kid that walks in through these doors, and I feel like my healing experience has rubbed off on him. He now leaves all his dark work in New York, preferring to keep Philly for family.

My eyes flick back to Ivy. After a few rough months,

SAMANTHA SKYE

she has been going really well. Working hard at school and playing soccer again, hanging out with Abby, and making lots of new friends, but she is very quiet today, hardly looking at me, so I know something is up.

Dad's funeral happened within two days of the incident. I played the role of grieving daughter, as did Maggie, even though we were anything but. The who's who of New York came, and it was a long and exhausting day. Ivy didn't want to come, so she stayed at the compound with Carter and Abby as Maggie and I leaned on each other, her husband also tagging along, helping us field questions and keep people away from us when needed.

We heard all the whispers, of course. How terrible it was that intruders robbed his home and left him and Daniel for dead. The police are still on the hunt for them, since the security cameras and guards could not provide any evidence. At the time, questions were also raised about Daniel. One night, we were the sparkling new couple on the New York scene, and the next, I was the grieving daughter and fiancée, losing both men tragically.

Daniel's father held a funeral for him, which I didn't attend, citing exhaustion and grief. However, that day, Carter had Ivy and I on a private plane out of the city and back to Philly, where we stayed indoors, laid low and learned how to process what had happened. I still don't ask questions of the inner workings of the mob, but I know that whatever Sebastian and the boys have done, it is working, because I never saw or heard from Daniel's father again. He steers clear of me, my name is kept out of every media article, and his troubles are increasing, with his various businesses collapsing. He is fighting a losing battle for the first time in his life, and I don't care one bit.

But my heart bleeds for his daughter. Ivy's Aunt Emilia, who I need to reach out to, because she really has no one else.

Carter has been with Ivy and I every day ever since.

He is still a mafia man, still visits New York frequently, still works with Sebastian and the others. Sometimes Ivy and I go with him, and we get to spend time with Annie and Goldie while we're there. He is protective of us, and that is something that will never change, but he is softer. He has mellowed, and our life is a master class of domesticity, but we both love it.

About a month after the incident, I remembered something my father said before he pulled the trigger that night. About how I looked like my mother before she died. It stuck in my mind, and I mentioned it to Carter. It appears that when Sebastian and Carter investigated, we found out my mother's death wasn't an accident either. But rather, it was made to look like one. My father no longer needing her once she finished being of use to him in whatever business plans he had at the time.

That was a sad day for Maggie and me. Our mother was a beautiful woman, one who didn't deserve the ending she had.

I roll up the tape and pack away the scissors before wiping down the bed. After everything that happened, I couldn't return to the hospital. The high energy of an ED department was too much, and after nearly losing Ivy, I wanted more time with her. So Carter asked me to manage the medical clinic here at the gym. I expected to see men with lots of bruising, needing ice and painkillers, and I do see that, but there is so much more.

As soon as he announced free medical, the gym clinic has been a revolving door of a variety of ailments. So much so that we brought Ian with us too. So when I'm not here, he is. I can bring Ivy as well, make my own hours, and I feel good for doing something for the community.

"How is your homework, Ivy?" I ask as I peer over her shoulder, seeing her coloring in, rather than doing the maths that she is supposed to do.

I purse my lips in question, because this is not like her at all, but before I can say anything further, the clinic door opens.

"Cat, got a minute?" Carter asks as he closes the door and locks it.

"What's going on?" I ask as I see Ivy turn in her seat and look at Carter.

"Ivy," Carter starts, and he looks a little pale. "Did you know that the Macaroni penguins mate for life?" he asks her, and I wonder if she has yet another project on animals that I don't know about.

"Yep, they do!" Ivy says in glee, her smile wide, and I can't help but smile too at the way she lights up at seeing Carter. I also don't miss the small nod she gives him, and I wonder what the two of them are up to.

"How about it, Cat?" Carter says to me, making me whip my head back around to look at him. He looks weird. Almost nervous, and it takes me a moment to register that he asked me a question.

"What?" I ask, confused, not sure what I missed.

"Want to be my Macaroni penguin?" he repeats, looking like he is about to throw up, and I wonder if he got hit in the head or something.

"Carter, what's wrong? You don't look so good. What do you mean about penguins?" I ask as I take a small step toward him, stopping when I see him get down on one knee and pull out a small black velvet box.

"Want to mate for life?" He opens the box and the large yellow diamond sparkles in the light.

"Carter!" My hands fly to my mouth, my eyes watering, and my voice gets lodged in my throat.

"I thought about taking you to a fancy restaurant or somewhere nice, but in a medical room is where we first met, and I wanted Ivy with us so, yeah... How about it, Cat? Are you going to be my Macaroni?" he says, fear now totally overtaking his features.

"Oh my God. Yes! YES! I will be your penguin!!!" I squeal and hop from one leg to the other, excitement making my palms sweat as I rub them on my jeans before he slips the ring on my finger. He is quick, the color now back to his face as he jumps up, grabbing me in his arms, kissing me long and hard.

"YES!" I hear Ivy say next to me, before Carter places me back on the floor and looks at my daughter.

"Ivy, I have this for you." He produces some paperwork from his back pocket.

"What is it?" she asks, grabbing it from him.

"It is an amendment to our contract. I have rewritten

the contract to promote us from Best Friends to Family. You just need to sign the bottom," he says, his face serious, and a tear runs down my cheek as I watch them.

My breathing halts as I look at Ivy, whose small face, which was full of a watermelon smile just moments ago has taken on Carter's previous pale color as shock settles on her features.

"That would be awesome," she says quietly, and I see her eyes welling up as well.

"Good, now come here," Carter says, opening his arms wide, and she runs into his embrace. He hugs her for a beat before pulling me in close, and my new little family has a special moment together that we will surely never forget.

"I'm going to find Benji. Maybe I can promote him to Best Friend status now!" she says before stepping out of the room, closing the door behind her.

Carter pulls away from me slightly, looking deep into my eyes. "I'm so fucking glad I found you, Cat. We talk a lot about the night that I saved you, but really, you are the one that saved me. The moment you walked into my hospital room, the moment you touched my body, held my hand, walked into this gym, looking like every inch the beautiful woman you are, so much so that I wanted to strip down and make mine the minute I saw you... you changed me, baby. You are everything to me. You and Ivy have both made me a better man, and I never ever want to let you go," he whispers, his hand cupping my cheek, pure love and joy in his face, and I melt further into his touch.

This man. He is everything I never knew I needed and everything I wanted and more.

He was worth the fight.

He was worth it all.

GRAB a **bonus scene** to get Catherine's point of view on what their life is like now.

DO YOU WANT MORE?

My Chance

Nico Molenti has been in Sebastian Romano's shadow for years. He has learnt everything from his boss and has a good head for business.

Now as he starts investigating who is responsible for trying to take away their foothold, it is his chance to step up to the challenge.

Until *she* gets in the way.

Grab a copy of My Chance now!

https://books2read.com/My-Chance-Samantha-Skye

ALSO BY SAMANTHA SKYE

Boston Billionaires Series

Coming Home - Now **FREE**

Finding Home

Leaving Home

Building Home

Men of New York Series

My Legacy

My Destiny

My Fight

My Chance

ABOUT THE AUTHOR

Samantha Skye is a contemporary romance author from Melbourne, Australia. A country kid turned city slicker, Samantha writes characters that are as diverse as they are devilishly handsome.

Her unique brand of suspenseful spice deftly combines the risky and the risqué, setting hearts pounding for more than one reason! When she's not plotting her next novel, Samantha can be found chatting on podcasts, or anywhere there's sunshine. An avid traveler, Samantha is just as comfortable in gumboots as she is in Christian Louboutins...but she's usually having more fun in the latter.

To learn more about her and what comes next in her author journey you can find her on;

WEB: samanthaskyeauthor.com

Manufactured by Amazon.ca
Acheson, AB